Something Special

Selim Ulug

Copyright © 2021 Selim Ulug All rights reserved

The characters and events portrayed in this book are fictitious. Any similarity to real persons, living or dead, is coincidental and not intended by the author.

No part of this book may be reproduced, or stored in a retrieval system, or transmitted in any form or by any means, electronic, mechanical, photocopying, recording, or otherwise, without express written permission of the publisher.

ISBN: 9798598057650

Cover design by: Johannes Chazot

*This book is dedicated to Betty Scarlett
in gratitude for her encouragement
and for making her house my home away from home.
And for all the great meals.
Especially the fish pie.*

Contents

INTRODUCTION	v
LIZZY AND ME	1
DON'T EVER CHANGE	14
REMEMBER ME?	44
A VOICE	63
PROTAGONIST PURGATORY	108
SOMETHING SPECIAL	132
A QUESTION OF JUDGMENT	142
THE KNIFE	162
LAURA WILCOX	166
TRUTH TO POWER	185
TOO CLOSE	207
UNDER THE SAND	226
UNFINISHED BUSINESS: A WHITE ROSE MYSTERY	243
THE RIGHT TIME	264
WHERE THE DRAGONS SLEEP	292
ACKNOWLEDGMENTS	309

Introduction

Welcome to *Something Special*, my first collection of short stories. Herein you'll find a mix of fantasy, horror, and mystery. My writing, you see, reflects what I read.

I wrote the oldest of these stories, "Where the Dragons Sleep," in 2002, back when my plan was to focus on children's stories. Plans change. Using the pseudonym selimpensfiction, I began to write fan fiction in 2011 and continued to do so through 2016. Along the way came "The Right Time" (2014) and "Protagonist Purgatory" (2015). Thank goodness for fan fiction, as it gave me the opportunity to grow as a writer in a friendly, encouraging environment. By the time I posted my last fan fiction story, I felt ready to take the next step in my writing journey.

In 2017, my *Doctor Who* story "Landbound" was selected by Big Finish Productions as the year's Paul Spragg Memorial Short Trip. It's available for free if you care to give it a listen. Big Finish released my second *Doctor Who* story, "Battle Scars," in 2019.

The stories in this collection are my original works. The fantasies are mostly of the urban variety, set in our world, except for "Protagonist Purgatory" and "Where the Dragons Sleep." Of the horror stories, "Too Close" and "Under the Sand" are Lovecraftian; the others are not. Then there are the mystery yarns, or "weird mystery," by which I mean mysteries that may or may not contain an element of fantasy, depending upon your interpretation.

Introduction

However, "A Question of Judgment" has nothing weird, with the possible exception of the detective.

A few stories are sequels to or are set in the same world as previous stories. Sometimes I'm just not ready to leave characters behind. The following stories are pairs: "Laura Wilcox" and "Truth to Power," "Too Close" and "Under the Sand", and "The Right Time" and "Protagonist Purgatory."

The collection is not organized by genre, but if you prefer to focus on one genre at a time, you can make use of the list below.

Horror
Don't Ever Change
Something Special
The Knife
Too Close
Under the Sand

Fantasy
Lizzy and Me
Remember Me?
Protagonist Purgatory
Laura Wilcox
Truth to Power
The Right Time
Where the Dragons Sleep

Weird Mystery
A Voice
A Question of Judgment
Unfinished Business: A White Rose Mystery

If you're in the mood for something light-hearted, try "A Question of Judgment" and "Protagonist Purgatory."

Introduction

I hope you enjoy reading these stories. If you do, look me up on Twitter @selimpensfctn and let me know.

Lizzy and Me

I started writing this story as I sat on a bench at Roker Beach in Sunderland, UK. My mother was from Sunderland and, over the course of several family visits as I was growing up, I came to find Britain, and Sunderland in particular, quite magical. This story is the inevitable result.

> Life can only be understood backwards;
> but it must be lived forwards.
> Søren Kierkegaard

It was here at the seafront that I passed my happiest days as a child, and after all these years, it really hasn't changed. The air is scented with seaweed, the waves lap at the long, sandy beach, gulls squawk as they dart about, children play, and dogs scamper. From tiny tin booths, vendors provide all-day breakfast, chips, and ice-cream cones.

Sometimes, after gazing for hours at the sea, as it's coming on to dusk, I can almost hear the old foghorn. The lighthouse is still here, at the end of the long, curved pier, but its light no longer shines and its horn is silent.

It's late afternoon, and from my sand-dusted bench upon the boardwalk I see that families are packing up to return home, the parents gathering up toys and pets and consoling their children with the promise of returning another day.

I also see, I think I can see, two children, a boy and a girl, running about the sand, each with a plastic pail and shovel, chasing each other, chasing dogs, chasing seagulls. The shovel tumbles out of the boy's pail and he stops, gets to his knees, and fills the pail with sand. The girl turns and joins him. It's hard to make out any details. I blink and wipe my eyes.

Movement to my left distracts me—a tall, thin man wearing an open brown trench coat over a black T-shirt and jeans. His face is gaunt, unshaven; his long blond hair a haphazard mess. Brushing the hair away from his blue eyes, the man looks out at the sea, notices me, or the bench, and takes a seat.

Have I seen him before?

After exhaling audibly, he says, "I don't know how you do it."

I wait for clarification, but none is forthcoming. The man rises, stuffs his hands in his coat pockets, and continues his shuffle along the seafront.

He is soon forgotten as my thoughts drift towards my childhood. Eventually, the chill of the oncoming evening reminds me of the time. With a sigh, I zip up my windbreaker and take my leave.

I drive home and cannot hide from my friends that I remain listless, disconsolate. And so, by degrees, they drift away, and I am left with my memories. Emma remains loyal. Her friends tolerate me, cast half-hearted smiles my way. I wonder how long it will be before Emma goes the way of my other relationships?

Wednesday evening, and as usual I'm at the care home where my mother resides. Going on eighty-six, she has advanced dementia. If it's a good day she remembers me. Today, it seems, is not a good day. She looks blankly in my direction as I enter her room.

"Evening, Mum. How are you today?"

Her watery eyes squint a bit, and her thin lips shift left and right. Finally, she brushes back her unkempt hair—it doesn't look as though the staff have paid her much attention today—and says, "Oh, I don't think I'm your mother, pet."

"Not my mother?" I say. Having already prepared myself to behave in as jovial a manner as possible, I reply, "Well that's a shame, 'cause I bet you were a great mum."

"Oh, howay with you," she says, with a hint of a smile that tells me she's pleased I said so.

The unit in the memory care facility is as it always is. A bathroom and small living room decorated with as many items from the family home as I could fit. There's the old Turkish carpet, a small settee, a coffee table, a reclining chair, a family portrait, a collection of small oil paintings, and a few Royal Doulton figurines set upon a shelf above the foot of her bed.

"Would you like anything?" I ask. "Some tea?"

"No, pet, I'm fine," she says, shifting slightly on the reclining chair.

I take a seat on the settee and my gaze drifts towards the family portrait. Father had already left us when it was taken. Mum is seated on a chair, with Lizzy sitting on her lap. I'm standing on her right, my hand resting on Mum's shoulder. Pointing to the portrait, I ask, "Who are those good-looking people? Do you remember?"

The neutral expression on Mum's face works itself into a frown as she gazes blankly at the portrait. "I don't like that picture," she says, and looks away.

After an hour spent talking about my day and the people I work with, I say goodbye and close the door behind me. Wiping away a tear, I wonder whether the mother I knew is gone completely, or simply buried so deep within as to be near unreachable. Since Lizzy, I've spent a great deal of time lost in my memories. What must it be like, living moment to moment, with no memory of yesterday, in a state where the past dissolves into tendrils of mist before disappearing altogether into a dense fog?

Emma is waiting in the lobby, having finished her shift a little while ago. After air kisses, we confirm our dinner plans. In half an hour, we are at the restaurant.

We complement each other well, I think. I am quiet, self-contained. Emma draws me out with her effervescent, bubbly personality. Tonight, I feel particularly withdrawn. My mother has stirred a jumble of thoughts and memories, and it can be hard to disentangle myself from the past. So it takes time for me to notice that Emma is unusually quiet. Our meals have arrived and we are on our second glasses of wine before I say anything.

Emma tells me of her concern regarding what she calls my obsession with the past. "I love you, Randy. But at some point," she says, raising her head to make eye contact, "we need to get on with our lives. We *all* do." She holds eye contact a moment longer, then returns to the business of cutting her food. With a sigh, I do likewise. Her message is crystal clear.

According to Emma, I'm neglecting my life for the sake of the past, and she's right. Nevertheless, I'm back at the seafront the first chance I get, on a bank holiday weekend, sitting on the usual bench, and once again the hours pass as I gaze at the beach and the sea and the lighthouse.

Ostensibly, I'm here seeking inspiration for my new novel. My second. My first published novel, *Now What?*, has been, as my agent put it, moderately successful. She's encouraged me to consider writing full time and to spend more time and care crafting the prose. She's awaiting some sample chapters from my next work.

Unfortunately, all I can think about is Lizzy.

When we were children, our family often came here to visit our aunt, Mum's sister. Auntie Maggie's house was a narrow three-storey affair, oddly organized and chock-full of nooks and crannies and hidey-holes. My favourite room was the top-floor library, with its floor-to-ceiling shelves stuffed with books and its piles of books upon the floor. We'd find treasures here, Lizzy and I, and spend hours reading to each other. Our bedroom was on the second floor. We slept in twin beds separated by a small chest of drawers upon which sat an old-fashioned alarm clock with bells and a hammer. After lights out, we would tiptoe to the window, and if we stretched and craned our necks to the right, we could just make out the lighthouse and watch the light spin endlessly through the evening fog. When we returned to bed, the foghorn, with its two mournful, stentorian tones, would lull us to sleep. In the mornings we would creep down the stairs, cover ourselves with a blanket, and watch *The Tom and Jerry Show* and other cartoons until the adults woke and hustled us into the kitchen for breakfast.

That home is now a bed and breakfast. I stay in the old bedroom when I come here. From the house, it's a short walk to the nearby park where we spent many an hour playing and chasing each other. It's a pleasant stroll past the tennis court, the pond, and the gazebo to the faded brick archway that empties onto Roker Beach. Odd to think how my childhood self walked upon this very pathway. Sometimes the past seems so close, and yet . . .

Though lost in thought, I notice him again, the tall man in the trench coat. He seems more haggard than before, his hair more matted, and his eyes have sunk deeper into his face.

As before, he takes a seat beside me and gazes straight ahead at the surf and the gulls. I'm not sure whether he's noticed that I'm here.

"I don't think I can do this anymore," he says abruptly.

Uncertain as to whether he's speaking to me or simply giving voice to his own despair, I look at him and wait for him to continue. Turning to me, his eyes widen. "You can… see me?"

"Of course," I answer.

He nods then doesn't speak for a while, seemingly turning his attention back to the sea.

"Are you all right?" I finally ask.

"I've been trying to understand what it is to live in this world."

"*This* world?"

Smiling slightly, he says, "Imagine a vinyl record, and you're the phonograph needle. You're placed in a groove and have the illusion of moving forward, though it's the record that's actually turning. This is your world. Now imagine that you can move about the surface of the record to any location you choose. That is my world. Being here, being so constrained as you are, it's . . . difficult.

"But you, you're time sensitive. You've seen things, haven't you? And heard things. And you're looking for something from another time." It was a statement, not a question. "Something, or someone—someone you associate with this place. And you think that being here will bring you closer to them."

To my surprise, my eyes begin to tear up, and I look away.

"You're not far wrong," he adds gently. I turn to him again. "If you let me, I can help you find what you're looking for. Then one day, if you keep looking, you'll find your own way."

I nod. "Help me."

I'm Randy Hodgins and I'm eight years old. I'm chasing Lizzy on the beach, but I'm not really trying to catch her, that wouldn't be any fun. It's more fun just to chase.

When the shovel falls out of my pail, I stop, get down on my knees, and scoop sand into the pail. We can build a sandcastle.

Where's Lizzy? Oh, there she is. She was still running, but now she's come to join me and is shovelling sand into her own pail. The tide has gone out and the sand is still wet.

I look up after a while and see that people are leaving. I glance at my watch. It has a shiny red strap and a large face.

"Lizzy," I say, "we're supposed to be home now."

Lizzy continues to work.

"Lizzy."

"No!" she declares, throwing her pail at me. "I want to finish the castle!"

I'm Randy Hodgins and I'm eleven years old. Mother is washing the dishes. Father is reading his newspaper on the chesterfield in the sitting room and glancing at *Top of the Pops* once in a while. I'm sitting on the floor, watching the television, when I feel Lizzy's arm grab me from behind and pull me down. "Time to fight," she says, and we wrestle.

I see Father glance at us. With a sigh, he shakes his head and then continues to read.

I forget myself in the excitement and pin Lizzy down. As she struggles, and I see the red in her face and the fire in her eyes, I remember. I feign that she's managed to get me off balance and roll off of her. Lizzy says loudly that she's won. She usually does.

It's not very nice when she doesn't.

I'm Randy Hodgins. I'm fifteen. Lizzy is getting ready to go out on a date. This makes me feel strange. I don't think I like it.

Lizzy is different now. So am I, but I mean she's different towards me. She ignores me most of the time. Doesn't look in my direction unless she has to. I've asked her why she's like this, but she just rolls her eyes and says, "We're growing up."

Growing up sucks.

I ended up half a block behind Lizzy and her friends while walking home from school once. Lizzy whispered into the ear of one of them and the girl turned to look at me and giggled. I didn't like that.

I want Lizzy back.

I'm Randy Hodgins at eighteen. Tomorrow Mum is driving me to uni, where I'll spend most of the next four years. Lizzy isn't going, and we'll be separated for the first time in our lives.

I begged her to come with me, but she says uni isn't for her and besides, the day had to come sometime. Now I think I don't want to go, but she's consoling me, telling me we can talk anytime on the phone.

What are you going to do, I ask? She says she'll continue working at the record store for now. She enjoys it and when she's saved up enough money, she'll get a flat on her own or with a friend.

For the past few months, Lizzy hasn't ignored me and we've become close again. Not inseparable, like when we were children, but we share lots of things. We've had a really nice talk this evening, but it's getting late. Lizzy gives me a big hug, kisses my forehead, and tells me to get a good night's sleep and that everything will be fine.

I hope so.

Randy Hodgins, twenty-four, living and working in London as a contract programmer. I'm on the train home to visit Lizzy. After some frantic phone calls from me, she's admitted herself to rehab. I've promised to visit.

The haggard, unshaven man sitting opposite to me seems familiar, but my thoughts remain on Lizzy.

Once she got hooked on barbiturates, Lizzy began having more and more trouble keeping up with daily life. She was nearly fired from the store, but her boss, with whom she's been friends for years, agreed to a leave of absence.

As the train continues northward, I find myself grinding my teeth. I try to force myself to relax; I have to admit that I'm very worried.

I'm at the clinic with Lizzy. The sun takes some of the chill out of the fall air and we sit at a picnic table on the grounds. She looks thin and pale but tries her best to smile and assures me that she will beat this and get back to her life. She brightened at the sight of me, which was lovely to see. My heart aches for her. I miss her so much.

Please let her get better.

I'm Randy Hodgins, twenty-eight, and Lizzy has gone missing. She hasn't shown up for work and her roommate hasn't seen her for three days. Her friends haven't seen her for longer, but even before Lizzy withdrew it was obvious that she'd relapsed after eighteen months of sobriety.

She hasn't taken anything with her. Her clothes are still in the apartment, as is her purse, her money, and her phone. We've notified the police but they say there's little they can do.

I've never felt so helpless.

I'm Randy Hodgins, twenty-nine. Today we heard—

"No!" I scream. I'm back on the bench by the seaside. Passersby are staring, but I don't care. I can barely see them for the tears streaming down my face. My body shudders uncontrollably.

As I begin to recover, I notice that the man beside me has a concerned look on his face.

"How?" I ask. "Hypnosis?"

He shakes his head. "This is what it is to visit your own past. You relive events with some awareness of your future self. You were actually there. I thought that was what you wanted."

"So did I," I say. "But it wasn't all as I remembered. I'd forgotten about the anger Lizzy carried with her. She'd try to bottle it up but it would finally, inevitably, erupt. Forgot how she'd been so cool, so aloof towards me during our early teen years. And the end, her end, I couldn't bear to live through that again. She relapsed and then died of an overdose after living on the streets for months.

"I don't know how you did that, but thank you."

Some time passes, during which we sit in silence.

"I saw you," I say. "In the past. At least once, on the train. And here at the seafront, I've seen you at least a couple of times."

"I will visit you in your past," he says. "For you interest me greatly—you and your potential."

"For so long I've felt tied to the past. Tried to recapture it. Now that I've seen it, I'm not sure what to do anymore."

Nodding, the man says, "With your permission, I'd like to show you a glimpse of a future. A possible future."

"You can really do this? But how . . . ?"

"For now, it doesn't matter. May I?"

I look at him and see no malice in his expression, just concern. "Why not. My future can't be any worse than my past."

I'm Randy Hodgins at thirty-seven. How I came to be so old I've no idea. But no time to think about that. I have to chase after Lizzy.

I'm at the seafront, and five-year-old Lizzy is darting about the pockets of seaweed, avoiding dogs and people until she's breathless. I'm not really trying to catch her. The chase is more fun. As she stands, laughing, cheeks red with the exertion, I find that I'm bursting with more love than I've ever felt before. I pick her up and embrace her. Then I hear a whistle behind me. Emma has her new camera and wants to take a photo of us. Lizzy and I pose.

My heart aches with joy, and I hate that the vision is fading as I return to this reality. The man is gone. There's no sign of him. I get up to leave. There's something special I need to take care of.

We're sitting at our usual restaurant, Emma and I. She's looking at me strangely.

"What?" I ask.

"You seem different. Brighter. Happy even. What's happened?"

With a smile, I reach across the table and take her hand. "I've realized that I'm ready."

"Ready for what?"

"For the future. For us."

Eyes wide, she tilts her head, smiles, and squeezes my hand. "In that case, so am I."

I'm Randy Hodgins and I'm thirty-two. I've learned how to travel to my past and have done so a few times, to relive some precious moments, but I no longer live for the past. Today I live for the moment. And the future. I haven't travelled to my future since that day at the seafront. I think it will be better to simply enjoy the journey.

I've learned there's more to the past than rosy remembrances. It's messier. Happy moments seasoned with routine and unhappiness. But that's okay. The happy moments make it all worthwhile.

Mum passed away seven months ago. At the end, she seemed ready, and I think I saw relief in her face. Relief that it was finally over. At times I feel sad, at times it doesn't seem real, that she couldn't possibly be gone. But in the end, I realize that it's what she wanted.

Emma and I have been married for a year, and she's pregnant. The ultrasound shows that it's a girl. Our discussion of what to name her was brief. It was Emma who immediately suggested we call her Lizzy.

Don't Ever Change

This story came about after attending Ottawa Comiccon and noting that some celebrities never seem to age. Shreya was a late addition to the story. I added her during an aborted effort to turn this story into an audio-play. I really liked Shreya, so when I abandoned the play, I incorporated her into the written version of the story. The theme here is the inevitability of change—even if we don't want change to come. Despite appearances, there are no vampires in this story. Not really. Unless there are . . .

"You don't belong there. This is a waste of time and money. For the last time, come home."

The message was from her father. It was the latest in a string of messages and conversations in which he'd repeatedly warned that she was going to fail and should never have embarked upon this path.

Plus ça change, *the more things stay the same*, thought Shreya Chandra. And yet, just a few weeks into the fall term, she felt different from her high school self. She could no more go back to those constraints and limitations than she could go back to the womb.

Never happier than when she was busy, Shreya put aside thoughts of her father and smiled as she bustled, unpacking boxes and setting items on shelves and in drawers. Her father's warnings be damned, the engineering program fit her like a glove and was quite successfully keeping her about as busy as she could manage. And now, to finally be in residence on campus—

Before she could finish the thought, the dorm room door swung open and a young woman about her age stood and gaped at her. "What the . . ."

After a moment Shreya clued in. "Oh," she said. "You must be Mindy Travis. Hi, I'm your new roommate, Shreya, and I'm so glad to be here! You wouldn't believe where I was living before. I was late applying for rez and ended up off-campus. I was sharing with two others but the only space was, literally, a walk-in closet! So, we set up a cot and stand-up lamp and that was my room. I felt like Harry Potter before he went to Hogwarts. But then this room, well this half of a room, came up, and I was so, like, relieved? What happened to the other girl? Just curious. Did she drop out or something?"

"She died."

"She . . . what? Oh. My. God. I'm so sorry, I had no idea. I had a grandmother who died. That was last year. It was so sad. They had a big funeral for her—"

"Sorry, but could you stop talking?" Mindy closed the door behind her, shuffled to her bed, and sat heavily.

"What? Oh, of course. I'm sorry. I just prattle on, don't I? I try not to do it but I still do. Sorry."

With her coat and shoes still on, Mindy lay back on the bed and gazed upwards. "I don't mean to be rude, but I'm just back from the funeral and I'd like to have some quiet."

"Sure, I understand."

Feeling admonished—though, after all, how *could* she have known, and of *course* it was natural to ask why someone would leave residence a few weeks after term started—Shreya continued to unpack and organize and tried to do so as quietly as possible.

The desk drawer seemed like a good place to put her pens, highlighters, and sticky notes, but, upon opening it, Shreya saw something that gave her pause. It was an eight-by-ten photo. Picking it up, she saw that the subjects were a man and a woman, and the man looked like . . .

"Oh my God," said Shreya. "This is Alan Fitts. He's going all vampire on this lucky girl. Oh, wait. This isn't your friend, is it?"

"Let me see that," said Mindy, sitting bolt upright. She swung her legs around to sit on the edge of the bed and accepted the proffered photo.

"I haven't seen this since the day it was taken," said Mindy, studying it. "It was the best day of her life, she said. And mine, as it turned out. Brooke was such a fangirl. She dragged me to the con in Toronto so she could meet Alan Fitts. She wasn't planning to get the photo, but couldn't help herself once she was there. This was probably her last photo. Thanks for finding this. It means a lot."

Shreya, noting the tears welling in Mindy's eyes, said quietly, "Can I just see it again for a sec?"

Mindy held it out.

"Wow, she was really beautiful, wasn't she? Even when she was surprised like that. I guess she didn't know he was going to dip her. Look at Fitts's eyes! They're almost glowing. And his mouth is wide open, just an inch from her, like he's really going to bite her. She could probably feel his breath on her neck. What a great memory that must be."

It is a great memory, thought Mindy. She let her thoughts stray to the days before she and Brooke had become close. Mindy hadn't wanted a roommate, but roommates came with the territory when you were a student living in residence. Still, she had promised herself that she would have nothing to do with whoever she was saddled with.

They were in different programs, she and Brooke, which was promising. Less to talk about that way. Brooke had enrolled in biochemistry, Mindy in computer science. But they were both taking calculus, and one day Mindy couldn't keep her mouth shut. While Brooke was out, she'd glanced at her roommate's desk while getting a book down from the shelving unit. That's when she'd noticed the assignment on top of a jumble of papers.

Brooke Winbush, a bit light-headed from lack of sleep, stepped up to the counter at the campus Tim Hortons and ordered a large double-double dark roast. She thought about what had kept her up the previous night and shook her head. Calculus. It really wasn't her thing. If it were, she'd have gone into math! Or physics. Or maybe computing, like Mindy.

Hmmm. They'd been roommates for a month now and still Brooke wasn't much the wiser. What made Mindy tick? As far as Brooke could tell, Mindy never went out. All she did was work. But there had to be more to her than that. *Maybe she doesn't have many friends*, she thought. *Or any friends. Maybe it's time I stepped up.*

"Actually," Brooke said to the barista, "could you make that two?"

Brooke quietly opened the door and entered the dorm room. Mindy, as usual, was hunched over her desk, which was, well, organized. Clean. Laptop, a handful of textbooks arranged between metal bookends, a neat stack of notebooks, pens and pencils upright in a jar, and a pad of foolscap.

She stepped softly towards Mindy's desk, set down one of the coffees, then returned to her own desk. She was scarcely seated when she heard, or perhaps felt, Mindy jump.

Turning her head, Mindy looked in Brooke's direction, a question written on her face.

"I needed a caffeine boost and thought you might like one as well," Brooke explained.

Mindy grunted. After a moment, she said, "There's a mistake in your assignment. Question three." She spoke the words quickly, as if she needed to blurt them out before thinking better of it.

Brooke blinked. "She speaks."

"Fine," said Mindy, turning back to her work, her cheeks colouring slightly. "Never mind then."

"No, wait," said Brooke, getting to her feet. "I'm just really glad you spoke up. Honestly."

Mindy turned again and studied Brooke's face. "Your answer is almost right. But there's an error in your simplification of the derivative. Two plus five doesn't equal six."

Brooke laughed and ran a hand through her hair. "Well I guess it doesn't. That's really great of you to say that. I appreciate it."

"No problem," Mindy mumbled. She turned back to her work again.

"You don't say a lot, and maybe that was hard, speaking up just now. I really do appreciate it, just so you know." When Mindy didn't respond, she added, "Hey! You owe me two bucks."

Mindy turned and searched Brooke's face.

"Gotcha," said Brooke, and laughed. After placing a hand on Mindy's shoulder for a moment, she sat at her desk and picked up the assignment. She was pleasantly surprised to hear a slight giggle behind her.

One day, as Mindy worked, the silence felt particularly heavy. She became aware of a snuffling noise behind her. Turning, she saw that Brooke was lying on her bed, her back to Mindy, her shoulders heaving.

"Brooke?" Mindy whispered. There was no reply. Mindy crossed the small room, hesitated, then gently touched Brooke's shoulder. As Brooke turned her head, Mindy saw that her eyes were red and tears were streaming down her face.

Getting to her knees on the bed, Brooke pulled Mindy into a tight hug and began to sob openly. Mindy, taken aback, wasn't sure what to do. She didn't really like to be touched. Despite this, she tentatively, then more firmly, put her arms around her roommate and let her cry.

Her tears finally exhausted, Brooke released Mindy, blew her nose in a tissue, and talked. She talked for quite a while. It was her parents. They were divorcing. It was as if they could barely wait for Brooke to leave home so they could finally split up. And Brooke, who'd been so homesick, felt that she no longer had a home.

Mindy, uncertain as to what to say, said little. Later, Brooke told her that this was the best thing she could have done. She'd needed a sympathetic ear, not someone to tell her that everything was going to be all right, or that she was making too big a deal of it.

Brooke became Mindy's first close friend. It took her some time to process this. Sometimes Mindy experimented—she'd tell Brooke something just to see if she would make fun of or belittle her. Brooke never did.

As time passed, Mindy found herself happy in a way that she'd rarely, if ever, felt before. At least, she was pretty sure it was happiness. There were two things Mindy found difficult: reading other people and understanding her own feelings. Up until now, she'd coped with the latter by shutting them down. Pushing them aside. Yes, she was almost certainly happy, but she was puzzled by her reaction when her roommate touched her shoulder in her casual way, or when she watched Brooke absently stroke her own cheek as she studied.

As for reading other people, well, she'd tried to be analytical about it, the way she was with most things. She'd read that forty-three muscles were used to create facial expressions, and these muscles were controlled by five branches of the facial nerve. Then there were the eyes: where they looked, how quickly they blinked. And as if that weren't enough, there was posture, hand movements, tone of voice, word emphasis.

Simply put, there were too many variables. Mindy could distinguish neutrality from anger from hilarity, but subtle expressions were most often beyond her.

One day, distracted by these thoughts, Mindy sighed, gave up on studying, and stood to look out the window. It was a warmer than normal fall day. In the courtyard, a few students stood and talked. Three were playing with a Frisbee, and a couple of others sat under a tree, reading. The geese, as usual, were nearly everywhere—the walking paths were a mess.

Brooke glanced at Mindy as her roommate took a rare break. How, Brooke wondered, did Mindy manage to work for such long stretches? All Brooke knew was that if she didn't get out of this room for a while, do something different, she would lose her mind.

"Let's get out of here and blow the stink off," she said.

Mindy blinked and turned towards her. "Blow the . . . what?"

Brooke smiled, knowing that Mindy was putting together the dictionary definitions of the words to try to make sense of the expression.

"It's something one of my aunts used to say," said Brooke. "I guess it means let's get some fresh air. A change of scene will do us both good about now. And I don't know about you," said Brooke with a grin, "but my brain could definitely do with a caffeine jolt."

Mindy hesitated. Coffee shops weren't among her favourite places. With so much conversation all around, she found it hard to focus on the person she was with or, for that matter, on anything at all. Still, she said "Okay" and grabbed her jacket.

After they'd settled at a table in the campus Tim's, Brooke noticed that Mindy's shoulders were hunched and she was looking down at the table. *It's the noise*, Brooke thought. *She can't deal with it. Maybe something to distract her . . .*

"Could use your help with this," Brooke said, as she produced a book of sudoku puzzles from her bag. After flipping through the pages, she said, "Ah, yes, this one."

Mindy put down her coffee. "You play sudoku?"

"Don't act so surprised. Even biochem majors like to exercise their brains from time to time."

Mindy gulped. "I didn't mean . . . I'm sorry . . ."

"Got you!" said Brooke, a big grin on her face. Then she became serious. "No, *I'm* sorry. I give you such a hard time. You must think I'm terrible."

"No!" said Mindy, her eyes wide. Brooke smiled again, and Mindy relaxed. "Here. Just give it here."

Taking a pen from her purse, Mindy glanced at the page and began to fill in numbers. She glanced up when she was about halfway through and looked at Brooke's face. "What?"

"How do you do that? You're filling it in about as fast as you can write."

Mindy shrugged. "I'm good at patterns."

"No shit."

She pushed the finished puzzle back to Brooke.

"Thanks," Brooke said. "That one really stumped me." Putting the book away, she added, "Hey, you remember that Fan Expo is this weekend?" She smiled as Mindy rolled her eyes.

"God, Brooke, I'm your roommate. How could I not know?" Mindy flinched, and Brooke could see that she was worried she'd said the wrong thing.

"It's important to me, is all," said Brooke, reaching across the table and patting Mindy's hand. "I've been an Alan Fitts fan forever."

"Well, I'm not so much into vampires, I guess."

"You could still get a ticket at the door," said Brooke. "It's not just vampires. Robert Englund will be there."

"Who?"

"What do you mean *who*? Freddy Freaking Kreuger, that's who." Brooke chuckled, took a sip of coffee, and pondered how it was that Mindy could make her laugh so. Then something occurred to her. "Oh, but you don't like crowds, do you? I keep forgetting. Don't worry about it."

Mindy shook her head. "It's not just that. There's a computing midterm coming up and . . . No, you know what? Maybe I will go, push my boundaries a bit. I should have enough time to prepare after, and besides, it'll be nice to do something special together."

Brooke's eyes widened. "Really? Hey, that's great. Alan Fitts, here we come!"

Mindy forced her hands to unclench. She needed to distract herself from the number of people in the auditorium and the noisy buzz of conversation. There must have been at least a thousand people in the room. The chairs were arranged in two sections with an aisle down the middle. An empty podium was placed in the middle of the raised stage, flanked by a microphone stand. A large screen covered the wall behind the podium. Mindy and Brooke, after a long wait in line, had obtained seats in the fifth row from the stage on the right. "Oh boy," said Mindy, turning to her roommate. "The anticipation! I can't wait for it to start."

"Oh, stop it," said Brooke. "You know you're an Alan Fitts fan. Deep down."

"Sure . . ." After a moment's thought, she gave Brooke a light poke in the ribs with her elbow.

Brooke chuckled but then sucked in her breath as the lights dimmed and darkness enveloped the audience in its inky blackness. A video illuminated the screen.

> A slow knock at the door. Angelika Labelle's eyes widen. She is seated upon a divan in front of the hearth, her face illuminated by the blazing fire within. The camera pulls back, and we see that the apartment is lit with candles, yielding areas of light and shadow. This is accentuated by the stark black-and-white photography. Decorations include antique cabinets and clocks, a hand-woven Turkish carpet, an intricately carved coffee table, and small Renaissance-era oil paintings. Another knock and she stands, adjusts her close-fitting dress, and sashays to the door.
>
> She opens the door slowly. There is a man standing in the corridor, hands folded behind him. He wears a black suit with a dark-grey shirt and a grey-and-black-striped tie. The corridor light is garishly

bright, causing the woman to blink and raise her hand over her eyes.

A smile comes to Angelika's face. She lowers her head slightly and looks up at the visitor, eyes half lidded. "Well this is a welcome surprise."

"May I come in?" says Charles Bardell.

Angelika steps back and waves her arm. Charles enters, and she closes the door behind him.

Stepping in front of the hearth, Charles regards the flames; the light dances in his dark eyes.

"Wine?" asks Angelika, moving to the buffet. She reaches for a decanter filled with red liquid.

"No," says Charles. "No, I'm here on business."

"Business," says Angelika, as she moves towards Charles. "Well now I *am* intrigued."

Charles turns rapidly and grasps Angelika by the forearm.

"Charles!" Angelika's eyes widen. "What are you doing?"

"You killed them. Those men. Why?"

Angelika blinks and her mouth opens slightly. Then, composing herself, she looks away. "I'm sure I've no idea what you're talking about."

"You seduced Doctor Boreanaz and blackmailed him. He provided you with the insulin and syringes you needed."

"My, you are fanciful. Why on earth would I do such a thing?"

"They uncovered the truth about your past. As have I."

Charles lets go of her then, and Angelika backs away, eyebrows raised. "What are you going to do?"

"Deliver justice."

Angelika laughs. Moving to the buffet again, she pours a glass of wine, giving away a slight tremor in her hand, and takes a sip. "So," she says, "you're a policeman now?"

"I'm no policeman." His words sound like a low growl. Approaching her once again, his face is dark with both anger and sadness. And something else. Hunger?

Angelika tries to back away but bumps into the buffet. Setting down her glass, she rests her shaking hands on the surface behind her. Charles approaches and bends so that he is very close to her neck. The camera closes in, showing the pores of her skin and his open mouth with its white teeth.

"Charles, this is hardly the time," Angelika says weakly, her body trembling.

> "This is the only time," Charles whispers.
>
> His canines grow, and when they reach full length, Charles bites down on her carotid and drinks deeply. The camera moves to his eyes. They're alight with energy. The camera pulls away and focuses on the roaring fire in the hearth.

The video faded to black, and Mindy and Brooke blinked as the auditorium lights came on. The audience erupted into applause, and Brooke clapped and cheered and whistled with the rest of them. Mindy remained unimpressed.

The applause faded as a man walked across the stage and raised his hands. "And now," he said, "without further ado, here he is, your favourite justice-dealing vampire, Charles Bardell himself!"

"So here we are," said Mindy. "In another queue."

Brooke didn't mind standing in a queue. She felt totally in her element. It was crowded, everyone was upbeat, and there were a lot of cosplayers. One of these days, she'd build up the nerve to come in cosplay herself. A couple of Daleks rolled past, threatening to exterminate all humans in their path.

When Brooke remembered what she was in line *for*, she thought she might throw up. Or faint. Possibly both. *Deep breaths*, she thought. *Deep breaths*. "Are you sure you won't join me?" she said to Mindy.

"I'm sure, thanks. I'll be waiting for you when you're done. Um . . . just don't let him anywhere near your neck."

"Not much chance of that. Oh my God! It's nearly my turn. I can't believe this is going to happen."

"What happens next?"

"There's another queue—don't worry, just a short one—inside the tent. When you're up, they take your photo and then you go and wait for the printout. It won't take long."

Brooke handed Mindy her bag, gave her a hug, and joined the short queue inside the photography tent. She could hear his voice now, which sounded exactly the same as on TV. Should she be surprised? Probably not. And there he was, wearing blue jeans and a black hoodie. He was posing with the woman who'd been in front of her, arm around her shoulder. The photographer said, "One, two, three!" and snapped the photo. Alan Fitts thanked the woman and turned to Brooke.

A moment of eye contact, then Brooke took a deep breath and moved forward, feeling that this was happening in slow motion. There were two Xs marked on the floor. As Brooke moved to her position, the actor took her hands then twisted and dipped her, as if they had just finished a tango.

Unable to breathe, Brooke heard the photographer say, "Look this way, please."

She did, then felt Alan Fitts's hot breath on her neck. Feeling almost faint, she heard the photographer call out, "One, two, three!"

Brooke left the actor in a daze. When she picked up her photo, she nearly swooned again. A small crowd formed around her, admiring, jealous. In the photograph, Brooke was nearly parallel to the ground, her mouth open. The actor was bent over, his head near her neck, his teeth visible, his dark eyes facing the camera.

Clutching the photo to her chest, she looked about for Mindy.

Mindy saw her first. "Brooke, you look . . . happy."

"Mindy! You won't believe this. Take a look at the photo. Everyone was so envious."

After gazing at the photo a moment, Mindy said, "What did I tell you about letting him near your neck?"

Brooke giggled. "Couldn't help it. He kinda took me by surprise."

"Jeez," said Mindy, "how old is this guy?"

"Fifty-two. Can you believe it?"

"Not really. More like midthirties, I'd say. It's a great photo. You must be happy."

"Come on," said Brooke. "Let's get out of here. I think I've had enough excitement for one day."

After walking the short distance to Union Station, they caught the 4:50 to Waterloo. Both passed the journey in silence. Brooke, still wide-eyed from her Alan Fitts encounter, frequently retrieved the photo and stared at it lovingly, which made Mindy smile.

Back in their dorm room that evening, Mindy watched from the window as Brooke skipped along the path on her way to pick up some coffee. Turning, she noted Brooke's side of the room. It was a mess, as usual. Bed unmade, textbooks and notebooks scattered all over, laundry on the floor, a stack of Coke cans on her desk in roughly the shape of castle ramparts. *Different strokes*, she thought, an expression she'd often heard Brooke use.

No sooner had she sat down to work than there was a knock at the door. With a sigh, Mindy got up and opened it. It was two students from her computing class. The boy was Jay, the girl was . . . Cynthia. Mindy regularly absorbed and retained all sorts of information, useful or not.

"We were wondering . . ." Jay faltered under Mindy's icy glare.

"What we were wondering," continued Cynthia, "was whether you'd be willing to host a review session for us. For some of us from the computing class. We're getting a bit bogged down and the exam is in just a couple of days."

"You've left it pretty late, haven't you?" said Mindy. So had she, to be honest. Taking the day off hadn't been the absolute smartest strategy. Now there was little time to get organized for the midterm.

"We'd really appreciate it . . ." said Jay, faltering again.

"We would," said Cynthia. "It'd be a great thing to do."

Mindy hesitated. No one had asked her for help before. Not here. But she had her own grades to consider and time was tight. "So, I'm supposed to let my grade suffer to help you cram at the last minute? Sorry. No."

Jay opened his mouth but Mindy interrupted. "I said no." As she closed the door, Mindy paused and opened it again. "Look, if there's something specific, right now, I could help with that."

"Forget it," said Cynthia. "Far be it from us to waste your valuable time."

She and Jay turned and walked towards the elevators. Mindy could just hear Cynthia say, "I told you she wouldn't go for it. Thinks of nobody but herself. She'll never change."

About an hour later, Mindy, engrossed in the intricacies of Scheme, scarcely heard the door open. She was jolted back to reality when a cup of coffee appeared on her desk.

"Oh my God, Brooke," she said, whirling around. "You nearly scared me to death."

Giggling, Brooke picked up the photo from her desk and passed it to Mindy. "What do you think? I mean, really. Isn't it great?"

Mindy stood and passed the photo back to her roommate. "Yes, it's still a great photo. And I'm sure one day your feet will touch the ground again." Mindy noted the light in her roommate's eyes, the flush in her cheeks, and saw that Brooke, generally quite laid-back, was so consumed with excitement that she could scarcely stand still, shifting her weight from one foot to another.

Resting her hands on Brooke's shoulders, Mindy said, "Slow down, girl, you're making me dizzy." They held eye contact for a moment, then Brooke pulled her close and held her tight.

"Oh, thank you for being you," said Brooke. "There's no one I'd rather share this with. Don't ever change."

Mindy caught her breath and then, inexplicably, she found herself crying, then sobbing as she hugged her roommate back.

Brooke pulled away and looked at Mindy, a puzzled expression on her face. "Mindy? I don't think I've ever seen you cry before. What is it?"

After Mindy summarized the visit from her classmates, Brooke said, "Screw them. You were absolutely right. They *did* leave it to the last minute. And I hope you never do change. As far as I'm concerned, you're perfect."

Wiping the tears from her face, Mindy said, "It's just that nobody likes me. No one ever has."

"Then they don't know what they're missing. All they need is to spend a bit of time getting to know the real you. I'm glad I did."

Mindy felt tears forming in her eyes again, and this time she pulled Brooke into a hug and held her. Brooke squeezed her in return. After a while, Brooke slowly pulled back, her cheek gently dragging along Mindy's. And as she continued to pull away, their lips brushed against each other, just for a moment.

Electricity shot through Mindy. Brooke, like her, was wide-eyed, but Mindy couldn't quite read her expression. There were too many cues to grasp and resolve.

Brooke moved her lips slowly towards hers, her eyes closing. In a daze, Mindy did the same.

They kissed, softly, briefly.

"What just happened?" said Mindy.

"I'm not sure," said Brooke. "Was that okay?"

"I . . . I think so. What about for you?"

With a smile, Brooke said, "I'll tell you after you kiss me again."

The photo fluttered to the floor.

"You're not getting up today?" said Mindy.

"Can't. Too sick. My mum is coming to take me home."

"Oh, Brooke. The campus doctor couldn't tell you what's wrong?"

"No, and I'm getting worse every day. Mindy, I feel so weak. I've got to do something. I don't want to leave you, but . . ."

"Don't be silly. You need to get healthy. And you will. You'll be back here before you know it."

"I hope so. But if I'm not, I mean, the way I feel, if I don't make it for some reason—"

Mindy touched Brooke's lips with her forefinger. "Don't even think it. You'll be fine. I'll stay with you until your mum gets here. Just get some rest."

"Thanks, love."

"Hmmm? What?" said Mindy, coming back to the present. How long had she been lost in her memories? "Sorry, what did you say?"

"No, it's okay," said Shreya. "I was just saying that this must be such a great memory."

"Yes," said Mindy, "but I was trying to remember. What did I say to her before she got this photo?" It was something obvious, something that made Brooke laugh. "Oh, right. I told her, 'Don't let him anywhere near your neck.' She thought this photo was the best thing ever. Couldn't take her eyes off of it."

"When was this taken?"

"Not long ago, actually," said Mindy. "Though it feels like forever. It was at the con in Toronto, just a few weeks ago. Then she got sick and—"

"What?"

A thought had come to Mindy. A ridiculous, terrible thought. Ridiculous, but what if . . .

She glanced at Shreya. "Sorry, but I've got some work to do."

Shreya, who'd been trying to work her way through an obtuse lab assignment, finally gave up. "Jeez," she said, turning around in her chair. "Mindy, your laptop is chiming up a storm. What gives?"

There was no answer. She seemed transfixed by her laptop's screen. "Mindy? What's the matter?"

"I just . . . I just got the results back," Mindy said, without turning.

"Exam results?"

"Results from the bot I wrote."

"Sorry, what?"

"I programmed a bot to search the Internet and correlate encounters with Alan Fitts and subsequent death notices."

Shreya considered this. "You mean, in case Brooke wasn't the only one who died after meeting him?"

"Exactly. Look at what it found."

She got up and peered over Mindy's shoulder. "Let me see? Oh . . . shut up. But, what does it mean?" Shreya could see full well what it meant but needed Mindy to say it.

"It means that a lot of people who get their photo taken with Alan Fitts die." She opened up a new browser window and entered a search. "He's going to appear at a con in Vancouver this weekend. I think I'm going to have a little chat with him."

"Mindy, you think he's involved in the deaths of these people and you're going to confront him? Seriously? Why?"

Mindy finally turned towards Shreya. "It doesn't matter why. I just have to do this."

Shreya could see that Mindy was deadly serious. "I see. I think." But to let Mindy go alone? Shreya didn't see how she could sleep at night if she did. And yet, Shreya was already flouting her father just by being here. If she did what she was thinking of . . .

Well, might as well go all in.

"I'm coming with you, Mindy."

"When was the last time you actually slept? You look like crap."

Mindy thought about it. She hadn't slept more than an hour or two per night for . . . actually, she wasn't sure how many nights. All she knew was that, after an interminable flight to Vancouver and a night tossing and turning at the hotel, the wait for Alan Fitts's first autograph session was almost unbearable. This morning she'd skipped breakfast, grabbed some coffee, and arrived at the Convention Centre way before opening time. Shreya, who hadn't skipped breakfast, had joined her later.

"I don't know. I can't sleep. Not until this is over."

Shreya's phone rang. Taking it from her back pocket, she groaned.

"Who is it?" said Mindy.

"My mother. I shouldn't answer, but if I don't, I swear she'll be calling the police in an hour." With a sigh, Shreya took the call. "Mummy. How are you?" She moved a few steps away.

"What was that about?" said Mindy, when Shreya returned to the queue minutes later.

"Long story short, my father doesn't think engineering is any place for a woman. The only reason I'm in the program is that my uncle is the patriarch of the family and I'm a favourite of his. He laid down the law and told my father to support me. Poor Mummy is stuck in the middle."

In her exhausted state, Mindy felt her eyes become teary. "And you still came here with me?"

"Hey, it's important right? Besides, we ladies have to stand up for one another. So, don't sweat it."

There were twenty people ahead of them. Mindy looked at her phone. Ten minutes to go. Assuming he arrived on time. She shifted her weight from one foot to the other and blinked repeatedly to try to stay awake.

They were lined up in tidy rows—over one hundred fans so far. A table with two chairs was set in front of a row of black curtains. An assistant was already seated. Next to her was a metal box for the fifty-dollar fee and eight-by-ten photos of Fitts in various poses and costumes. Coloured markers were placed on the table near the empty chair.

Finally, the curtains parted and Fitts emerged to a round of applause. With a wave and a grin, he took his seat and the first in line approached him.

After taking a gulp of coffee, Mindy held out the cup to Shreya. "Would you hold this, please?"

"No problem. Last chance—are you sure about this?"

"Very sure. Just let me do the talking, though, okay?"

When their turn came, Mindy found herself not angry, not nervous, just cold. Ice cold.

Fitts smiled and extended a hand to shake. Mindy simply took a photo from the folder she held and set it down in front of him. Fitts looked at the photo then at her. "If that's you, then you weren't wearing nearly enough sun block back then."

"That's Brooke Winbush, my friend. You met her in Toronto. She's dead."

Fitts blinked and looked up at her. Mindy continued, setting down five more photos. "Susan Stanford, Calgary. Rachel Thompson, Chicago. Flo Jenkins, Houston. Kate Saunders, San Diego. Mary Robins, Nashville. All dead a few weeks after meeting you. In all cases, the cause of death was unexplained. And this is just going back three years."

Fitts's mouth started to open then closed.

"See a pattern?" said Mindy.

Fitts glanced at his assistant, who appeared concerned. Shaking his head slightly, he turned back to Mindy. "Look." He reached for one of his own photos and scribbled on the back. "I can see you're upset. Let's talk. Give this to one of the volunteers. They'll let you into my dressing room after this session is over." He looked up at her. "Okay?"

"Sure," said Mindy. *So far, so good.* She collected her photos and left, trailed by Shreya.

The volunteer in the celebrity area seemed to be expecting them. She didn't say a word as Mindy presented Fitts's note, just beckoned them to follow. When they reached Fitts's dressing room, the woman knocked and entered, and then closed the door behind them. Fitts asked the volunteer to stay in the room, which suited Mindy fine. *We've both got our witnesses*, she thought.

Taking a seat, Fitts beckoned Mindy and Shreya to sit opposite him. "We weren't introduced properly before," said Fitts. "Alan Fitts."

"Mindy Travis."

Fitts turned his gaze to Shreya, who narrowed her eyes. "I'm with her."

"I see." Turning back to Mindy, Fitts said, "I just want to be sure that we're on the same page about something. You know, right, that Charles Bardell is a role that I play? That I'm not actually him? Not a vampire?"

Mindy nodded.

"Ah. Okay, good. But you'd be surprised by some of my fans."

"I'm not actually one of your fans," said Mindy. "Sorry."

Fitts blinked. "Refreshingly honest. I like that." He flashed Mindy what she assumed was one of his patented grins, until he saw that it had no impact on her. "So, what? You think that I'm involved in the deaths of these girls?"

"Aren't you?"

"Um, no."

"Yes, you are. You didn't drink their blood. Of course not. But you did *something* to them. It's a bit of a coincidence otherwise, don't you think?"

"Tell me something. How did you get this information in the first place?"

"Brooke was my roommate. My friend. As for the others, I programmed a bot to search the Internet for mentions of you and correlated those with obituaries."

"Clever. I'm impressed. You're probably good with math, then, right?"

Mindy nodded.

"So, here's some math for you. During one day at a con like this, I'll have at least four hour-long autograph sessions with, let's say, twenty seconds per fan. I'm usually at a con for three days. On top of that, I have up to three photo-op sessions with, say, 150 fans each, half of whom, don't also get an autograph. How many do we have so far?"

"Over 2,300," said Mindy without hesitation.

"Right. Now, let's say I do six cons per year. That's over fourteen thousand. And if we go back three years, that's over forty thousand. And out of all of those, six people passed away?"

"I . . ." Mindy didn't have a comeback. She was so lacking in sleep that she felt as if her brain were short-circuiting.

"How did these women die?"

"The doctors couldn't explain it. Complete internal organ failure. No one knows what caused it."

"And how do you think I might have caused this? I mean, exactly?"

"You tell me. It likely requires physical contact, and likely you have to want it to happen, otherwise everyone who touched you would die. That would be too obvious. Somehow you can sap a person's life force. You feed upon it. It's how you keep yourself so young."

Fitts chuckled. "Thanks for the compliment. About looking young. But it might have more to do with exercise, diet, and genetics. I mean, life *force*? I think you'll find that, biologically, there's no such thing."

"But it's a pattern," said Mindy. "It's still a pattern."

"A pattern," said Fitts. "Tell me. Did you ever see that movie *A Beautiful Mind*?"

She had. Russell Crowe played the brilliant, though occasionally delusional, John Nash.

"He was good at seeing patterns," continued Fitts. "Too good. He saw them even when they weren't there."

Mindy didn't answer. She couldn't. It was all she could do to keep from shaking uncontrollably. Glancing towards Shreya, she thought her roommate's face spoke of… Anger? Concern? As usual, she couldn't work it out.

Speaking up, Shreya said, "It's not just the number of death's though, is it? It's the fact that they died within a few weeks of meeting you, and that the cause of death is unknown."

Fitts ignored Shreya and focused his attention upon Mindy. Taking her hand and holding it in both of his, he said, "I'm sorry. I'm very, very sorry that your friend is dead. That all these people are dead. But I promise you, it had nothing to do with me."

"Mindy, I wish you'd talk to me," Shreya said, when they were back in their dormitory. "You've said nothing since Vancouver."

"There's nothing to say."

"What I really don't understand is, you thought he was killing people by touching them and then you let him touch you? What if you were right?" When Mindy didn't respond, Shreya considered this further. "Or were you hoping to make yourself a martyr? To expose him? Do you really think you've nothing left to live for?"

Mindy, still silent, sat at her desk and opened her laptop.

After staring at Mindy for a moment, Shreya said, "Well, I won't pester you. But I'm here if you feel like talking. Okay? You could at least nod . . . Fine, never mind!"

Frustrated, Shreya was about to sit at her desk when there was a knock at the door. She opened it with an abrupt "Hi."

"Hi. I'm Cynthia. I'm in one of Mindy's classes. Can I speak to her?"

"Sure," said Shreya, "she's right here."

Mindy sighed and faced the door but didn't get up. "This really isn't the time—"

"I'm not here for help. I just wanted to say . . . I wanted to say I'm sorry about Brooke. She seemed nice. She spoke to us about you, you know. Told us that you were pretty wonderful. That we'd never given you a chance. So, I wanted to apologize for that. And I wanted to ask, do you think we might become friends? You and I? Would you like to give that a try?"

Mindy stepped forward and studied Cynthia's face.

"What?" said Cynthia.

Mindy started. "Sorry. Sometimes I look at a person's face and try to . . . Never mind. Sure, why not?"

Cynthia brightened. "Great! I'd really like that. When you're ready, I'll be here."

"Thanks," said Mindy, and closed the door. "And thanks to you too, Shreya. I'm sorry about just now. It's the way I get sometimes. I try not to be like that, but it's hard. I do appreciate your coming with me all the way to Vancouver. And you're right. I was thinking about making myself a martyr. For Brooke. But that was silly, wasn't it? You must think I'm a fool."

"Of course not. Anyway, you've been through so much. I can't even imagine."

"Did you know that Brooke and I were . . . lovers? Yes, I thought you did. That day, after she and I came back from the con, she said I should never change, that I was 'perfect.' And yet, I am changing. But she was the one who set me on this road, so I think that's okay. I don't think she'd mind."

"I didn't know Brooke," said Shreya, "but no, I don't think she'd mind at all. I'm sure she's proud of you, wherever she is."

Glancing at the wall calendar, Shreya wondered how it could be the end of March already. "That snow we had yesterday?" she said, moving to the dorm room's window, "it looks like it's pretty much gone now. Spring is definitely in the air."

"What's that? Snow? Sorry, I was just thinking that it's time to get organized for exams."

"Of course you were . . ." said Shreya, trailing off as she heard her phone buzz. Oh Lord, a text message from her father. Although tempted to ignore it, she didn't.

"Oh, shut up!"

"What is it?" said Mindy.

"It's from my father. I can't believe it. Listen to this: *Daughter, your grades in the engineering program have been excellent and I may have been hasty in my advice to you. It is my sincere wish that you continue to excel. Best of luck with your exams.*"

"Wow," said Mindy. "A bit stiff, but that almost resembles an apology."

"Right? I mean, who is this man and what has he done with my father?"

Mindy giggled, and Shreya regarded her. "I've been meaning to tell you that you seem much better than when we first met. Happier, I mean."

Mindy gave that some thought. "I think I am. Brooke's death was a fresh wound then, and I didn't think I'd ever have another friend. I guess I needed to blame somebody, so I blamed a TV vampire of all people. Now there's you and Cynthia in my life. I'll always miss Brooke, but I've a lot to be grateful for."

"Well, I'm sorry that you lived a life where having friends was a novelty," said Shreya. "I hope those days are gone for good. You do have a lot to offer, you know."

"Thanks. And—" Mindy was interrupted by a ping from her laptop. "Now what could that be? I don't think I have any calendar events for today."

"Mindy?" Shreya frowned. "What is it? You've turned pale as a ghost. Bad news?"

"I . . . I can't . . . Come see."

"What is it? How bad can it . . ." Shreya's eyes widened. "Oh no. No way."

Mindy read aloud: "*Keya Chadha: died March 25; age twenty-one; met Alan Fitts March 3.*"

Remember Me?

The way in which Will meets Sam (the cat) is similar to something that happened to me. I was walking by the waterfront in Kingston and a cat came out of the darkness. It walked alongside of me, slowing when I slowed, picking up the pace when I did. Finally, I knelt down and said to the cat, "I can't take you home with me." Which I couldn't. The cat's eyes widened, and then it turned and disappeared into the darkness.

I'm writing this on May 8, 2019. When are you reading this, I wonder? Oh, I'm not talking about just any reader. No, if you're not *her*, and by that I mean if you haven't met me and taken me . . . places, then you're not the *you* I mean.

When you left, you said that you'd be right back. That was two years ago. Obviously, "right back" has a different meaning for you than for me. Mind you, you told me once that, sometimes, time works differently *there* than *here*. So maybe only minutes have passed wherever you are. It's also possible that something's happened, that you're injured somewhere, or worse. But I choose to believe that you're simply . . . distracted. And I know from our travels together that there are a lot of distractions waiting for you.

I'm not sure what I'm supposed to do now, after the marvels you've shown me, knowing that they're out there but beyond my reach. I feel like I've been in limbo. Yes,

Remember Me?

I've done some work, but only half-heartedly. And as for relationships, I've neglected the people I know and haven't sought new friends or acquaintances. Perhaps I haven't yet accepted that you're not coming back any time soon, if at all, to whisk me away. I know it's not healthy to live like this, so I'm writing you this letter. Perhaps it will act as a kind of therapy.

Before we met . . . funny, but it's hard to imagine that there *was* a time before we met. But there was, and before we met, I was doing all right. I wasn't rich but had enough to get by, with some savings on the side. Socially, well, I was content enough, though not overly happy. I'd recently lost a friend, and I've never had many of those, especially the close ones. I don't mean that they died; it was more like they woke up one morning and, as they were brushing their teeth, thought we might as well not be friends anymore. All I know is that they dropped out of touch, ignoring messages and phone calls, making their intent abundantly clear in the resounding silence.

This wasn't the first time that this had happened, and I wondered sometimes, what was the point in getting close to another person if, in the end, they were going to abandon you. Or was there something the matter with me? Did I drive people away? Did I drive you away? Did I matter to you? Or was I just one of countless people you've encountered, befriended, and more? It didn't occur to me at the time, but that's most likely the case, isn't it?

Do you remember the day we met? I'd been gazing at the marina in Confederation Park, contemplating the ephemeral nature of friendship, and was quite lost in thought. Behind me, I heard you say, "Well, that was close." I turned in your direction. You seemed to have staggered, or tripped over something.

I'd neither seen nor heard you coming. The park had been near deserted. Steadying yourself, you looked around and noticed me standing a few feet away, and I'm sure I was regarding you with a curious expression. After all, you were naked.

With a tired smile, you said hello.

I blinked and asked, "Are you okay? Are you in trouble?"

"Oh, right," you said. "People normally wear clothes in this world. Don't worry, I can fix that."

And with that, you pulled clothing out of your leather backpack and dropped it onto the ground around you. "You can turn around if you're bothered," you said. "Sorry if I embarrassed you."

I did turn. "I'm not so much embarrassed as worried."

"Thanks," you said. "But don't mind me. I'm fine. There. How do I look?"

I still remember what you were wearing: a Panama hat with a black ribbon tied in a bow; a blue long-sleeved crewneck shirt; khaki trousers; and red-leather shoes. Your curly auburn hair, which glinted in the sun, dropped to almost shoulder length. There was something about your hair. I couldn't put my finger on it at the time. Later, I realized that, somehow, your hair was always in motion, even if there was no breeze, as if it had a life all its own.

"You look fine," I said, and I turned to leave once you'd assured me that you were all right.

That's when you said, "Actually, can you hang on a second? I'm looking for someone, and you're not them, but there has to be a reason why I've come upon you."

"Does there?" I said. "Have to be a reason?"

"I think so. You know what? I would love a coffee. Is there a shop nearby where we could chat for a few minutes? Would that be okay?"

I regarded you, an apparently unassuming, guileless woman. Your expression was sunny and your smile infectious. I really didn't know what to make of you, but I was curious.

"Sure," I said. "There's one just a couple of minutes away."

As we started off, you said, "My name's Susan. Susan Follows."

"I'm Will Fallon. Nice to meet you, Susan."

"Oh, this is good," you said, sipping your dark roast. I'd chosen my favourite, an Americano, which was an indulgence, but it seemed like that kind of day.

As usual, the shop was bustling with patrons coming and going, and the tables were jammed with people talking or working on laptops. Throughout the space, the delicious smell of coffee mingled with the sweet odour of chocolate.

"You said you were looking for someone," I reminded you.

"Right. Yes, I am. And you're the link, but I'm not sure how."

I was probably looking at you expectantly, waiting for you to say more. After taking a couple more sips of coffee, you did.

"Have you heard of the multiverse theory?"

I smiled. I was getting the sense that keeping you fixed on one topic at a time was going to be a challenge. "Changing the subject?"

"Not really, no. Have you?"

"Yes," I said.

"Great. So somewhere out there, there are other places, other realities, reflecting different choices, different events, and even different laws of physics."

"Okay, sure."

"And sometimes, there are cracks between the realities. And sometimes, people can fall into them."

You seemed quite serious, so I went along. "So, people literally fall through the cracks. From one reality to another?"

"Exactly! Well done. The person I'm looking for has done just that. I'm here to help them get back to their own reality."

"And you think I can help?" I said.

"I'm fairly sure, yes."

"So what happened, exactly?" I said, deciding to suspend my disbelief for the moment. "How did you end up here?"

"I came upon a crack in reality. It was closing. And the way it was humming, I could tell that somebody had passed through. The only way that I'd be able to help bring them back was to follow them before the crack closed, so that's what I did, and I barely made it. Half a minute later and it would have been too late."

"So that's why you said 'that was close' earlier."

You nodded. "Sometimes, the crack, the doorway, whatever you want to call it, it takes me right to the person who crossed over. Other times, not so much, and some detective work is called for. I've done this enough times now that I'm turning into a regular Sexton Blake."

"Sorry, who?"

"Ah. Never mind. Just me showing my age."

We were both quiet for a time. "Well," I said, resting my head on my hand, "I'm not sure what to say to all that."

"You don't believe me. Never mind, I can prove it to you after. But for now, tell me about yourself."

Honestly, I thought about just getting up and leaving. But I was curious, and I remember thinking that maybe I could use a character inspired by you in a story. But how much of myself should I reveal to a perfect stranger? There wouldn't be any harm, I supposed, in telling you what you could find out by doing a Google search.

"There's not too much to tell. I consult as a technical writer, I've published a couple of short stories, and I write the odd book review for the *Globe and Mail*."

"I need you to think. Has anything out of the ordinary happened to you lately?"

That gave me pause. I lived a fairly quiet life. I had a lot of acquaintances and ran into them all the time. Kingston is that kind of town. But I had few close friends, fewer all the time it seemed, and I rarely went out. As for odd things happening . . .

"I won a hundred dollars in the lottery," I said. "My first lottery win."

"Congratulations," you said. "But that's not it. Anything else?"

I considered, then it came to me. "You know, the only truly odd thing was when I met my cat."

You perked right up, so I continued. "I was walking by the lakefront one evening a couple of months ago when a small cat, little more than a kitten, came out of the darkness. She kept pace with me, stopping when I stopped and walking when I walked. I finally stopped and bent down to pet her. Noticing that she had no collar or tag, I figured someone must have abandoned the poor thing. So, I said to her, 'I guess there's nothing for it. You'll have to come home with me.' The thing that was odd wasn't the way she emerged from the darkness to join me, but the way her eyes widened when I said that."

I remember that you just about jumped out of your seat. "That's it! That's who I'm looking for. What's your cat's name?"

"Um, it's Sam. Short for Samantha. So you're telling me that you've been looking for my cat? Did you lose her?"

"I think she lost herself. Will you take me to see her?"

"Just wait a second. You said you were looking for a *person*."

For a moment, you looked puzzled. Then I saw realization in your face. "Of course. You think she's just a cat. Except she's not. First, I had no idea who I was looking for, just someone who had accidentally come into this world. Second, where she comes from, cats are considered to be 'people' as much as you or I."

Remember Me?

It was at this point that I decided this had gone far enough. "No, I'm sorry, but I don't think I will be taking you to see her."

"Ah. Right. You want proof. Tell you what: This evening, say at dusk, come back to the park where we met. I'll show you something special that will change your life."

"I'll think about it," I said. "Meanwhile, it's been fascinating to meet you, Susan. Enjoy your day."

And with that, I rose, we shook hands, and I left the shop. I turned when I got to the door and saw you sipping your coffee, your eyes closed, your face full of contentment.

Do you remember where I live? It's on the top floor of a beautiful old house, a short walk from the courthouse. My living space is quite idiosyncratic, with sloping ceilings, alcoves, and oddly shaped rooms. It has a unique personality and I love it.

When I sat down at my desk after returning from the coffee shop, Sam leaped onto my lap and settled herself down, her claws digging slightly into my legs. I've still no idea what breed of cat she is. I don't really care. I think she's a mix. All I know is she has a white belly and the rest of her is alternately white, orange, and black.

"Were your ears burning?" I asked her. "I was talking about you with someone, and they were very interested. I wonder if I should have thrown caution to the wind for once and invited her here?"

Sam purred while I scritched. "Where *did* you come from, I wonder?" With that, Sam turned her head towards me for a moment, then lay it down again on my lap. That's when I made up my mind to meet up with you again.

The day droned on and I found myself restless, unable to focus on the story I'd been writing. I had no better luck getting into the book I'd promised to review for the *Globe*. It was near dusk when I set out from my unit. As I walked, I wondered why I was doing this. It made no sense, so I supposed it was pure instinct. Something told me I should. And knowing myself, if I didn't, I'd always wonder what would have happened.

Having reached the park, I sat upon the reconstructed Market Battery wall and looked around. There was no sign of you. After a time, I'm not sure how many minutes, I saw you strolling up the path in my direction and looking around like a tourist who'd arrived at her favourite destination.

"You came!" you said with a big smile. "Fabulous."

As you approached and took a seat beside me, you said, "First, a question. Are you sure? Are you sure you want to see this? Because once you do, nothing will ever be the same. Are you ready for that?"

I shook my head and you looked disappointed. "I think you believe what you've been telling me," I said, "but yes, I really do need to see something pretty amazing to be convinced. So go ahead. Amaze me."

There was a tall, old tree near one corner of the park. You led me there, and I realized it was because we'd be sheltered from prying eyes, at least for the moment. After telling me to stand back, you positioned your hands in the air as if you were about to pry open a sliding door. Then you opened it.

Remember Me?

Beyond the entrance, I could see another world. What struck me first was the light, it had a distinct magenta hue. There were mountains in the distance, their peaks disappearing into blue clouds. The ground was covered with tall bright-yellow grasses, and upon the grasses were creatures I'd never imagined, large and small, buzzing, singing, chirping. Some were as large as elephants and had round orifices, mouths I assumed, on the sides of their bodies. Some were as small as golf balls. In fact, they looked like golf balls, white and round and dimpled, but they jutted about purposefully, changing direction willy-nilly.

I stepped back, stunned, and stumbled, falling backwards, never taking my eyes off that incredible sight. "Enough," I croaked.

You let go of the door and it closed. Sitting down beside me, you patted my hand. "All right?"

I nodded, speechless. My heart was pounding in my chest. I swallowed and took a breath. Finally, I said, "How?"

"How? You mean, how did I do that?"

Again, I nodded.

"No idea, really, I just can. Look, you've had a shock. Shall we head to your place, give you a chance to recover a bit? Then we can talk some more."

I fumbled with the key as I let us into my unit. You insisted I take a seat in the living room, then you made a pot of jasmine tea and set it on a tray with a couple of large mugs.

After taking a few sips, I came back to myself and took a good look at you. I'd deliberately not done that since the park, feeling a need to ground myself in reality.

Sam, who'd been hiding up until then, came up and rubbed against your leg. You knelt down and said, "Hello, you beautiful thing. May I pick you up?"

She seemed to look right at you then, and you lifted her and held her close, petting her between the ears and under her chin. "I've come to take you home. What do you think of that?" Seemingly in response, Sam purred contentedly.

"Look," I said, feeling that I was losing control of my sanity. "Who are you? Where are you from?"

Setting Sam down, you said, "I'm from Toronto. Whether this world's Toronto or not, it's hard to tell anymore. I was born in 1903. Time can pass differently in the other worlds. When you spend time in them, sometimes much more time has passed here. Or less. It depends. I honestly don't know how old I am at this point. Sometimes it feels like I've been doing this forever.

"As for travelling to other worlds, it started when I was twenty and came across a homeless man. He seemed, I don't know, out of place somehow, bewildered and lost, like he couldn't believe where he was. It was near dawn, and I was on my way home from a speakeasy, still dressed in my breezy black dress. I knelt down beside the man and found that the closer I got, the greater the feeling that he didn't belong.

"'You poor thing,' I said. 'You're really quite lost, aren't you?' I patted his arm then stood quickly. I thought I heard a humming. I moved in its direction and realized that it wasn't a hum, not really. I was just interpreting the sensation as a hum. I came to the source of it and, after some trial and error, pulled at something in the thin air, like a heavy curtain. That's the best way of describing it. And there was another world, but not just any world. It was the world that the man had come from. Taking his hand, I helped him to his feet and, together, we crossed over.

"I spent some time there. I'm not sure how much. But when I returned to my world, it was the late 1940s. I'd missed the Great Depression and World War II. My parents were dead, and my brother had aged twenty years and had a family of his own. I didn't go to him. How could I have explained where I'd been or why I hadn't aged? So, with nothing in my world to tie me down, I set off exploring, helping displaced people whenever I could. Trying to do some good with this gift I had."

I got up and paced around the room. "I feel I must be dreaming," I said to you. "Like I'm going to wake up and none of this will have happened."

"Speaking of dreaming," you said, "maybe a good night's sleep will help. And sex. I love sex, don't you?"

"What?" I said stupidly.

"I mean, let's both sleep in your bed, if that's all right with you. I'm not fond of sleeping alone. And if we feel like having sex, we can do that, too. You don't have to marry me or anything. Sorry, I'm not sure what the norms are in this world for this kind of thing. Have I said something very shocking?"

"No," I said automatically, and realized it was true. I was shaken, my sense of what was real and what wasn't, shattered. I needed comfort. The reassurance of simple human warmth. I realized that you were both the cause of my distress and the cure. "I don't think I want to spend the night alone either."

Sam had always been happy enough to stay indoors, but not all the time. When she was ready, she would scratch at the door until I let her out. Sometimes this was in the evening, sometimes during the day. What she did outdoors I'd no idea, but I was thankful she wasn't the sort to bring back dead animals as a prize. She began to scratch at the door while we breakfasted the next morning, and I let her out.

"She may want to say goodbye to her mates in this world," you said.

At this point, the sad reality hit me. I was going to lose my cat. But, you pointed out, I would want to return home even if a family in some other world had taken me in. And of course, you were right.

It would be best, you said, to wait until dusk. There was something about dusk and dawn. They were the easiest times to open a doorway. In the meantime, you said, perhaps I could fill you in on what life was like in this world.

Just then I got an alert on my phone, and this piqued your curiosity. We talked about smartphones, the Internet, and social media. We talked about how enlightenment ebbed and flowed in society over the years, and about how, at the moment, it seemed to be ebbing. We had lunch and watched *Star Wars: A New Hope* on my OLED display. I think it's safe to say you were as enraptured by that as I was stunned by your demonstration the previous day. We went out afterwards, looking at clothing shops and bookstores; we walked through the university campus and took a stroll along the waterfront.

Looking out at Lake Ontario, you said, "This reminds me of Toronto when I was growing up. When we were children, my parents used to take us for walks along the waterfront and then we'd stroll through High Park."

To my surprise, your eyes became teary. Up until then you'd been endlessly cheerful and excited, but of course you're only human. You were robbed of your early adulthood, weren't you? You hadn't asked for the gift you have or for what happened the first time you helped someone. Honestly, I wasn't sure how to behave towards you that day. I knew that we weren't in a relationship, and yet we'd passed such a warm, loving night. I'd kept my distance since the morning, content to follow your lead. Now, with you so sad, I tentatively put my arms around you. You hugged me tightly in return.

Hand in hand, we started walking again, and you remarked on the beauty of blue jays, the cute skittishness of chipmunks, and the universal truth—you'd seen this in world after world—that all creatures love their young.

In the late afternoon, we grabbed some Indian takeout and went home, in case Sam was waiting to be let in. She was, and she sipped water and nibbled on cat food while we ate. It was your first time eating Indian food, and I couldn't help but chuckle at your reaction to the spicy dishes.

At dusk, the three of us gathered in Confederation Park. I'd already told you that I wanted to come with you, at least for a while. I had autopay set up for my bills and enough savings to keep things going for a while. You warned me that I might be gone for longer than I hoped, that there were no guarantees. You also warned me that sometimes it wasn't safe. Yet I longed to see some of the wonders you'd seen, and, if I was honest, I wasn't ready to say goodbye to you yet.

You looked at me when you were ready, and I nodded. You turned then and opened the door.

I asked you how it worked. After all, there were so many other worlds out there, how could you find the right one? You weren't sure but knew that if you opened the door with one hand while touching Sam with the other, we would get to the right place. And you were right, because as soon as we crossed over, Sam said, "Home."

I thought that nothing would ever shock me again, but I fully admit that this was a surprise. You laughed when you saw my face. All I could do was gape in your direction.

"Sam's not really talking," you said. "Cats and other nonhuman creatures use a nonverbal language here, and now that you're in this world, your brain is interpreting that as sound. You'll get used to it. Meanwhile, there's something we need to do."

Ah yes. You'd warned me. We had to remove our clothing since, in this world, humans remained nude unless the weather was cold or wet. We took off our clothes and stuffed them in our respective backpacks. I felt self-conscious at first, and was relieved that I'd made a point of trying to stay in decent shape. But before long I thought nothing of it.

Remember Me?

Sam rubbed against my leg. I knelt down, and she looked up at me. "Thank you," she said. With that, she turned and left. Standing, I was surprised by the tears in my eyes. Bless your heart, you hugged me, took my hand, and said, "Let's have a look around this world for a while, shall we?"

We'd emerged in a park. Or so it seemed. In fact, this world was preindustrial; I soon saw that people lived simply and happily, growing their own food, their small dwellings fashioned from wood and stone and grasses. Children played, women and men worked on gardens, repaired rooftops, sewed clothing for the brief winters.

We strolled through a village where people bartered for goods, trading seeds for tools or baked goods for woven material. Animals such as dogs, cats, and ponies roamed freely and entered into conversation with each other and with humans. I understood it all, somehow. We came upon a small lake on the other side of the village and lay on a grassy area near the beach, where we watched the birds and the buzzing insects and the clouds.

"It's not always this peaceful," you said. "But I've learned to just enjoy worlds like this when I find them."

I don't think I've ever felt so rested and at peace as I did that day.

We boarded with a family on the outskirts of the village, receiving food and lodging in exchange for stories. I spoke about my world, with its technology, geography, and politics, and you spoke of some of your adventures. I was as spellbound as they were as we listened to you. Despite the comfortable bed they found for us, I slept little that night. Instead, I watched you sleep, brushing my hand through your hair occasionally, and considered the impossible wonder of being in a different world.

The following morning brought a pleasant surprise. Sam was waiting for us as we emerged.

"Sam?" I said.

"Hello, Will."

"Are you all right?"

With a sigh, Sam said, "I was just a kitten when I left here. Too much time has gone by, and my littermates have gone their separate ways. This is my world but . . . I don't think I can be happy here. Not without you."

"Sam," I said, getting down on my knees and lifting her up to my chest. "Oh, I can't tell you how happy you've just made me." And it did. Her coming back to me seemed like the greatest of gifts.

"So, you'll come with us?" you asked her.

"Yes," said Sam.

That day, we left for another world. And the next day, another. And many more after that. Sometimes I saw wonders. Other times I saw things that I wish I hadn't— things I couldn't unsee. On some worlds Sam could speak; on others she couldn't. Or, perhaps more correctly, I wasn't able to hear her. It was exhilarating and mind expanding and exhausting.

Finally, there came a time when I began to get homesick, and I think you sensed this before I spoke about it. I asked, finally, if you could take me back for a little while, just so I could get my bearings and a bit of rest. You did, and the three of us found ourselves back in Confederation Park. I glanced at a newspaper as we walked and was relieved to find that only two days had passed in this world. We were about to enter my building when you said you thought you heard a familiar humming and needed to check it out. You gave me a hug, told me you'd be right back, and dashed away.

I wonder if you'll ever come back? I hope so.

Until then, I remain your faithful friend,
  Will

Postscript. I've sold this letter to you as a story. The publisher considers it fantasy and I don't blame them. My hope is that someday you'll come back and, if you can't find me, you'll look me up and find this story. At least you'll know that I never stopped thinking about you. Because I never will.

I won't lie. It's been hard since you left. But I think writing this out has helped. I realize that, as much as I miss you, and miss our adventures, I'm much better off for having known you. I watched you closely on our afternoon together in my world, and was taken by the way you saw the extraordinary in the most ordinary, everyday things. I think that, now, I appreciate the little miracles all around me in a way I never did before. The buzz of bees, the happy play of children, the warmth of the sun.

And then there's Sam, and the fact that she chose to come back with me, out of love. Not only did she not abandon me, she gave up her world to be with me. You've both made me realize that I shouldn't be afraid of relationships, even if they turn out to be fleeting. There is so much to gain from being close to someone.

Something Special

There's a woman at work that I like. That I think I like. We're meeting for supper this evening. Who knows what will come of it? But that's really the point, isn't it? It will be another adventure.

A Voice

What does it mean to have a voice? And what if there were a voice helping you when you needed it the most?

Katy LaPointe shifted in bed, clinging to the heavy warmth of sleep, until her foot touched ... something. She tentatively moved her foot again, realized what the something was, and groaned.

"Morning, babe," said a masculine voice behind her.

As she turned and sat up, Katy tried to remember the previous night. It was a bit of a blur, but she did remember one thing. The thing she always insisted upon.

"I thought you promised to be gone before morning," she said, her voice raspy with too much drink and not enough sleep.

"Sorry, babe, I guess I fell asleep. But now that we're both awake ..." He stroked her arm.

"Look," said Katy, "last night was great. I think. Actually, I can't remember much of it, but I'm sure it was great. We had an understanding, though. You come over. We have sex. You leave. And unless you're okay with losing an important body part, don't even think about calling me 'babe' again."

The man laughed. He was handsome, and his voice was rich and pleasing. She had to give him that. But still.

The laugh faded as he regarded her face. "You're serious."

By way of answer, Katy got out of bed, grabbed the sheets and blanket, and dragged them with her. As she did so, she thought, *This guy's body is actually very easy on the eyes.*

"I'm going to have a shower. I expect you'll be gone by the time I'm finished." With that, she sashayed, unselfconscious of her nakedness, towards the bathroom. Until she stopped and lowered her head. *Oh, what the hell.*

Turning, Katy ran her hands through her hair and approached the bed. "Actually, since you're still here . . ."

The headache wasn't helping. And, given how she'd started her day, her head wasn't the only thing aching. Katy took a deep breath. That didn't help, either.

Raymon Corporation's Canadian headquarters, located in Kanata North, was an eight-storey glass tower with a circular drive and canopied entrance. This part of the building, on the top floor, east wing, was known as Mahogany Row. It featured dark hardwood floors, mahogany wall panelling, portraits of previous CEOs, an elaborate break room with futuristic coffee makers and cozy chairs, and the boardroom where Katy was now seated. The long oval table was mahogany—no surprise there—the plush carpeting maroon, and the walls panelled with, yes, mahogany. The whole thing was an anachronism, an artifact of a richly profitable past, when the directors, all men of course, smoked cigars and went for long martini lunches. Some things were slow to change, and an entitled, male-dominated culture was ingrained in this company. The grudging admittance of female

A Voice

engineers and management had more to do with HR obligations and public perception than a change in the corporate culture.

Jim Coban, the marketing director, had just finished an overview of product features he'd promised to their chief client, Breze, an Internet and mobile phone service provider. The room was quiet and all eyes were upon Katy, except for those of her boss, a VP of product development, who was conspicuously engrossed in a printout of the presentation.

Katy sighed. She hated playing to type, but someone had to say it, and it always came down to her.

Yesterday, she and the other section heads had received a copy of the presentation. After opening the file, she'd sat back and begun clicking. The proposed product features were actually coherent, sensible, and well specified. Katy was pleasantly surprised, having expected the usual turgid mess that constituted Jim's proposals. But as she continued past the product features, alarm bells started going off in her head. Jim had already communicated these features to a customer without a proper internal review. And then she got to the proposed delivery schedule.

It hadn't taken long before a string of colourful language erupted from Katy's office, causing snickering laughter from the nearby software developers. The sole exception, the resident Christian, promptly dialled the number for HR.

At 4:00 p.m., she'd stuffed her laptop into her satchel, grabbed her jacket, and left, shoulders hunched, ignoring anyone who tried to grab her attention. Her destination was a bar in the Glebe, the Tik Tok, a couple of blocks from her condo. The bartender was a middle-aged man named Joe. Joe the bartender. To Katy, it was almost too good to be true. Joe had gotten to know Katy a bit—enough to know that when she came by before the end of the business day, it was usually because the day wasn't going so well. He mixed a glass of her usual, a Canadian Club and soda, and it was ready before she took a stool. As she drank in silence, Joe continued to wipe glasses with a white cloth.

Several drinks and a still-empty stomach later, Katy had decided that further distraction was required. Unlocking her phone, she'd opened the dating app and selected a suitable mark. After leaving the bar, she'd picked up some takeout and a fresh bottle of Canadian Club.

And this morning she was paying the price.

"For fuck's sake, Jim," said Katy. Her voice was controlled. She was pretty sure it was controlled.

"Here we go," someone whispered. More than one someone. She ignored them.

"Do you not think that, for once, it might have been a good idea to consult engineering before making promises we can't keep?" Katy took a breath and continued. "Saying a thing, having the words come out of your mouth, doesn't make it true. The fact is, we won't be able to deliver on this. Do I really need to point this out? Again? And why on earth would you present this to a customer without holding an internal review?"

A number of attendees shifted uncomfortably in their seats, avoiding her gaze. *Oh no*, she thought. *Don't tell me.*

Jim smiled in that infuriating, condescending way of his. He did so whenever he and Katy butted heads, hoping to draw her out and make her seem less credible. "Thanks for your input, Katy. Granted, there was no *formal* review, though there were internal discussions."

Without me, obviously, Katy thought. "But you don't think I get a say? You don't believe I have a voice?"

"Of course, Katy, but I think if we take emotion out of the equation, we'll see that . . ."

She stopped listening. *And there it is. Again. I'm a woman and therefore a creature of pure emotion, scarcely capable of rational thought.*

Katy got up and left.

Things only went downhill from there.

Work on the release had commenced, a preliminary design had been approved, and development was underway. This was all good. The problem was that Katy had refused to sign off on the marketing schedule. Marketing, in turn, had refused to sign off on the engineering schedule (time-to-market was critical); would not prioritize the new product features (they were all equally important); and had shrugged off the evidence Katy presented—a history of product features and development time—that backed her up. Facts, an irrelevant and inconvenient distraction, were to be discarded.

The project lumbered along. The marketing deadline came and went. Katy did her best to shield her people from the pressure she was facing.

They were a month from product release when the shit hit the fan. Davidson Networks had announced the imminent release of a product that bore a striking resemblance to Raymon's. They'd been scooped. Or Davidson almost had.

Three weeks later, seated in her office on a Monday morning,, Katy sipped coffee as she prepared to add to a lengthy chain of emails about the "marketing fiasco" (her term; marketing referred to the situation as "engineering intransigence"). But she was interrupted by a terse high-priority message from the company president. The RCMP had launched an official investigation into suspected corporate espionage. All employees were expected to cooperate fully. With a sigh, Katy realized that this had to be related to her product, Pegasus. The customer—well, potential customer, maybe former potential customer at this point—had denied leaking the product specs.

Watch yourself, a quiet voice whispered in her ear.

Swivelling her head, Katy confirmed she was alone in her office. The door was open as usual, but there was no one outside. As far as she could tell, there weren't any apps open on her laptop that could have spoken. Besides, she remembered, the volume was turned all the way down.

So who or what had it been?

"Jim," she said aloud, "so help me God, if you've bugged my office . . ."

All quiet. Katy, though an engineer, was not above attributing things like this to magical, electronic jiggery-pokery. She mentally shrugged and got back to work. A few minutes later, a knock at the door caused her to look up over her monitor. It was Angela, her HR rep, with two men she didn't know dressed in black suits. One was middle-aged, the other seemed younger, thirtyish maybe.

A Voice

"Katy," said Angela with a nervous smile, "these men are from the RCMP. They'd like to speak to you."

Blinking, Katy realized that they'd likely made tracks for her office the minute the president clicked Send on his email. Which meant . . . *Lovely*.

"Of course," said Katy. "Please come in."

"I'll leave you to it, then," said Angela, closing the door behind her as the officers took seats opposite Katy's desk.

"How can I help?" said Katy.

The older man took out his ID. "I'm Detective Ragip Okur. This is Detective Paul Lamoureux. We're investigating a potential case of corporate espionage."

Katy said nothing. *Let them make the first move*, she thought.

Clearing his throat, Okur unlocked his phone and opened an app. "You've been working at Raymon for how long?"

"It will be ten years this August."

"And what do you do here?"

"I'm the engineering director for the Pegasus product line." Prompted by the detectives blank looks, she added, "I oversee the software and hardware development of a family of products used by telecom service providers."

"And are you happy working here?"

"The answer to that depends on which day of the week you ask. But generally, yes."

"And what about your coworkers? Your peers and subordinates?"

"What about them?"

"Do you enjoy working with them?"

"Most of them. The ones who are actually, you know, competent."

"And how do you think they feel about working with you?"

"I would hope the feeling's mutual."

"You say you're happy to work here, and yet there are reports that contradict that. In fact, it's been alleged that you're quite disaffected with the company."

"Really? Well, I can't imagine where those reports come from." She paused. "Oh, wait a minute. Jim Coban, maybe?"

"Why do you say that?"

"I've had the audacity to rain on his parade from time to time. I'm sure he'd like nothing better than for me to be gone from this company."

"Ms. LaPointe, you got your degree from Queen's University, is that correct?"

"Yes."

"And your degree was in . . ."

"Computer engineering."

"I see. And while you were in the computer engineering program, you met a Mr. Marvin Benett, did you not?"

"Marv? Yes . . ."

"Mr. Benett happens to work at Davidson Networks, the company that allegedly received information about your product."

Katy couldn't help but laugh. "Seriously?" she said. "Do you have any idea how small this town is in the IT world? Everyone in the business knows people at other companies."

"When did you last make contact with Mr. Benett?"

Katy had to think. "It was a couple of months ago. We met for lunch."

"During your meeting, or at any other meeting with Mr. Benett, did you discuss privileged information?"

"No! I did no such thing." Feeling that she was about to lose her temper, Katy said, "Look, as pleasurable as this conversation has been, can we close the book on this for now? I've got a lot of work to do."

The two men looked at each other, and Okur nodded. "Thank you for your time, Ms. LaPointe. We'll be in touch."

As they were leaving, Katy muttered, "I can't wait," not caring if they heard or not. Then she took out her phone and opened WhatsApp.

The next day, Katy entered Brenda's Bistro just before noon. It was quiet, as it often was, making it a favourite of Katy's for meeting friends. Glancing around, she noted Marv at a table in the back corner and joined him.

He hadn't changed a lot since graduation. Hair just a bit thinner, hints of laugh lines around his eyes when he smiled, maybe a few pounds heavier. She used to know that body pretty well, way back when, when they were a thing. Not so much lately.

"So," said Marv, "shit hitting the fan?"

"I was questioned by the RCMP yesterday, so yeah."

"They've been to our place as well. Haven't spoken to me yet, but I'm sure they'll get around to it."

"You can count on it. They strongly implied that you and I were the culprits."

"I wouldn't worry. They probably did that just to see what reaction they'd get. Um . . . what reaction *did* they get?"

"I might have invited them to leave my office."

"Good. Well, that certainly won't arouse any suspicion."

"It seemed better to do that than to call them a couple of idiots. Speaking of idiots, they must have spoken to your marketing director."

Marv chuckled. "Oh yeah. But he maintains that our features and design were developed independently, and that you guys must have borrowed our work."

"Naturally," said Katy. Spotting the server heading their way, she added, "We should order."

Between bites, they talked about friends in common, family, and politics, an endlessly diverting source of discussion. Their conversation, as always, was effortless. It was one of the reasons they'd been friends for years.

When they'd finished their post-meal coffees, Katy regarded Marv without speaking.

"What?" said Marv.

"I've something you might be able to help with. An itch."

"I see," said Marv, setting down his cup. "That sounds like something in need of immediate attention. Tonight?"

"Definitely," said Katy.

It was Friday of the same week, and Katy was at work, just finishing some prep for a meeting, when she received an urgent WhatsApp message. It was from Gabrielle, a former Queen's classmate with whom she was still close.

A Voice

The message was to the point: *911 CALL ME!!!* Her meeting was in just a couple of minutes, but screw that. Katy tapped the video-call icon.

As soon as the video kicked in, Katy knew it was serious. Gabrielle was crying.

"What's going on?" said Katy.

"You haven't heard?" said Gabrielle.

"Heard what?"

"Oh God. I'm so sorry, Katy. It's Marv. He was found dead in his apartment."

Katy blinked. "No. No way. I just saw him the other day."

Shaking her head, Gabrielle wiped her eyes. "It's true. The police have made a formal announcement. They're treating the death as suspicious."

After swallowing, Katy said, "Thanks for letting me know. I . . . I have to go." And with that, she terminated the call and sat at her desk, shaking.

As she gathered up her things—there was no way she could work now—a colleague poked his head into her office and pointed to his watch. She shooed him away. Once she was in her car, she pulled up a local news site on her phone and confirmed the news.

> Marvin Benett, 34, has been found dead in his Westboro apartment after coworkers notified police that he was missing. Police are treating the death as suspicious and have urged the public to come forward with any information that might assist the investigation.

Katy couldn't remember the last time she'd cried. It wasn't her style. But without warning the tears came, and she found herself sobbing uncontrollably. Some minutes later, after drying her eyes and blowing her nose, Katy was about to start the car when her phone rang. She glanced at the display.

Oh no, not now. She briefly considered letting it go to voicemail but took the call. "Hello?"

"Ms. LaPointe, this is Detective Okur. We met on Monday of this week."

"Yes, I remember."

"We'd like you to come to headquarters for a follow-up interview."

"I see."

"Can you come in this afternoon?"

Katy sighed. "I can be there in an hour. Just text me the address."

At the reception desk in the RCMP building, Katy received a visitor's badge, and then an officer escorted her to a small meeting room on the second floor. Okur and Lamoureux stood as Katy entered and beckoned to a chair on the opposite side of the table.

When they were all seated, Okur opened a file folder and looked pointedly at her. "Are you aware, Ms. LaPointe, of the news concerning Mr. Benett?"

"Yes, I heard just before your call," she said, feeling pale, as if all the fight had been knocked out of her.

"We're very sorry for your loss, Ms. LaPointe," said Lamoureux. "Had you seen him since we last met?"

A Voice

You know perfectly well I did. "Yes, we had lunch on Tuesday." The detectives regarded her with stony silence. With a sigh, Katy continued. "He came over to my place that night. Around 10:00 p.m. We had sex. He left at 1:00 a.m."

As Okur scribbled on a pad of paper, Katy said, "Can I ask how he died?"

Lamoureux glanced at Okur, who nodded and continued to write. "It was an overdose of fentanyl," Lamoureux said. "He may have committed suicide."

"No!" said Katy, shocked. Feeling colour returning to her face, she said, "There's no way. Marv wouldn't have committed suicide, and he certainly wasn't a drug user."

"Are you sure?" Lamoureux asked. "On both counts?"

"Jesus, yes. I've known him long enough. He was in a good place. When I last saw him, he was happy and looking forward to a holiday in Cancún with some of his friends."

"How would you describe the nature of your relationship with Mr. Benett?" said Okur.

"We were friends. We have been since university."

"It seems you may have been more than friends."

Fighting the urge to roll her eyes, she said, "We dated for a few months when we were students. Once in a blue moon, if we're both single and in the mood, we have sex. Had sex. You can attach any label you wish."

"Did you discuss the investigation with him?" said Lamoureux.

"Yes, of course. At lunch. He was expecting you to question him. And no, he wasn't worried. He had nothing to hide."

"Did you follow him home when he left your condominium?" said Okur.

"What? No. I went to bed. Why would I do that?"

"Perhaps," said Lamoureux, "you wanted to be sure he wouldn't identify you as a perpetrator of corporate espionage. You followed him, he let you in, you injected him with a lethal dose of fentanyl."

Katy straightened. Did they really think . . . ? She thought back to what Marv had said. They were likely looking for a reaction. As her face began to flush with anger, she felt that she just might give them one.

"Are you fucking kidding me? I mean, are you out of your freaking minds? Let me be really clear about this. No, I did not leak corporate IP. No, I did not kill Marv. If you think for a second that I would or could, you're barking up the wrong hardwood. So why don't you spend our tax dollars just a bit more effectively and find out who actually did this. I'm done."

With that, Katy rose and went to the door. Looking back at the pair of detectives, she said, "Either arrest me or get me an escort the fuck out of here."

The Tik Tok was bustling, Katy noted as she stormed into the bar. Not unusual for a Friday at quitting time. Some eighties pop was playing, but not at a volume that made conversation difficult. Not that she was looking for conversation. Not today. Most of the tables and seats at the bar were occupied. A group stood at the far end, mostly men, and they erupted into laughter periodically. Most people seemed to be happy. She was not.

A Voice

Joe had her usual drink ready by the time she took her seat. Downing the drink, she beckoned for another. In short order, she was through her second and had nearly finished her third when a man took the seat next to her and ordered a Guinness.

Turning to Katy, he began to speak. Katy cut him off. "Don't even," she said, glancing at him. "Try to hit on me and you'll have your nuts in a sling." He seemed about forty, was in fairly good shape, and though his tone was light, his posture was erect and she sensed a hardness in his eyes.

"I'm not going to hit on you," he said. "Promise. I'm here to warn you."

"Warn me. About what? Talking to strangers in bars?"

Lowering his voice, the man said, "Warn you that someone might be out to kill you. The same someone who killed Marvin Benett."

Katy slammed her glass down and glared at the man.

Better listen to him.

Swivelling her head, Katy couldn't see who had spoken. It had been a woman, but which one?

When she turned back to the man, he was smiling. "You heard her? Good."

"Who was that? And, for that matter, who the fuck are you?"

But before the man could answer, Katy finished her drink and got up. "On second thought, I don't care. Say goodbye to your friend, whoever she is." And with that, Katy left the bar.

The cool evening air felt delicious. Despite her misery over Marv, she was grateful to be alive. But poor Marv.

Was she wrong to have had such a casual relationship with him? Should she have given them another chance? Well, it was too late now. *Of all people*, she thought, as she approached her condo. *Why would anyone want to kill him?*

Her unit was on the second floor of a newish building in the Glebe. It was a great location and it was quiet. Nothing like living atop a bar, which she'd made the mistake of doing a few years ago. Her current unit was above a taekwondo dojang. She'd taken advantage of this and was now a red belt. This had been home for five years now. From the entranceway, a corridor ran the length of the unit, off of which was a decent-sized kitchen/dining area, a living area, a bathroom, and two bedrooms. The smaller bedroom doubled as an office and, with its futon, a guest room.

The unit was dark as she entered. Flipping on the entranceway light, she hung up her jacket and started down the corridor to the living area. She had just passed the kitchen when someone grabbed her from behind and held her fast, one arm encircling her waist, the other her neck. Shocked, Katy struggled and flailed to no avail. She tried to grab his nuts, but he was pressed too close. She threw her head back, hoping to break his nose, but only grazed his chin. He was tall, and his grip around her neck was tightening. She needed to do something soon or she would lose consciousness. A thought came to her, almost as a whisper in her ear.

The vase.

Next to her was a side table, on top of which sat a heavy crystal vase filled with flowers. Reaching blindly with

A Voice

her right hand, she found the vase, raised it, and brought it down hard on her attacker's head.

Emitting a loud grunt, the man released his grip just enough to allow Katy to squeeze out of his reach. Turning, she aimed a kick at his groin, and the man doubled over with another grunt. He was dressed in close-fitting black garb, and a black balaclava covered his face. Still gripping the vase, Katy approached, intending to repeat the blow to his head. Rising slightly, but still bent over, her attacker swung his right arm, knocking the vase out of her hand and delivering a blow to Katy's head. Katy fell to the floor and then backed away from him, crab-like. With a sharp intake of breath, he turned and stumbled out of the unit. Katy stared at the open doorway in disbelief. She was hyperventilating and in shock. At some level she knew that. But she also knew that he might come back. Forcing herself to her feet, she locked the door with trembling hands and dialled 911.

While the police questioned her, a paramedic bandaged the raw bruise that her attacker had left on the side of her face. Soon after, Detectives Okur and Lamoureux arrived. Katy, exhausted, stumbled to the living room, and let herself drop onto the sofa.

The detectives approached her after conferring with the police officers. "How are you doing, Ms. LaPointe?" said Okur.

"Oh, you know. Beat up and nearly strangled. Fine apart from that."

"Can you describe him for us?" said Lamoureux.

"Not really. He was dressed all in black and his face was covered. He was tall. The top of my head just grazed his chin."

"Can you think of why someone would attack you?" said Okur.

Katy was impressed by the detective's ability to keep a straight face. "Are you kidding?" When the detectives said nothing, she continued. "So, let's see. Marv is killed, then I'm attacked later the same week. Coincidence?"

"You believe this to be related to Mr. Benett's death?"

"You're the detectives. You tell me."

Lamoureux spoke up. "If you think the attack is related, why do you suppose you're still alive?"

Allowing herself a small smile, Katy said, "A kick to the nuts might have had something to do with it. He was nearly doubled over when he left. Plus, he saw that I was going to put up a fight. Maybe he wasn't expecting that."

"If we can clarify one more thing, Ms. LaPointe," said Okur. "You said that the attacker was already in your unit when you arrived. You're certain of that?"

"Yes, I'm certain."

"What is puzzling, then, is how the attacker gained entry. There's no damage to the door or lock."

Katy hadn't thought about that. "I don't know . . ."

"Does anyone else have a key to your unit?" said Okur.

"Well, the condo manager has a spare, of course . . ." She trailed off and her eyes widened. "Marv! He had a spare key."

Nodding, Okur said, "We'll look into that. Excuse us a moment." The two men retreated and spoke in hushed tones. Katy couldn't make out what they were saying.

A Voice

When they returned, Okur said, "We'll need you to find other accommodations tonight while we scan the unit for forensic evidence. Is there anywhere you can go?"

Checking her watch, Katy saw that it was past ten. "I'll just go to a hotel. I assume that I can come back tomorrow?"

"We should be finished by then, yes. Can we give you a ride?"

"No, thanks. I'll gather a few things and get out of here."

Just then, a forensic team in white overalls and shoes entered the unit.

"Before you do that," said Lamoureux, "we'll need you to give us the clothes you're wearing. We'll also need to take samples from under your nails for analysis."

A female forensics examiner accompanied her to the bedroom, where Katy placed her clothes and shoes into a large plastic bag. After she'd dressed, she let the examiner scrape under her nails. The woman then placed the cotton-tipped scrapers into labelled bags.

Still feeling too shaken up to drive, Katy took an Uber to a high-end hotel with a view of the Rideau Canal. *I'm still alive*, she thought. *Might as well celebrate.* After checking in to a suite, she ordered champagne and pâté and started a movie. But she hit pause part way through as a thought occurred to her—she'd forgotten all about the man in the bar and his strange warning. Maybe not so strange after all. She needed to speak to him again.

After retrieving her car from her building's parking garage in the morning, Katy drove to the office. Her work day, it turned out, would be shorter than usual. Her badge wouldn't allow her through the turnstiles at the employee entrance. With her heart sinking, the security guards took her aside, checked their screens, and informed her that she'd been placed on mandatory paid leave of absence pending the results of the corporate espionage investigation.

There was no point arguing with them. Instead, Katy called her manager. The call went to voicemail. Angela took her call, but the HR rep could repeat only what security had told her. At least she had the decency to sound regretful.

Part of Katy felt that she should be furious. But after the attack, after the unsympathetic questioning from the police, and the skepticism in their faces, she simply felt deflated. Beaten. There being nothing else to do, Katy left. At least Okur had texted her to let her know that they'd finished with her condo unit.

Back home, she tore off her bandage and made some coffee. As it brewed, she thought about the events of the past few days and tried to make sense of them. She realized she needed more information. Taking her coffee to her home office desk, Katy sat and combed through Internet news sites. There weren't many reports concerning the alleged corporate espionage, and Marv's murder had been reported by only a few media outlets. No one had connected the dots. And as far as she could tell, there was no coverage of her attack. That suited her just fine.

She was thankful that her vase, an antique, was undamaged, though she would gladly have shattered it to

A Voice

pieces over her attacker's head. Thinking about the vase, she remembered the voice. She could swear that someone had whispered to her, reminding her that the vase was right there. Had it been her subconscious or something else? She thought again about the man with the warning, and the voice she'd heard then. Who was he and what did he know about all this?

One thing she knew for sure—she needed to be able to defend herself if her attacker showed up again. While she had training in martial arts, she'd have to get lucky to take down an opponent so much bigger than she was. A while ago, after a particularly vigorous bout of love-making, Marv had tickled her until she was breathless. It wasn't fair, she'd said, because he wasn't ticklish, and told him she might have to beat him senseless next time. A week later, he'd given her an expandable self-defence baton as a joke gift. It didn't seem so funny now. Retrieving the baton from the bottom drawer of her dresser, she gave it a flick and smiled as it expanded to its full length. It felt solid and hefty and might be just the ticket. After stuffing it in her purse, she went back online and ordered more of them. She'd hide them in the kitchen, living room, and bedroom.

She needed to change the lock, of course. It also seemed like a good time to invest in an alarm system, though that might take some time to put in place. After identifying a supplier with mostly positive reviews, she got on the phone with a sales rep and explained the urgency of her situation. The rep promised that they would install a system by the end of next week. In the meantime, he suggested, Katy could pick up some indoor motion-detection cameras.

Good idea, she thought. That she could do this afternoon. Then she'd just have to check her phone before entering the unit.

Rising from her desk, she poured another cup of coffee, sauntered into the living room, and looked out the window. It wasn't much of a view. Street parking directly below, and a coffee shop and attached homes with tiny lots and tall trees across the street. At least she wasn't looking at a sea of concrete and asphalt. The sky was blue. She considered going for a walk along the canal to clear her head. Then again, maybe He was out there. Waiting for her. He'd probably wanted her death to look like suicide, but he'd blown it. So what now? Would he leave her alone, or just kill her outright? It all came down to one question: Why?

Still. Was she about to live in fear? Hell no. Lots of men had thought they could intimidate her, one way or another. She'd always held her own and more. This time would be no different.

The question of why was still on her mind when she walked into the Tik Tok late in the afternoon. That man at the bar had warned Katy that she was a target. She needed to know what that guy knew, and the Tik Tok was the only place she knew where she might find him.

Glancing around, she spotted him. He was seated alone at a quiet table in a corner. After getting a drink from the bar, she walked toward him and hoped that this wasn't a big mistake. How could she know for sure that he was on her side? She should be safe enough in a bar, but at this point she needed to be extra careful. Taking a deep breath, she sat as his table.

"Are you okay?" he asked.

"Heard about my little adventure, did you?"

Nodding, the man said, "We did. Couldn't help but notice the police and ambulance outside your place last night. And then there's that welt on your cheek."

Katy touched her face and winced. It was still tender. "Yes, well, you should see the other guy. Speaking of which, as a token of goodwill, do you mind if I examine your scalp?"

His eyes widening a bit, the man nodded and smiled slightly. "Let me guess. You gave your attacker a goose egg and you want to make sure I'm not him."

"Correct. Now be quiet for a minute."

Standing behind the man, Katy ran her fingers through his thick hair and satisfied herself that he couldn't be her attacker. Sitting again, she asked, "So who are you?"

"I'm Ray. Ray Bolger."

Katy blinked. "Ray Bolger. Like the Scarecrow guy?"

"Yes," he replied, with a small, sad smile. "I've discussed my parents' name choice with them a time or two. It's often a good conversation starter, though, so there's that."

Katy assessed Bolger, noting that his eyes darted about, rarely staying still, as if scanning for threats. Was he ex-military? A spook? She had a lot of questions.

"You warned me yesterday. How did you know and why do you care? Who's 'we'? And while we're at it, what the hell is going on?"

"Let's start with the last question first. The short answer is, we're not completely sure. But clearly, you've been set up as a fall guy for the espionage case. If both you and Marvin Benett had appeared to commit suicide, the police could say job done and close the investigation. Someone wanted to make that happen. The question remains, who? And why? And why are the stakes so high that it's worth taking lives?

"As for your other questions, I guess you could say that we're investigators of sorts. We identify people who could be headed for trouble and try to help. That's what we do. My partner . . . well, this is tricky. You've heard her at least a couple of times now. Once while you were here with me, and once when you were attacked."

"So, what? She was in my condo unit? Hiding somewhere? Or she bugged the place?"

"It's not as simple as that. To put it bluntly, I don't know who she is. Or, for that matter, what she is. You'll never see her. You'll simply hear her voice from time to time. What I do know is that she's committed to helping people. She helped me once and I've been working with her ever since."

Looking at him steadily, Katy saw no sign that he was pulling her leg. "So you're telling me your partner is Tinkerbell? And you expect me to take you seriously?"

She heard a soft peel of laughter to her right. But beside her was only an empty chair.

"Wow," Katy said, getting to her feet. "Bravo. You've got a concealed microphone somewhere. Look, for all I know you're working with the people behind all this. Or you're certifiable and a danger to yourself and others. Maybe both. Thanks for the chat."

"I'll be here if you need me," Bolger called after her.

Katy turned, gave him the finger, and left the bar. She needed to visit an electronics store.

Sunday morning came, and Katy's phone roused her from a particularly pleasant dream.

"Hello," she croaked.

"Detective Lamoureux, Ms. LaPointe. Sorry if I woke you."

She'd stayed up late the previous night watching a movie after thoroughly scanning her unit with her new metal-detector wand. She'd found no concealed listening devices and no microphones.

"Forget it. What time is it?"

"Eleven a.m. We'd like to discuss the results of the forensic examination of your condo. Can you come see us at one today?"

Katy was suddenly wide awake. "Sure, I'll be there."

"We'll see you then."

"See you then," Katy repeated and disconnected the call.

Please let there be something, she thought. *Anything that'll help make sense of all this.*

A couple of hours later, she was seated in a conference room in the RCMP building with Okur and Lamoureux.

"Well?" she said.

Okur didn't open the file folder in front of him. "I'm afraid the results were negative. No fingerprints besides yours, no fibres, no DNA. Nothing to corroborate your version of events. Also, I should note, there's nothing to disprove your version of events."

"My *version*?" Katy said, disbelief heavy in her voice.

"Regarding the means of entry, the condo manager's key is accounted for. He keeps it locked in a safe, and the safe has been undisturbed. The key is not among Mr. Benett's possessions, so again, we cannot confirm or refute your assertion that he had a key."

"And what about this?" said Katy, pointing to the bruise on her face.

"Our medical experts concede that the bruise might have been caused by a fist," Lamoureux said. "However, they cannot rule out the possibility that the bruise was self-inflicted."

Katy closed her eyes and took several breaths before continuing. "So, what? You think I'm lying? You think I faked getting strangled and beaten up?"

"Let's review what happened," said Okur. "Why don't you go over the events one more time, in your own words."

And so she did, with all the patience and calmness she could muster. It didn't take long. After all, Katy figured, the attack couldn't have lasted more than thirty seconds from start to finish. It had seemed much longer at the time.

When she finished, Okur and Lamoureux remained stoic. With a sigh, Katy said, "Please tell me that you're at least *considering* the possibility that I'm telling the truth."

"We're certainly considering all potential avenues of investigation, Ms. LaPointe," said Lamoureux.

A Voice

"But there is the issue of Occam's razor," said Okur. "Are you familiar with this?"

"I'm an engineer. Of *course* I'm familiar with it."

Okur nodded. "The simplest solution is most likely the right one. And in this case, the simplest explanation of events is the following: You leaked your company's IP to Mr. Benett; you attacked and killed Mr. Benett, making it appear as a suicide; and you faked an attack on yourself to draw suspicion away. That's one explanation. Other explanations, in which you are entirely innocent, are possible, but much less simple."

"And yet you have a witness: me."

"Yes, there is one witness, but with no corroborating, independently verifiable evidence to back her up. You seem to believe in what you're saying. But just because you speak those words, even if you speak them in a convincing way, that in and of itself doesn't make them true."

Katy was stunned. "Sonofabitch." Seeing Okur cock his head in question, she added, "My own words have come back to bite me in the ass."

After a moment of silence, Katy continued. "Okay, I understand where you're coming from. But still, it's not up to me to prove my innocence. It's up to you to prove my guilt. And since I did none of the things you're suggesting, the more you try, the more time you're going to waste. If there's nothing else, I'd like to go."

Back home, Katy grabbed her laptop, curled up in a corner of her sofa, and formulated a plan for Monday. When she was satisfied, she closed her laptop and remembered that she'd promised, ages ago it seemed, to call her mother.

Something Special

"*Bonjour, Maman, c'est moi. Comment vas-tu?*" And then came the usual question. With a sigh, Katy said, "*Non, je ne suis toujours pas fiancée. Dans deux ans.*"

It was late Monday afternoon. Parked in the Raymon lot, Katy kept watch for her target. About forty-five minutes later she spotted him. She let Jim Coban drive out of the lot and then followed him. He turned left and got into the left-hand turn lane at the lights. Katy approached cautiously, allowing someone to manoeuvre between them. When they got the left-turn signal, Jim swung into the inside lane, keeping to the speed limit. Three blocks on, he turned into a subdivision, a bedroom community popular with tech workers with families. As she drove past home after identical home, Katy thanked her lucky stars she didn't live in this wilderness of suburbia with nothing but more of the same within walking distance.

She was puzzled, though, because as far as she knew, Jim was single. It was when he took another right that she understood. He wanted to live close to the golf course. What better way to keep up with the old boys' network?

Staying half a block behind him, Katy saw him turn into the driveway of a two-storey home with brick and aluminum siding. The lot was so narrow she imagined she could stand between his house and his neighbour's, stretch out her arms, and touch both outer walls. What was the point? Putting that thought aside, Katy pulled up to the curb a few houses down, walked up to Jim's front door, and rang the bell.

Jim's eyes widened at the sight of her, partly in surprise, it seemed, and partly in fear. *Good*, she thought.

A Voice

"What are you doing here?" he said, trying to rouse some bluster to his voice. But if he was selling intimidation, she wasn't buying.

"Just popped by for a chat," she said, flashing him a sunny smile.

Jim blinked. "It's not appropriate for us to be talking. Not with a police investigation in progress."

He started to close the door, but Katy stuck her foot in its way and gave the door a push. As Jim stumbled backwards, Katy entered and closed the door behind her. "On the contrary, not only is it appropriate to talk, it's long overdue."

The living room was to her right; it held a central fireplace, an armchair, and a couple of love seats. She sat in the armchair, crossed her legs, and folded her hands in front of her.

"Have a seat," she said, beckoning to him.

After glaring at her for a moment, he sat on the nearest love seat. "What do you want?"

"I want to know what the hell is going on. One person is dead, and another, me, was nearly killed."

"I know nothing about that."

"Bullshit. It all started with Pegasus. You didn't come up with those features. You know it and I know it. So spill. Where did they come from?"

The expression on Jim's face shifted from outrage to one with which Katy was all too familiar, having seen it at far too many meetings: condescension in the form of a smirk.

"Now, Katy," said Jim, "I can see you're feeling very emotional about this. Let's just look at this rationally."

"Oh no you don't," said Katy, rising and moving to stand in front of him. "We're not in the boardroom now, you asshole, and your golf club buddies aren't here, so don't try to give me that BS." She bent over so that her face was level with his, and that was when she felt something whiz past the top of her head. A sound had come from her right. There was a hole in the living room window, and glass scattered on the ground. Putting two and two together, she dove to the floor, dragging Jim with her.

"What do you think you're doing?" said Jim, disbelief in his voice.

"Someone is shooting at us, you dumb fuck. They just missed me."

"Nonsense," said Jim, as he started getting to his feet. "Your paranoia has no bounds does it?"

"Get *down*!" Katy hissed.

"I've had enough," said Jim. "I'm going to call the—"

There was a crack, and then a hole appeared in the side of Jim's head. He crumpled to the floor.

"Shit!" said Katy. "Shit, shit, shit!" She had to get out. Now.

There's a door at the back.

She crawled out of the living room on all fours. As soon as she was out of sight of the front windows, she got to her feet and ran to the back of the house, where a glass patio door led to the backyard. She unlocked it, yanked it open, and dashed through the yard. After climbing the fence, she ran through the neighbour's property to the street behind.

A Voice

There was a car alarm going off somewhere. She ran down the street, between two houses, and called 911.

She'd just finished the call when a car pulled up. The driver looked right at her.

"Shit!" she said again, but as she prepared to run, the driver lowered the window and she could see it was Ray Bolger. At the same moment she heard an explosion. With the sound bouncing off the houses, it was hard to tell where it had come from.

"Get in!" said Ray.

"How do I know it wasn't you shooting at me?"

"Because I think the shooter just blew up his car. Come on. We don't have much time."

There was no way she was getting in. Instead, she paused about six feet away from the car.

"Are you okay?" he said.

"Yes, I'm fine. What are you doing here? Were you following me?"

"Like you followed that guy? Yes. I saw the shooter enter the house. I punctured one of his tires, then gave his car a little nudge to set off the alarm. I figured you'd headed out the back, so I drove around the block looking for you. When he saw the flat tire, he must have figured he needed to destroy any evidence, so he blew it up and escaped on foot. Who keeps explosives in their car? Anyway, whose house was that?"

"Jim Coban's. He didn't make it. Did you see who the shooter was?"

Bolger shook his head. "He was dressed all in black, and his hoodie covered most of his face. Look, the police will be here soon. As soon as you hear sirens, head back to the house and tell them what happened. I'd appreciate it if you kept me out of it. I'll contact you when the police are done with you."

"Thanks," said Katy. "Thanks for your help." As she watched him drive off, Katy wondered what to make of him. Crazy? Probably. But was he trying to help her? *Maybe*, she thought. *But I'm not ready to count on that quite yet.*

Back in the RCMP's meeting room, Katy found her adrenalin fading and shock kicking in. An assistant brought her a mug of tea with lots of milk and sugar. After Katy had taken a few sips, Okur and Lamoureux came in and sat across from her.

She'd already told the police officers at the scene what had happened. She repeated her account a second time for the detectives. When Katy finished, Okur asked, "Why did you go to Mr. Coban's house?"

"Because all of this started with the IP theft. Jim proposed a set of product features that he couldn't possibly have come up with on his own. He's not that smart. Wasn't that smart. Someone gave them to him and suggested pointing to me as a scapegoat. If he'd confessed, I'd be a step closer to understanding what the hell was going on."

"And did he?" said Lamoureux? "Confess?"

"No. He just blustered, as usual."

"Do you own a gun, Ms. LaPointe?" said Okur.

"What? No. I've never had one. Never wanted one."

"We've impounded your car and have warrants to search it and your condo unit. If you have a gun, we'll find it."

A Voice

"Well good luck with that. You think that I'm the shooter? Seriously? The bullet just missed me. If I hadn't bent over at just the right moment I'd be as dead as Jim. Poor Jim. He was a dick, but I wouldn't wish this upon anyone."

"The car that exploded in front of Mr. Coban's house," said Lamoureux. "What do you know about it?"

"Just that I heard the explosion. I was already on the other street by then."

Okur regarded her in silence for a moment. "I don't believe that you're telling us everything," he said.

Katy crossed her arms. "I'm sorry you feel that way, but there's nothing I can do about it."

"Okay. We're going to hold you overnight while we review the evidence and complete the forensics. In the morning, you may wish to contact a lawyer."

"Wow. I get to spend the night in a cell. There's that bucket-list item checked. Can I make one suggestion first?"

"What's that?" said Lamoureux.

"You'll want to protect Hitesh Varma. He's the marketing director at Davidson and the likely next target."

Okur and Lamoureux glanced at each other. "We'll take that under advisement, Ms. LaPointe."

With that, they left the room and an officer escorted Katy to her overnight accommodations.

It was late the next morning when an officer escorted Katy to one of the meeting rooms. A few minutes later, a bedraggled Okur and Lamoureux joined her.

"All due respect," said Katy, "but you look more like crap than I feel."

Okur didn't respond, simply opened a file folder and arranged several reports in front of him. "Mr. Hitesh Varma was killed last night," he said. "We'll be releasing you this morning."

"You've got to be kidding," said Katy, suddenly furious. "Did you just ignore my warning completely?"

"Mr. Varma lived in a condominium near Dow's Lake," said Lamoureux. "We placed an officer outside overnight. The killer gained entry nonetheless and escaped undetected."

"Unbelievable."

"Forensics and witness statements back up your account," Okur said, ignoring her comment. "The shooter seems to have used a silencer as no one, including you, heard gunshots. However, two bullets were retrieved, one from a wall in Mr. Coban's living room, and the other from within his skull. The kill shot was fired from some distance, it seems. Witnesses saw a tall man wearing all black. The car he arrived in was reported stolen earlier in the day. No usable forensics survived the blast. The man escaped on foot."

"And he's still out there," said Katy.

"There's only one gap in our understanding of events," said Lamoureux. "The shooter's car alarm. Neighbours report hearing the alarm. One reported seeing a car hit the shooter's car and drive off. Do you know anything about that?"

"No," said Katy, "I was gone out the back by that time."

A Voice

"That incident may have saved your life. What's not clear," said Okur, "is why the shooter didn't simply silence the alarm and drive off."

"Like I said, no idea. It's just a shame the asshole wasn't in the car when it blew up."

"Very well. That will be all, Ms. LaPointe. I'd like to assign an officer to you, as it seems you may be a target."

"No shit," said Katy. Then she glanced down. "Sorry, I shouldn't give you a hard time. I know you're working hard on this. But no thanks." There were things she wanted to do, and the last thing she needed was the police getting in the way. When she saw Lamoureux about to voice an objection, she said, "I insist."

The police did give her a lift to her condo and promised to have her car back to her by late afternoon. No sooner was she in the door than she collapsed on her bed, fully dressed, and slept for hours.

The following morning, she found a text message from an unknown number on her phone: "2:00 p.m. Tik Tok. RB." Ray. She wasn't sure how he got her number, and at this point, she didn't care.

Ray was sitting at the same table as before. "Sorry to keep asking," he said, setting down his Guinness as Katy joined him, "but how are you?"

"Fine." Noting his raised eyebrow, she added, "Really. Except for the fact that everyone around me keeps getting killed. Maybe royally pissed is a better answer."

"Anger is good," said Ray with a nod, "as long as you channel it and don't let it drive you."

"I heard your mysterious friend again. In the house. She roused me from the shock of being shot at and reminded me there was an exit out the back."

"Well, as I said, we're trying to help."

"And I probably owe you my life. Both of you. Unless I'm suffering from the same audio hallucinations as you."

"As far as that goes, I'm afraid I don't know what to say. I do have objective evidence that she's real. But that's not important right now."

"Fine," said Katy. After taking a sip of her Canadian Club and soda, she added, "In the meantime, what do we do about all these people dying?"

Ray regarded her. "You're willing to work with me now?"

"Look, I know squat about you. But that can wait. So, for now, yes."

"Well, I think what we need to do is look at who benefits from all this. Because I imagine that both your company and your competitor will be in chaos about now."

"Good idea. Well, I can't think of who in my company would benefit. If it was personal, I can't imagine why they'd target both Jim and me. We had nothing in common, certainly no friends in common."

"And what about at Davidson?"

Katy shook her head. "I could see why Marv and me would be targeted by the same person. But then, why Jim? No, that makes no sense. So again, not personal. And as a corporation, well, I can't imagine how either company benefits."

A Voice

"If it's not personal, and it's not either corporation, then perhaps another company. Who benefits from the two big players being taken out of action for a while?"

Katy had to think. "Someone up and coming maybe, hoping to fill the vacuum. Telecom contracts can be ginormous. The stakes are really high. Especially . . . especially if you're a hungry young company trying to get your foot in the door. Hmmm."

Rubbing her chin, Katy sat back. "S&J Networks have their headquarters here. They started up in 2010, cobbling together staff from people who'd been laid off. They're small, but growing. And they seem to have deep pockets. Must have some sort of angel investors. They're still private, so no one outside knows what their finances actually look like."

"So," said Ray, leaning forward, "suppose you showed up unannounced at S&J tomorrow and hung out in their lobby for, say, half an hour. Think you'd get anyone's attention?"

"What? You want to use me as bait?"

"Are you game for that? It's a bit risky, but they won't know that I'll be around to back you up."

"Actually," said Katy, "I like it. And I think I can do one better than just visiting their lobby."

The uppermost floor of S&J's headquarters was refreshingly low-key, at least in comparison to the top floor at Raymon. The corridors were wide and bright, the polished floors gleamed, and tasteful art decorated the walls. It looked modern and clean. An assistant guided

Katy along the hall and knocked on the door of the office at the end before opening it.

"Katy!" said Robert Johnson, as he stood from his desk and approached her. "What an unexpected pleasure this is. Good to see you!"

"Good to see you, too, Robert," said Katy.

"Can we get you anything?" said Robert. "Coffee? Tea?"

"Coffee would be great, thanks. One cream, no sugar."

"Of course," said the assistant, before closing the door behind him.

Robert, one of S&J's founders, had been Katy's first manager. They'd worked together for a few years on an enterprise communications product before he left to start up the new company. S&J had wisely focused on products for wireless service providers. Their business had taken off almost immediately.

Robert gestured for Katy to sit in a chair across from his desk. "So, what brings you here today?"

"Well, I might be in the job market in the near future so thought I'd check in and see what's available here."

"Really? Well wouldn't that be nice? I'd love to work with you again. 'No-nonsense Katy,' that's what I used to call you. Remember?"

"I do. Must say, I love the facilities. You guys must be doing something right."

"We've got good people here, so that helps. We try to keep an eye on what's coming down the pipe so we can be ready for it. We see some rapid growth opportunities coming up, so there may well be a spot for you here."

A Voice

"That would be great. And there's one more thing you guys have got going for you."

"Oh?"

"Your people aren't getting killed off."

"What?" said Robert, his eyes narrowing.

"Raymon's marketing director was shot dead, as was Davidson's. And another Davidson employee, a good friend of mine, was killed." Observing that Robert's face denoted shock while his eyes expressed anger, Katy continued. "Oh, yes. And someone's tried to kill me. Twice. Seems like they're desperate to tie up loose ends. Now let's see, who would benefit from all this chaos that's consumed the established telecom suppliers? Oh, right. You guys. And did you just say there were rapid growth opportunities coming up? Funny coincidence. Anyway, I've a meeting with the RCMP this afternoon. The latest of many. Do you know they thought that I was behind all of this? At least until Hitesh Varma was killed while I was in custody. Someone's getting sloppy."

Katy sat back and smiled sweetly.

Just then the assistant entered the office with two steaming mugs. Robert rose. "I'm sorry. Katy was just leaving. And I don't think she'll be back."

"Oh, what a shame," said Katy, rising as well. "Well, I'll say hello to the RCMP for you, shall I?"

"Get out of here," Robert growled.

Katy gave Robert the finger on her way out.

In her car, Katy called Ray and set the phone to speaker.

"Do you think you got his attention?" he said, by way of greeting.

"You could say that. On the downside, he might send an entire platoon after me rather than just one guy." After a moment, she added, "Actually, I really hope it's him because I don't think he and I can be friends again after this."

"One problem at a time," said Ray. "I can hear you loud and clear and your location is coming through. I suggest waiting a few minutes before proceeding to the next step. That'll give them the time they need."

After taking the highway from the Kanata office, Katy exited at Barrhaven and pulled into an outdoor shopping plaza containing a grocery store and several restaurants.

She got out of her car and strolled towards the Vietnamese place. "Where is he?" she asked Ray, who was still on the line with her.

"Just pulling in. Give him time to see you before you enter the restaurant."

"Roger Wilco, boss. Has he made you?"

"I don't think so. I've been well back of him, with other cars between us. I'll enter the lot by the far entrance just to be safe."

"Okay. I'm just about to go inside. He should have seen me by now. Do be careful, Ray."

"Always."

Inside the restaurant, Katy ordered a noodle soup to go and then asked the server if she could freshen up. Walking past the washrooms, Katy left the restaurant through the rear exit. She crossed a strip of pavement and slipped through the row of hedges that bordered the parking lot's east side.

A Voice

"I'm behind the hedges," said Katy. "What's he doing?"

"He's outside the restaurant smoking a cigarette and looking at his phone. Once in a while he'll glance inside. At some point he'll get tired of waiting."

"Okay, I'll stand by until then."

A few minutes later, Ray spoke again. "He's just gone in. We're coming up to the dangerous part. You still okay?"

"Ready and waiting. I'm going to send Okur a text now. Keep the video rolling. Hopefully this guy will try his luck with me before they get here."

"Hopefully?"

"Oh, I so want to hand this jerk his ass. I have something special waiting for him."

"Remind me not to get on your bad side. Just a minute. Yes, it's him coming out, and he looks pissed. Now he's looking around for you. Hah! And now he's heading towards his car. Imagine his reaction when he finds his tire flat. Again."

Katy emerged from the hedges. The killer was dressed all in black, as before, but his hood was down. He was Caucasian with close-cropped hair and a thick, muscular neck. She was close enough to see his eyes nearly bulge out of his head when he noticed his tire.

Though about to put herself in great danger, Katy couldn't help but laugh. "Are you ready?" she said into her phone.

"Oh, I'm ready, but please, please be careful."

"Sure," said Katy. "See you on the other side." She hung up and pocketed her phone. "Hey, asshole!" Katy yelled as she approached the man. "Having trouble with your stolen car?"

"You," the man growled, and began making tracks for Katy.

"What? Are you coming to kill me? Better get on with it, scumbag. The cops are on their way and you don't have a car."

The man stopped. "You do."

"Yes, I do. And I even have car keys. Somewhere. Now where did I leave them? Oh my, I've simply no idea. Isn't that silly of me?"

He resumed walking steadily towards her. "I am so going to enjoy doing you."

"Do you say that to all the girls? Pretty brave of you, you dickless coward, with me being able to see you coming."

Reaching into his leather jacket, he produced a large knife. Katy reached behind her with her left hand and gripped the baton she'd tucked into the back of her jeans.

When he was almost close enough to stab her, Katy screeched, "No! Please! Please don't hurt me."

With a chuckle the man lunged forward. But Katy was faster. As he moved, she sidestepped while freeing the baton and brought it down hard on his wrist. She heard a satisfying crack. With a scream, he dropped the knife and tried to catch her with a left hook. Blocking it with her right arm, Katy shoved his chest while he was off balance, pushing him back a couple of steps.

His face full of fury, his right arm dangling at his side, the man charged. Katy pivoted, planting her left foot on the ground, and delivered a side-piercing kick with her right, the same kick that had broken several boards at the Ontario taekwondo tournament, winning her a bronze medal.

She heard another satisfying crack that told her she'd broken some ribs. His face spoke of surprise and pain as he doubled over. It looked like the fight was out of him but …

Oh, what the hell. For the second time, Katy delivered a swift kick to his groin, and he collapsed in a heap on the ground just as several police cars, sirens blazing, entered the parking lot. The man moaned piteously. Katy laughed. "Just be grateful I'm not wearing stilettos."

The following evening found Katy and Ray back in the Tik Tok. After the server had brought their drinks, Guinness for Ray and Canadian Club and soda for Katy, they clinked their glasses.

"So?" said Ray.

"Well, first off, Okur and Lamoureux berated me for being an idiot. I didn't argue. They confiscated my baton, but on the plus side, they didn't charge me for using it. I let them know that was very decent of them, considering I was defending myself against a serial killer. That actually got a smile out of them—the first one I've seen."

She sipped her drink and continued. "The killer's name is Bernard Ladouceur. He's head of a group of security consultants hired by—guess who?—S&J. Apparently, he tried to tell the police that he was acting in self-defence, that little old me had attacked him without provocation. But it turns out that someone uploaded a video to YouTube anonymously. It showed the whole thing, and apparently it's gone viral, so hats off to whoever it was who shot it."

Ray raised his glass in salute and took a sip.

"Ladouceur finally came clean and pointed the finger at Robert Johnson directly and they brought him in, so yay. They're still working on him and checking out his work and home electronics. I pointed out to the detectives that S&J would benefit from taking out the two major contenders in its space. The way I see it, I told them, is that Jim Coban and Hitesh Varma were cut from the same cloth: they could talk and look the part but fell short when it came to actually doing anything. Their real strengths were in laying the blame for their shortcomings on others. They were hungry for success, short on ethics, and ripe for the picking. Johnson would have used an intermediary, maybe Ladouceur, maybe someone else, to slip them some valuable product specifications that fell off the back of a truck. They both grabbed the opportunity, ignorant that their competitor had been given the same specs. Things started to fall apart when Ladouceur failed to kill me. They needed to tidy up all the loose ends."

"And that seems to conclude our business," said Ray.

"Indeed. So what does the future have in store for you?"

"I'm not sure. But I think I want to do something different. What that is, I don't know. Not yet. What about you?"

"Same. I've had quite enough of the toxic environment I've been working in. Guess I'll take some time to figure out what comes next."

"You were pretty impressive through all this," said Ray. "I wouldn't be surprised if you get a whisper of an idea in your ear one of these days."

Katy smiled. "Speaking of which, I had a very satisfying moment at RCMP headquarters."

"Do tell."

"As I was leaving my interview, Johnson passed by with an officer. He was handcuffed. He stopped and glared at me and spat out that I was 'nothing.' I just laughed. 'You're the one in handcuffs,' I said. 'And I'm not nothing. I have a voice.'"

Protagonist Purgatory

As I mentioned earlier, sometimes I'm not ready to say goodbye to characters after a story is told. So here we find several characters from other tales brought together in a place that is familiar to them and yet strange. Be warned that one of the characters drops the F-bomb rather frequently. In pretty much every sentence, actually.

When Michael Rousseau realized that he was here, wherever here was, or rather, when he realized that he *existed*, his first question wasn't "Where am I?" but "Which Michael am I?" He looked at his hands, jumped up and down a couple of times, and felt his face and hair. Young. *I'm the young Michael*, he thought. *Good. I much prefer being young.*

In the story, Michael had started off young, a first-year student in university. He grew old but in the end was young again.

Fantasy. There was no taking anything for granted.

With that decided, it was time to sort out just where he was. And after that, try to work out *why* he was wherever he was. Because, as far as he knew, his story was over. It had been told. So what was this? The sequel?

From his position next to the bank of a river, Michael turned in a circle, slowly, so that he could take in his surroundings. He stood in a meadow that extended about a mile from the river before yielding to hills and mountains. But the meadow was semicircular. To either side of him, the hills closed in until they were flush with the riverbank. On the other side of the river, the banks brushed against the base of a range of mountains, tall, rocky, and very steep.

The sun was almost directly overhead. The sky was a comforting shade of blue with a smattering of cumulus clouds. Michael turned his gaze earthward, to the meadow in which he stood, with its tall grasses, wildflowers, and buzzing insects. He approached the riverbank, knelt, and gathered up some of the red-tinged soil in his hands. It felt rich and loamy, a gardener's dream, and it brought to mind the large vegetable and herb garden he'd treasured in his middle years.

Standing again, he scanned the broad, slowly flowing river. It was a clean blue, almost turquoise, and when he looked closely he saw a school of fish swimming close to the surface.

It was a place he didn't know, but he revelled in the natural landscape, the sound of the river, and the sweet scent of the fresh air. There were no trees, birds, or animals, but it seemed like a thriving, healthy, normal ecology. He breathed a sigh of relief. Not a magical creature anywhere to be seen.

A sudden breeze prompted Michael to turn, and the feeling of calm that had come over him left rather abruptly as he stared, wide-eyed, at the two-storey rooming house where he'd lived during his university days and again at the end of his life.

This was impossible. It hadn't been there just a moment earlier. Michael started towards it but then paused. It was uninhabited. Empty. He wasn't sure *how* he knew, but he knew.

None of the neighbouring buildings from back home were here. There was no sidewalk, no road; there were no people, and no answers. Just more questions.

If there were no answers here, he'd have to go looking for them, and there were only two directions from which to choose: upstream or down. As he pondered this, a shadow caused him to look skyward.

The airborne creature was thin and long, perhaps some twenty feet from head to tail, and covered with dark scales. Its bat-like wings were broad with a considerable span, and its head was thin and bony; it contained large eyes and short, pointed horns, which jutted from its upper neck as well. It was flying fairly low, too low for comfort, maybe forty feet above the ground. Michael considered running to the rooming house for cover, but reasoned that if the thing was intent on killing him, there was no getting away at this point.

This could end up being a very short story, he thought. *What do they call that? Microfiction? No, flash fiction, that's it. Then again, maybe it's not actually a dragon. Maybe . . .* But before Michael could finish the thought, a flame erupted from the creature's mouth. Then it banked and turned back the way it had come, flying around the bend in the river upstream.

So, definitely a dragon. He noted with a sigh, *I'm in another fantasy.*

Although tempted to go in the opposite direction, some instinct told Michael that he should follow. He set off upstream. As he walked, the hills edged closer and closer until, by the time he reached the bend in the river, they were just about flush with the riverbank. Climbing was out; the hill was steep, almost vertical, and rocky. But he could just about squeeze past without having to get his feet wet.

Once round the bend he stopped short. If he hadn't, the sword that had appeared in front of him would have sliced his throat in two.

"What manner of wizard are you?" a man's voice asked.

The voice was thin and high pitched, a rather jarring juxtaposition to the man himself. He stepped forward so that Michael could see him. At least six-and-a-half feet tall, broad, and muscular, with shoulder-length light-brown hair. His attire consisted of a pale-green vest, tan leggings, and a leather belt that held a scabbard. The sword was the length of an arm and some three inches wide at the hilt. It gleamed like the sun, even though they were in the shade of the hills. Was the hilt of the sword made of diamond? Michael wondered.

"Wizard?" Michael said, moving his gaze from the sword to the swordsman. "No manner of wizard, actually. Just a guy. So, you'd be from an epic fantasy then, is that right?"

The sword moved away from his throat a little.

"Well, yeah, my story was pretty fucking epic at that. Yours?"

"More urban fantasy, really. With maybe a dash of sci-fi. We did save the world, though, so kind of epic at that."

"If you speak truly, and are not a wizard, and aren't fucking me over, then how did we arrive in this fucking place?"

"Beats me. I was hoping to find someone who could tell me. Maybe we could sort this out together?"

The swordsman stepped closer and looked Michael in the eye. "You might be telling the truth. But if you're not…"

"Let me guess," Michael said. "The consequence involves the sword?"

"Fucking-A," said the swordsman with a grin.

"Fair enough. I'm Michael."

"Dromhiller." He sheathed his sword. "And this dumb ape is, well, let's face it. Who cares?"

"Sorry, which dumb ape would that be?"

Dromhiller turned his head towards Michael. "The one staring at your face. Carrying me."

"Now you've completely lost me."

"Really?" he said, backing away from Michael slightly. "You've never heard of the Swords of Baakthrip?"

Michael shrugged.

"Well fuck me," said Dromhiller. "And what planet are you from?"

"Earth," said Michael. "Twenty-first-century Earth."

Dromhiller scratched his head.

"I'm going to guess that our stories were set in different worlds," said Michael. "Where I come from, you tend not to see a lot of people walking around with swords, and even fewer with glowing swords that have diamond-encrusted hilts. So, assuming I've no idea what you're talking about, why don't you fill me in?"

"Okay, look. See those rocks over there?" Dromhiller pointed to a rock formation some twenty feet away. "Notice anything unusual about them?"

Michael stepped up to the formation. From a flat granite base arose hundreds of conjoined octagonal stones at various heights, from three to five feet. The stones were such a deep black that there wasn't the slightest reflection on them. Though they varied in height, they were all the same circumference, around twenty inches. Running his hand along the sides and top of one of them confirmed what his eyes were telling him. The stones were perfectly smooth.

"This is amazing," Michael said.

"That's nothing," said Dromhiller. "I mean, these stones, they're fake. Back on my world, the stones are what give birth to us. So to speak."

And so the swordsman explained. Or rather, the sword explained.

In Dromhiller's world, swords, forged from magical lava, lived with their wielders in a kind of symbiosis. The swords were sentient and grew from the octagonal stones. Upon maturity, they glowed and pulsed with a heartbeat-like rhythm that attracted local tribesman. Immediately upon physical contact, the swords took control of their wielders.

The swords fed from the kinetic energy of being wielded. The more a sword was used, the more it fed. After absorbing sufficient energy, the swords returned home, like salmon returning upstream to spawn. Those swords ready to reproduce dissolved into clouds of magical elements and mixed with one another, resulting in a new generation of swords.

Swords evolved in the same way as ordinary creatures. Swords that were wielded more often returned to reproduce more often, and successful characteristics were propagated through the population. The wielders evolved in tandem with the swords. Wielders, at least, those who survived, were thought to be quite heroic by the females of the species. As a consequence, they reproduced with surprising frequency. Their offspring often became wielders themselves.

"Well that's all very... remarkable," said Michael.

"And the hilt?" Dromhiller said. "Solid magic. Not diamond." He tapped the hilt with his forefinger. Immediately afterward, Michael felt something pass through him, like a deep bass note from a good subwoofer.

Dromhiller grinned.

Michael gazed again at the rock formation. "Funny that it's here, don't you think? A piece of home for you. 'Cause back that way was the building I lived in. Except that it wasn't real. I'm sure it was solid enough, but it just wasn't *real*."

"Fuck me if it makes any sense," said Dromhiller. Grinning, he withdrew his sword and began spinning it about in the air. "But I've got a nice present waiting for whoever is toying with us."

"You know," said Michael, "I have trouble imagining how someone who created all of this and was able to bring us here is going to be worried about a sword. Even if it is magical."

Dromhiller scowled at him then started walking. Michael caught up to him, and they walked together without speaking.

After a few minutes, Dromhiller broke the silence. "Fuck, this is boring. Why can't there be some dragons at least?"

"You didn't see it?" Michael asked.

"What? You saw a dragon?"

Michael nodded. "It flew overhead just a little while ago."

"Well, that's more like it," said Dromhiller. "Now I've something special to look forward to."

"So there were dragons in your story?"

"Sure. Well, at least until I killed them. What about in yours?"

"No dragons," said Michael. "There was a unicorn, though. And a few other magical creatures."

Dromhiller nearly choked. "A unicorn! You've got to be kidding." Doubling over with laughter, he stopped moving until he could catch his breath. "A fucking unicorn! Let me guess. Story didn't sell, did it?"

"No," said Michael, his head drooping slightly. "Not to the best of my knowledge."

"No wonder," said Dromhiller. "With a fucking unicorn? What a surprise. Nobody cares, boy. It's dragons. Everybody loves a good fire-breathing dragon."

"Really. And you don't think they're overused?"

"How could they be? Dragons are great. How does a sword get a reputation if not by killing a few dragons?"

"And what about you?" Michael asked. "Did your story sell?"

Dromhiller cleared his throat. "Well, no, not yet. But it will, never fear. It's got dragons, after all. And me. It can't lose."

Eventually they came to another bend in the river and, as before, the steep, rocky hills crowded towards the bank. Dromhiller squeezed through first and called the all-clear. Michael was about to follow when he felt a tremor, like a mild earthquake. He stepped back and looked up at the hill, but there was no sign of any loose rocks about to tumble down.

Once he'd moved past the hill, Michael stopped and gaped at Dromhiller.

"What're you staring at?" Dromhiller asked.

"Um . . . Dromhiller?"

"Who the fuck do you think?"

"You look a tad different, that's all," Michael said. "Completely different, actually. You've got short, thin, curly hair, and you're wearing a pinstriped suit. I have to say that the belt and scabbard is an odd look with the suit."

With his eyes wide, Dromhiller looked himself over, felt his face and hair, and used his sword to examine his reflection. Then his face relaxed and he grinned. "This is all right," he said. "Pretty fetching, in fact. Means even better luck with the ladies."

Michael sighed. "Okay, but that's not the most important consideration right now, is it? I mean, *why* did you change? What does that tell us about where we are?"

"Tells me you think too much," Dromhiller said with a shrug. "I've had many wielders before the one you met. As far as I'm concerned, this is just one more. For now, all I'm looking for is a head to lop off."

Michael decided to ignore his companion and focus instead on their surroundings. Unlike in the previous two regions, the sky here was overcast, the clouds so thick and dark that it felt more like dusk than just past midday.

There were clumps of trees scattered about, their branches twisted and their leaves dried, and tufts of brown grass and shrub, but for the most part the area was a steaming, stinking swamp. The air was rank with the smell of rotting vegetation. Pockets of dirty fog drifted about the landscape, making it hard to see more than a short distance in any direction.

Picking up a fallen branch near his feet, Michael stuck it in the water and swished it around. The murky water cleared for a moment, and he could see small dark things, about an inch long, darting about beneath the surface. He was about to bend down for a closer look when some of them leaped out of the water and tried to bite him. Michael stepped back, shocked. He had to use the stick to dislodge the two that had a firm grip on his trousers.

What a nice place, Michael thought. *Still, might as well see who or what's here.*

There were rocks sticking out of the swamp, spaced such that it would be possible to step or jump from one to another. Michael set out in this fashion, not waiting for Dromhiller, who continued to examine himself.

"I'll leave you two to get better acquainted, shall I?" he called back.

After a few minutes, Dromhiller was lost from sight and Michael's courage and curiosity started to fade. He contemplated turning back until something, barely visible through the fog, caught his eye. As he approached, he saw that it was a small circular brick dwelling with a couple of windows and a wooden door.

The door opened and a man wearing tan robes stepped out, smiling, arms folded in front of his chest. He was tall and wiry, elderly, with short white hair and a closely trimmed beard.

"Ah," the man said, nodding. "Young Michael. Come inside." And with that, he went back into the dwelling. After hesitating for a moment, Michael followed.

The interior was sparsely furnished; there was a table, four wooden chairs, and a cot. A recorder, some seashells, and a vase sat upon a shelf mounted on one of the walls. The only other item in the room was a small cabinet.

Hearing a sound behind him, Michael turned and saw Dromhiller, sword drawn.

"And Dromhiller," the man said, nodding. "Good."

"Who are you?" Dromhiller said. "Did you bring us here?"

"Please," the man said, gesturing to the chairs. "Be seated and I will explain."

Michael sat; Dromhiller didn't.

Raising an eyebrow, the man seated himself and continued. "My name is Augura. To me, through untold ages, has been passed the prophecy. You, Michael Rousseau, have a destiny."

Dromhiller groaned.

"Yes?" said Augura.

"Okay, just how old is this prophecy?" Dromhiller asked.

"Ages."

"How many ages?"

Augura took a deep breath. "Untold. Ages."

With a sigh, Dromhiller sheathed the sword. "Fine. Go on then."

"My small role is to be your guide, Michael Rousseau, on this Great Quest that you and your"—Augura screwed up his face—"companion must undertake. There will be trials. Danger. Yet through it all, you must—"

But Augura stopped midsentence, which was unavoidable given that his head had suddenly flown off his shoulders. It came to rest at Michael's feet. Augura's eyes seemed to widen in surprise, his mouth started to open, then his tongue protruded slightly in Dromhiller's direction.

Stunned, Michael turned to see Dromhiller sheathing his sword again.

"Fucking boring old pot pisser and his 'Great Quest.' Give me a fucking break."

"Why did you do that?" said Michael, his voice rising. "What harm did he do?"

"He was boring me to death, that's what harm. I've seen old men like him before. Plenty of them. All prophecies and quests and destinies. Fucking useless. Maybe killing him was *my* destiny. Let's get out of here."

"Fine, but you may have killed the only one who could tell us what's going on here. Please, just promise me you won't kill anyone else. Not unless you have to."

Michael looked again at Augura's body and realized what had been nagging at him. "Why is there no blood?"

"Magic sword, remember?"

Michael exited the dwelling, making a mental note to try not to bore his companion. Together they worked their way through the swamp back to the river. Michael noticed that Dromhiller's head drooped a bit and that he was being unusually quiet. "Are you okay?"

"I don't even know what I'm doing here," Dromhiller muttered. "What use is a magical sword in a place where there are no worthy opponents?"

"You're not the only one wondering what he's doing here," said Michael. "Where I'm from, I'm a scientist, a renowned biologist, actually. But really, what's the point in being a scientist in a place where magic is real? Any time you ask 'How does that work?' the answer could well be that it works by magic. And then where are you?"

Dromhiller smiled. "And you think that magic cannot be studied scientifically?"

"What do you mean?" Michael asked.

"I mean, perhaps there are scientific principles behind the way magic has its effect on the world. Look at me. I feed off kinetic energy. Science, right there. The magical elements that comprise swords like me dissolve, recombine, and reform into new swords. How does that work? Seems like a perfect domain for scientific studies."

Michael stopped and gaped at Dromhiller.

"What?" said Dromhiller. "You think a sword is all brute force and pretty face? Inside of me is the accumulated wisdom of a thousand generations of swords. You pick up a thing or two."

Continuing along the path, Michael said, "There's certainly more to you than meets the eye."

"You're not fucking kidding," Dromhiller said with a wink.

A moment later, something caught Michael's ear and he stopped short, causing Dromhiller to nearly bowl him over.

"Watch where you're going," Dromhiller growled.

"Shut up a minute," Michael said. "Do you hear that?"

Dromhiller tilted his head as he listened to the faint sound—laughter. "Let me take the lead," he said.

They were within sight of the river when a figure emerged from the fog. It was dressed in black robes and black gloves, its face hidden by a hood. It held a large black sword—as black as Dromhiller's was bright. The little daylight that there was seemed to drain into it, as if the blade wasn't a blade at all but a hole in reality.

"Step forward and meet your fate," the figure said. Its words were well-enunciated and spoken slowly, in a deep voice that seemed to echo around him.

"Fuck me," said Dromhiller. "Seriously?"

"It is," continued the figure, extending a clawlike finger towards Dromhiller, "your *destiny*."

"Oh for—"

Michael interrupted him. "Sword," he whispered.

"What?" said Dromhiller.

"Might be a good time to draw your sword. Maybe this is your worthy opponent."

Dromhiller shook his head. "Even I have standards. No, I just can't be bothered." Turning, he set off upstream. Michael sped after him, glancing backward all the while.

The figure in black spoke more loudly and shook its fist. "You *dare* turn your back? On *me*? Revenge *shall* be mine."

"We've got to get out of here before I puke," said Dromhiller.

As Dromhiller and Michael vanished from sight, the figure screamed, "WE SHALL MEET AGAIN! AND WHEN WE DO . . . Oh, screw it."

And with that, it dashed the sword to the ground and stomped off in a huff.

When Michael and Dromhiller reached the next area, the sky was clear and the sun shone brightly. It was larger than the previous regions, the hills lying further in the distance, and it was heavily forested. A well-trod path led into the woods from the riverbank.

In silent agreement, they followed the path until they came to a clearing, in the centre of which was a large hole in the ground. Michael walked up to it and peered down. He could see nothing but noted that it smelled vaguely of sulphur.

Dromhiller joined him then grinned wickedly. "This is it!"

"This is what?"

"What I've been waiting for. The reason I'm here." Looking at Michael's blank face, Dromhiller continued. "Don't you smell the sulphur? This is the dragon's lair. Now we just have to wait for it to emerge, then . . . chop!"

"Chop?" said a new voice, rich and deep.

Michael turned abruptly. Right behind them was the dragon. It was resting on the ground, its head tilted slightly, looking at them with large, curious eyes. With a gulp, Michael took a step backwards. Then another.

Dromhiller immediately leapt to the side, rolled on his shoulder, and in one smooth movement withdrew the sword and took a defensive stance.

The dragon yawned. "Are you trying to intimidate me? Because, honestly, I don't feel very intimidated."

"That's because you've never faced a magical sword the likes of me." Dromhiller spun the sword in the air, faster and faster, causing it to glow more brightly and to sing dramatically, a clear, high note that seemed to penetrate to Michael's core.

"No, that's still not doing it for me."

"Nothing worse than a fucking lippy dragon," Dromhiller muttered. "Those will be your last words, Dragon!"

But before he could turn those words into action, a rock hit the back of his head.

"Ow," said Dromhiller, rubbing the injured area. "What the…?"

"Keep away from my dragon!" shouted the young woman who'd just emerged from the woods.

At the sound of the voice, Michael turned abruptly. But no, it wasn't her. This woman had long brown hair. She wore a simple beige dress tied at the waist with a sash.

"This dragon saved my life and is my friend," she continued. "So please, sheathe your sword."

Dromhiller blinked. "You're saying this is a *good* dragon? Well, fuck me if this isn't the most fucked-up place I've ever seen." With a skeptical look at the dragon, Dromhiller reluctantly sheathed the sword.

Eyeing him carefully, the woman dropped the stone she was holding. "I assume you're the ones who brought us here."

Michael and Dromhiller glanced at each other. "No," said Michael. "Afraid not. We're looking for answers, just like you. Since there's a dragon here, I'm going to assume you were in a fantasy story as well?"

"That's right," she said. "It was kind of a story within a child's story. The dragon was the only magical element. My name is Meribel."

"Dromhiller, beautiful." He grinned at her. "I'll keep you safe, never you fear. And this here is Unicorn," he added with a chortle, gesturing to Michael.

"Michael, actually," said Michael, searing Dromhiller with his stare.

"And I am called Dragon," said the dragon.

"Well that's a big fucking surprise, isn't it?" said Dromhiller.

Meribel frowned at him. "I don't think I'm going to like you very much."

Michael tried to steer them back to the task at hand. "Is anyone else here with you?" he asked Meribel.

Meribel shook her head sadly. "No, just Dragon and me. I've looked within this enclosed area but haven't explored any further."

Trying to swallow his nervousness, Michael turned to the dragon. "Dragon, have you seen anyone else? I saw you flying about earlier."

"There's a dwelling in the next area, upstream. I wasn't able to tell if it was occupied or not."

Meribel nodded. "Since we all have questions, I suggest we travel together to that dwelling. Perhaps the answers we seek lie there."

Michael smiled.

"What is it?" Meribel asked.

"Are you sure your name isn't Dorothy?" he said. "Because it would be great if it were. Then Dromhiller could be the Tin Man and I'd be the Scarecrow. You know, e pluribus unum and all that."

Meribel looked at Dromhiller, who wore the same confused expression.

"Don't worry," said Dromhiller. "I don't know what the fuck he's talking about either."

"Not to worry," said Michael. "Let's go. We're off to see the wizard."

Dromhiller took the lead while Michael and Meribel walked side by side. Once they were out of the clearing, Dragon spread his wings and took flight.

"I'm not actually crazy," Michael said to Meribel. "It's just that this place makes no sense. It's got me a bit giddy."

"This is indeed a strange land," Meribel said. "You need not apologize. I found myself here in a cabin identical to my own, but with neither my father nor Taar, my . . . friend. I was very distressed and was about to set out to seek them when I found you both with Dragon."

"There's no one else here from my life either," Michael said. "When I first heard your voice, I thought you might be… someone I knew. But of course, you're not. So you lived out in the woods?"

"Yes, my father and I had a garden, and once a month I walked to the village with produce to trade."

Meribel and Michael discussed their previous lives until they reached the next area, which was also bounded by rocky hills that jutted to the edge of the river. All three stopped cold. *This*, Michael thought, *has to be the most beautiful, the most intricately built mansion I've ever seen.*

Between the building and them was a broad marble terrace spotted with white statues of nymphs, cherubs, lovers, and lions. There were rose bushes that clung to ornately carved columns and pools adorned with marble urns and dotted with water lilies.

The building itself, set on a hill above the terrace and connected to it by a twisting staircase, consisted of several storeys of some type of seamless white material with turrets at all four corners. There was almost too much detail to take in. The decorations carved into the walls and columns gave Michael the sense that the building was a living, writhing thing. He shuddered at the thought.

Meribel was the first to speak. "I didn't know it was possible to build such a place as this."

"If there's a sorcerer in this land, this is where we'll find him," Dromhiller said, drawing his sword. But he'd scarcely taken a step when the ground shook violently, knocking all three of them off their feet.

As he sat up, Michael said, "Well, that was . . ." He fell silent before finishing his sentence.

Dromhiller, looking at his arms and legs and feeling his face, looked frantically back at Michael.

Michael blinked. Dromhiller had changed again and was now a nonhuman primate, some kind of chimpanzee, but about the same height as a man. Michael approached him cautiously.

"Dromhiller?" he said.

Dromhiller looked at him then craned his neck upward and screeched, "Is this some kind of fucking joke?"

Michael turned to Meribel and noted the shock on her face. "Still the Dromhiller we know and love, then. He changed once before, but it wasn't as drastic as this." To Dromhiller, Michael said, "You did refer to your wielder as a big ape before. I wonder if whoever brought us here took that to heart."

"Are you trying to be funny?" Dromhiller asked, approaching Michael. "Because I'm not laughing."

Backing away, Michael shook his head vigorously.

Dromhiller grunted then scooped up the sword, all the while muttering a string of expletives so foul that Meribel walked away, red-faced, holding her ears.

"Look," said Michael. "Take it easy. I know you're upset, but she's not used to this kind of language. She was in a children's story, remember?"

Dromhiller took a deep breath. "Fine. All I know is that whoever did this is going to be missing a few body parts by the time I'm through with him."

"Look, both of you," Meribel said, pointing. "The mansion. It's vanished. I was looking at it and then it was gone."

It was true. Now, in place of the expansive terrace was a dense forest. A broad path led from their position to a clearing, and in the clearing Michael saw...

"Oh, God," he said. "We can't go there. We'll die."

"How can you know that?" said Meribel. "It's just a cabin. Old and dilapidated, that's all."

"No," said Michael, his voice quivering. "It's a *cabin in the woods*. It looks just like the ones I've seen in a hundred horror movies."

Noting the blank looks on their faces, he clarified. "Stories. Stories meant to scare you. And in these stories, people go into a cabin just like that one and get killed, one by one, by something horrible. I thought we were in a fantasy, but maybe it's not. Maybe this is a horror story."

"Perhaps you should both stay here," Dromhiller said. Then, placing a hand on the hilt of the sword, he started towards the cabin. But he'd scarcely gone ten paces when another violent quake struck.

When the three travellers collected themselves, their surroundings had changed again.

They were lying on pavement. A street, Michael realized, as he got to his feet. Before them stood a house—a suburban two-storey house with white siding, a paved driveway, and a one-car garage. It was set off by a well-manicured lawn and shrubs. Steps at the side of the house led to a raised patio made of thick planks of cedar, beyond which was a large in-ground swimming pool.

There was only the one house. The street ran parallel to the river and there was nothing else but neatly cut grass all around them.

"What manner of dwelling is this?" Dromhiller asked.

"Where I come from," said Michael, "this is a normal dwelling. A family would typically live in a house like this."

They stood still, waiting for another earthquake.

There was none.

Michael and Meribel followed Dromhiller to the front door. He was about to kick it in when Michael turned the knob and it opened. They explored the first and second floors but found no occupants. Nor was there any furniture except in the sunroom at the back, where they found a chair and a desk on which stacks of paper had been placed haphazardly.

Dromhiller raised his head. "Show yourself, coward!"

There was no answer, just the echo of his voice off the bare walls. Dromhiller left in disgust.

Meribel picked up a sheaf of papers as Michael sank into the chair.

"Michael," said Meribel. "Listen to this." She read aloud. "*When Michael Rousseau realized that he was here, wherever here was, or rather, when he realized that he* existed, *his first question wasn't 'Where am I?' but 'Which Michael am I?'*"

"What?" said Michael, getting to his feet. He moved beside Meribel as she skimmed a few pages ahead.

"Here," said Meribel. "There's more." She continued reading. "*'If you speak truly, and are not a wizard, and aren't'*— Sorry, I can't say that word—*'me over, then how did we arrive in this ... place?'*

"*'Beats me. I was hoping to find someone who could tell me. Maybe we could sort this out together?'*"

Meribel was blushing from the strong language. Michael's eyes bulged. "That's exactly what happened when I met Dromhiller," he said. "What is this?"

Meribel looked at him. "It's a story. Our story. It's what's happening to us right now." She skimmed a bit further then pointed out some writing in the margin: "*Not a . . . beefcake.*" She looked up at Michael. "I don't understand that expression."

"This is where Dromhiller changed the first time. From really muscular, that's what a beefcake is, to the way he looked when you met him."

Michael took the papers from Meribel. "Let's see what happens at the end."

But before they could get that far, another earthquake struck, shaking the house wildly. Michael dropped the pages and they scattered about the room. With a sigh, he noted that the pages hadn't been numbered.

They were getting to their feet when Dromhiller's voice rang through the house. "WHAT THE FUCKING FUCK IS THIS? ARE YOU FUCKING KIDDING ME?"

After exchanging glances, Michael and Meribel dashed to the side door and stepped out onto the deck. Dromhiller was looking wide-eyed at his reflection in the pool.

Turning to Michael, he said, "Not one word. Not even one fucking word from you."

But Michael couldn't have spoken if he'd wanted to. He collapsed, helpless with laughter, holding his midsection and shaking.

Meribel just nodded and smiled in understanding. Dromhiller was now a small white creature with a shining mane and tail. But he wasn't a horse, for upon his head was a long, brightly shining horn. "This is still a draft," she said. "Michael, this story, our story, it's still a draft. That's why things keep changing."

Michael sat up and wiped his eyes while the unicorn stamped its feet and vigorously shook its head. Just then, Dragon, who'd been circling above, came down to land a few feet from Dromhiller.

"For what it's worth," Dragon said, "I think you look lovely."

"No one asked you, you mangy, fire-breathing fuck. Well, one thing's for sure."

"What's that?" Michael asked, approaching Dromhiller, hoping to console him somehow.

"This story we're in," said Dromhiller. "It's never going to get published now."

Something Special

This is an example of an epistolary story. These are stories which, traditionally, are based on a series of documents. Perhaps the most famous example is Bram Stoker's Dracula, *with its journal entries and letters. Here we have a sequence of posts on an online forum that become increasingly disturbing.*

Widowed18 June 27, 2018
Hi, I'm new to this forum. Actually, I'm new to all forums. But I've been having trouble coping since my wife's passing and someone suggested looking for support. You know, from people who have already (somehow) gotten through this. I've looked at some of the other posts here and can see that my situation is nothing new. And yet, it's *my* situation. It's new to me. So here I am near the end of June and my wife has been gone since February. And still, months later, I wake up every morning wondering where she's got to. Every night is, well, a nightmare. I haven't gotten a lot of sleep lately. I eat once a day or so. Kind people are still bringing me food. It's not that I *can't* cook. I was the chief cook and bottlewasher while we were married. It's just . . . well, I'm sure you know. So, I guess my question to you all is, how do I sensibly go on from here? Thanks in advance.

HeavyHeart10 June 27, 2018
So sorry for your loss, Widowed18. A lot of us here have been through something similar, but keep in mind that, just as every couple is different, so is the grief suffered by every survivor. Suffering comes in a lot of flavours. I wish I could tell you that it gets easier, but I'm not sure that's true. I've found that the paralysis and pain do subside a bit, but nothing about my day has gotten "easier." How to go on? That I can tell you. Get through today. Just today. And when tomorrow comes, get through that day. One day at a time. Just focus on that. Sending prayers your way.

StillSad98 June 28, 2018
I don't have much to add except to say that we're here for you, buddy. We're listening, any time you feel like talking.

Widowed18 June 28, 2018
Thanks, I really appreciate your thoughts and knowing that I'm not going through this alone.

NotFarAway18 June 29, 2018
So sorry you're in pain, Widowed18. Some people say it helps to talk about your happiest memories together.

Widowed18 June 29, 2018
Really? I've been trying *not* to think about things like that. But then, that strategy hasn't exactly been a roaring success. So I hope no one minds if I ramble on a bit. You don't have to read it all, but, I don't know, having read NotFarAway18's post, I feel a need to talk about my wife.

Something Special

I'll call her Eve. I first met her at an ice-skating rink. I hadn't skated many times at that point and was a bit wobbly. When I began to lose my footing, Eve came skating past, saw that I was going to fall, and grabbed my hand to steady me. It didn't work, and we both went down. Once the initial shock wore off, we looked at each other and started laughing.

I'd recently relocated for my first full-time job. I knew few people and rarely socialized. Then Eve came along, and we would meet up for coffee, then lunches, then dinners. We hit it off very quickly and were married about a year later. That was ten years ago.

We spent our honeymoon on the north shore of Prince Edward Island. The cottage had large windows that yielded spectacular views of the foam-capped waves lapping at the red-tinged beach. We took long walks along the shore, enlivened by the snap of the breeze and smell of the ocean. We ate a lot of lobster. At first, we had no idea where to begin, but our server was an "island girl" and showed us how to break the crustacean apart for the meat and marrow. When it rained, we got in the car and visited craft boutiques across the island. I learned at least one new thing about Eve—that I should never play Scrabble with her. Every game she wiped the floor with me. Did you know that *em* is a word that denotes the letter *m*? I mean, come on. And yes, we visited Green Gables. We both loved Lucy Maud Montgomery's writing and spent a few evenings reading *Anne of Green Gables* out loud to each other.

The following year we took a holiday in the UK's Lake District. We stayed in an old lodge on Lake Windermere and walked for miles over heather-covered hills and footpaths bordered by old stone fences. We toured Beatrix Potter's house and garden and went on canoe day trips. Although people complain about British food, we developed a love of Yorkshire puddings, roast beef, roasted potatoes, and hot apple pie with custard. Our love of books kept us entertained in the evenings. This time we took turns reading aloud from *Wuthering Heights*. Even though we'd lived together for a while by this time, we never seemed to run out of things to talk about.

I'd moved into her apartment after the wedding. A couple of years later, after saving for a down payment, we moved into a suburban home with a yard, garden, trees, the whole deal. Things were really good. Our careers advanced, we had friends, parties, holidays, and a lot of fun. I swear, we were still in the "honeymoon phase" after all those years together.

There were lots more good times through the years, at home as well as away. Sadly, the good times are gone, as they say.

StillSad98 June 29, 2018
Those are some golden memories you've got there, Widowed18. Maybe one way to look at it is, those memories, plus the pain you're feeling, they're your proof that your wife was HERE and will always be with you. At least, that's what I've found. Though I wouldn't tell people I know IRL, the fact is that I talk to her all the time.

NotFarAway18 June 29, 2018
How beautiful, Widowed18. You must have loved each other very much.

Widowed18 June 30, 2018
Yes, we did. We really did. Our tenth anniversary was going to be this year. We had talked about flying to Vegas and getting remarried by Elvis. From there, I'd hoped we could fly to Hawaii for a second honeymoon.

NotFarAway18 June 30, 2018
That sounds very special. I'm afraid that I suffered a loss this year as well when my husband and I were separated from each other by tragedy. He meant the world to me and I loved him very much.

Widowed18 June 30, 2018
I'm . . . well, I'm not sure what to say. I'm so sorry for your loss. And there you were consoling me. You must have a big heart, NotFarAway18. Do you feel like talking about it?

NotFarAway18 June 30, 2018
I know I said that sharing your happiest memories might help, but no, I'm just not ready for that. I guess I can dish out advice but I can't take it. What I feel most of all is angry. Angry that we can't be together. Angry that our life together is over and that all the plans we made, all the hopes we had, well, they'll never happen, will they? If he were here I'd really give him a piece of my mind. That probably sounds silly, but as someone in this thread

already said, the grieving process is different for everyone. But I'm sorry, this should be about you, not about me. Yes, I've suffered a loss recently, but I'd still like to be able to help if I can.

Widowed18 June 30, 2018
You know, you could be on to something. I wonder if the way to get through this is to stop thinking so much about my own troubles and try to focus more on others, and to make their lives a bit better somehow? I appreciate the support I've had from everyone here, but this suggestion could really make a difference!

NotFarAway18 June 30, 2018
I'm very glad, Widowed18. Do you mind if I ask how your wife died?

Widowed18 June 30, 2018
Man, this is hard. But sure. Eve had a severe peanut allergy. One terrible day in February, a neighbour found her on the kitchen floor. She'd called earlier and Eve had told her to come over for tea in the afternoon. Eve had baked some cookies to have with the tea and must have tasted one of them. Somehow, peanut particles had become mixed in with the dough. Eve didn't have her inhaler with her. It was in the bedroom. It looked like she was trying to reach it but didn't make it out of the kitchen. No one knows how it happened. We kept jars of mixed nuts on hand for guests, but Eve was extremely careful with them.

However it happened, she's gone, and I have to live with the fact that I wasn't there for her. I really hope she didn't suffer in the end.

NotFarAway18 July 1, 2018
Actually, Buttercup, I did suffer. A lot. But I'm much better now.

Moderator
This post is in extremely poor taste, NotFarAway18. Consider yourself warned. Another such post and you'll be banned from the site.

Widowed18 July 1, 2018
Is this what they call "trolling"? Do you think what I'm going through is something to joke about? I thought you were being nice. That you cared. Who are you? And why did you call me "Buttercup"?

StillSad98 July 1, 2018
OMG! So sorry that one of "us" added to your misery, Widowed18. You should be ashamed of yourself, NotFarAway18.

NotFarAway18 July 1, 2018
But that's what I've called you since "that night." You know, the night we . . . did it. For the first time. We watched *The Princess Bride* at your place. You made popcorn. We started to lick the butter off of each other's fingers and the rest just kind of happened. Remember?

Something Special

Moderator

Apologies to the group. We're trying to remove this user from our system but have been unsuccessful so far. We can't seem to delete posts from this user either. This is a top priority. I'll report back when it's done.

Widowed18 July 1, 2018

OK, NotFarAway18, so obviously you're a friend of Eve's. A close friend judging by what you're telling me. She wouldn't have shared those kinds of details with just anyone. Just so you know, I'm going to discuss this with my lawyer when we meet later today. Rest assured, I'll be taking action.

Moderator

Sorry to report that all efforts to remove user NotFarAway18 have thus far been unsuccessful. There's two more aspects to this weirdness: No one is able to create new user IDs at the moment, and screenshots of NotFarAway18's posts turn out blank. Please bear with us while we continue to work towards a solution.

StillSad98 July 1, 2018

Well I'll be damned. After looking at the moderator's post just now, I tried to take a screenshot of NotFarAway18's last post. It was blank. I've never seen anything like it . . .

NotFarAway18 July 1, 2018

I understand that you're upset, Buttercup. With me gone, you must find our house empty. We'd barely inaugurated the jacuzzi we installed in the en-suite bathroom. And on the front porch, there's that rocking chair for two we bought a few years ago. Now there's an empty seat next to yours. Perhaps Lilith could help with that.

Widowed18 July 1, 2018
What do you mean by that, NotFarAway18? Whoever you really are.

NotFarAway18 July 2, 2018
It's me, Buttercup. Evelyn. Or Eve, as you've referred to me. And you know perfectly well what I mean. After all, Lilith was, well, let's say she was very nice to you, wasn't she? Before I died, I mean. And after.

Widowed18 July 2, 2018
While we did have a friend by the name of Lilith, I resent what you're implying. I loved my wife. LOVED her. I wouldn't have hurt her that way.

NotFarAway18 July 2, 2018
Ah, that's sweet. But you did, though, didn't you? I mean, I didn't know before, not while I was alive. But I know it now. And I know other things.

Widowed18 July 2, 2018
What are you implying?

NotFarAway18 July 3, 2018
Well, for instance, BUTTERCUP, I know how you killed me.

Something Special

HeavyHeart10 July 3, 2018
Really, NotFarAway18, this has to stop. Can't you see that Widowed18 is in pain? Is this how you get your jollies? No one wants you here. Just leave. And take your misery with you.

NotFarAway18 July 3, 2018
Alright. I've said my piece, except for this: One day, BUTTERCUP, perhaps not so long from now, it will be your time. And when that day comes, I'll be right here, waiting. I've arranged something special for you.

A Question of Judgment

This light-hearted story derives from TV detectives who seem as keen to pass moral judgment on their interviewees as to solve the crime in question. "You had an affair? After five years of marriage? With a gymnast?" Extrapolate that a little bit and I present to you Detective Gumm.

Detective Ridley Gumm stood and rolled up his sleeves. He was just getting warmed up.

Vic Hapless, meanwhile, took out a handkerchief and wiped the spittle from his face. "You're getting awfully worked up about this," said Vic.

The interview room, bleak and grey, held a metal table bolted to the floor, a one-way glass mirror, and particularly uncomfortable chairs. Vic wondered if that was part of the strategy. Having to sit here for any length of time would be enough to wring a confession from the most hardened axe murderer. *I'll talk! But for mercy's sake, get me a comfortable chair!*

As for Gumm, Vic observed, he quite looked the part of an outraged detective: clenched, square jaw, close-cropped hair, tie loosened around his neck, faint odour of cigarettes. No, Vic decided. Cigars. He could just imagine the imposing, six-foot-tall man chomping on a cigar, guzzling whisky, and pacing as he worked out whodunnit.

"Now," said Gumm, leaning on the table with both arms, "let's start at the beginning."

Vic sighed. "I was walking down Bank Street."

"Which direction? Which side of the street? When?"

"Okay, okay. I was walking south on the west side of Bank Street. It was sometime after 2:00 p.m. I don't know when exactly. I had just reached the Book Company and was looking at the window display. That's when the clown came up to me."

"Description?"

"Pardon me?"

"What did this person look like?"

Nonplussed, Vic considered this. "He looked, you know, like a . . . clown. White-painted face, wide red lips, red nose, hair that stuck out in a couple of spots."

Is that a noise behind the glass? Vic wondered. *What's going on back there?*

He returned his attention to the interview when Gumm pounded the desk with his fist.

"What?" said Vic.

"I asked you what happened when this person approached you."

"He was doing some sort of mime act, moving left and right when I did. I couldn't get past him. Then he started to poke me with his left and right forefingers. So finally I slugged him."

Gumm's eyes widened, he clenched his right hand into a fist, and drew back his arm as if he were winding up to punch Vic then and there. "You're *admitting* that you *assaulted* him?"

"He assaulted me first, touching me without my permission, so I would argue it was self-defence. Besides, I never was overly fond of clowns."

As the interview continued, a half-dozen officers in the observation area doubled over with laughter.

"Oh, this is the best," said the first to recover his breath. "I would *pay* to watch a Gumm interview."

"How does he get these cases?" said another. "I mean, an assault on a clown? How does he keep a straight face?"

"Well, this *is* Gumm we're talking about."

There was silence for a moment. Then: "Gumm. What a bozo."

That was it. The officers were completely helpless.

Vic pulled into the driveway of his Stittsville home, his interrogation fresh on his mind. The detective had told him that the clown was declining to press charges, but Gumm had left Vic with a warning: "Watch yourself. If I see you again, I won't be so easy on you."

As he approached the house, Vic got the feeling that all wasn't well. His cat, Tommy, was invariably perched upon the back of the sofa, looking out the front window for him. Not today.

His next clue was when he set about unlocking the front door. It wasn't locked. Yet he would swear that he'd locked it that morning. Stepping inside, he called for Tommy and froze. The place was a shambles. And that was his last thought for a while.

His next thought was *Ow*. The thought after that was *Where am I?* Finally, *Why am I wherever I am?*

A Question of Judgement

After blinking a few times, he realized he was lying down. Strapped down, in fact. And beside him was the kindly face of a black-clad paramedic, stethoscope wrapped around his neck. Something jolted Vic up and down.

"Oh good, you're conscious," said the paramedic. "You've received quite a blow to the head. We're taking you to the hospital for tests. We'll be there in just a couple of minutes." As Vic processed this, the man continued. "Do you remember what happened?"

Shaking his head, Vic groaned in pain. "I've no idea. I remember walking up to the house, but nothing after that."

"Well, I'm sure the police will be following up with you later on."

Vic, who felt he'd had quite enough attention from the police for one day, was less than thrilled.

After X-rays and blood tests, Vic was admitted to a semiprivate room. Thankfully, the bed next to his was empty. There was no concussion or evidence of brain damage, he'd been told, but he would be kept overnight as a precaution.

After calling his boyfriend, who, as Vic predicted, freaked out (and then calmed down in due course), Vic found himself tired. Sometime later, through half-shut lids, he noticed a figure standing at the foot of his bed. Opening his eyes fully, he found his worst fear confirmed. It was Gumm.

He stood, hands on hips, glaring at Vic.

"What?" said Vic.

"What aren't you telling me?"

"I don't recall that you've asked me anything."

"Don't play coy with me. We've been through your house."

"Okay . . ."

Gumm didn't reply. Instead, he crossed his arms and continued to glare.

"Look," said Vic. "The only thing I know is that I was attacked. See the goose egg up here?" He pointed. "Why are you looking at me as if I'm guilty of something?"

"Aren't you?"

"No," said Vic. Deciding to wait Gumm out, he whistled to himself and let his eyes wander around the room.

"Do you think you're being *funny*?" said Gumm, his face reddening. He pulled out his phone, unlocked it, flipped through a few screens, and held it up for Vic. "How do you explain *this*?"

Squinting, Vic saw a photo of a bulletin board with attached newspaper articles and images.

"Sorry, what am I looking at?"

"This photo was taken in your house. In one of the bedrooms. It's full of photos and newspaper clippings about my cases."

"In my house? I don't think so. I never heard of you before today."

Before Gumm could continue, a nurse entered the room and gestured to her watch. "You should let Mr. Hapless get some rest now."

"Very well," said Gumm, as he put away his phone. He looked at Vic. "A police officer will escort you home once you've been discharged. I expect you to cooperate fully."

With a final, withering look at Vic, Gumm turned and left.

In response to the nurse, who cast him a questioning glance, Vic could only shrug.

"Thanks for the lift," said Vic, as Officer Reeves pulled into his driveway. "At least I didn't have to pay for a taxi."

The officer had told Vic that, in addition to escorting him home, she'd accompany him while he checked to see if anything was missing.

When they entered the house, Vic stopped short. It had been completely turned over.

"I take it you didn't leave it like this," said Reeves.

"No," said Vic, fighting the gurgling in his stomach. He wanted to throw up right there on the floor. "Not exactly. But I remember now. I saw this mess just before someone clobbered me." He gingerly touched the bump on his head.

In the living room, to the left of the front entrance, cushions, books, and magazines were strewn about the floor. Framed posters had been taken down, the TV placed on the sofa, and the side table's drawers all pulled out and emptied upon the floor.

"Someone was able to feed my cat, weren't they?" said Vic, feeling a need to say something. Anything.

"Yes, we set out food and fresh water yesterday evening," said Reeves.

It was the same throughout the house. The kitchen was especially bad. The odd thing, thought Vic, was that, although the place was a mess, it didn't appear as though anything was missing. The only things of value he owned were electronics—the home theatre, laptop, peripherals—but those were all present and accounted for. Of Tommy there was no sign. Vic assumed the cat was freaked out and hiding underneath one of the beds.

It was when they reached one of the spare bedrooms that Vic stopped short. The bed had been shoved against the wall, and where it had rested was a bulletin board full of clippings and photos. Glancing at one of the walls, Vic saw that it was likewise decorated with grainy photos and printouts.

"Um . . ." Vic was momentarily speechless. "This wasn't here before."

"Are you sure about that?"

"Are you kidding? This is my house. I know what I have and what I don't. I promise you, this wasn't here before."

"Okay, then I'd better get you to headquarters. Detective Gumm will want a word with you. While you're doing that, forensics will gather up the evidence and take it for analysis."

"The day just gets better and better," Vic mumbled.

"I really don't understand you," said Vic. "Yesterday I was accosted by a clown. Then I was attacked. Knocked unconscious. My house was broken into and tossed. And yet you're interrogating me like I'm the one who's done something wrong."

He and Gumm were back in the interrogation room at police headquarters. The chair hadn't become any more comfortable in his absence. Gumm, as before, was standing on the other side of the table. Regarding Vic with narrowed eyes, he rolled up his sleeves. *Probably in case he feels like roughing me up*, thought Vic. *Maybe I should invite him to give me his best shot.* On further consideration, Vic decided that was a bad idea.

"What do you do for a living, Mr. Hapless?"

Vic blinked. "I'm a project management consultant."

"So," said Gumm, "what do you *do*?"

Vic sighed. No one understood what project managers actually did. "A project is a set of inputs, a set of outputs, and a set of tasks that happen in between. A project manager identifies what tasks need to be accomplished and what inputs are needed to produce the desired outputs. Then they make sure that it all happens in accordance with applicable quality standards." In reply to Gumm's raised eyebrow, he added, "It's actually a lot of work."

"If you say so. Did it take a lot of work to put together that bulletin board?"

Vic exhaled. "As I've already said, the first time I saw it was when your officer escorted me through the house."

"Then why are your fingerprints all over it?"

"My . . ." *What?* "I've no idea. Look, would it help if you spoke to my boyfriend? He's been in the house lots of times. He'll tell you that I have never had a room dedicated to Detective Gumm."

Gumm lowered his head and jutted his neck forward. "Do you know what the penalty is for obstruction of justice? *Do you?*"

As Vic reached for his handkerchief, he noted some sort of commotion on the other side of the glass.

"Qik!" Staff Sergeant Baker barked from his office. Sied jumped in her seat then got up from her desk. Baker beckoned her in and closed the door. "Your paperwork on the Edison case was excellent, Detective," he said, as they both took their seats.

"Thank you, sir."

"I'd like you to join Detective Gumm on the Hapless case."

Sied couldn't help but groan out loud.

Baker raised an eyebrow. "Is that a problem, Detective?"

Yes. Really, yes. But Sied bit her tongue before saying, "Not at all, sir. Detective Gumm's a credit to the force."

"Quite right," said Baker, handing her a file folder. "You can start by delivering these forensic results from Ident Unit. That's all, Detective."

"Yes sir," said Sied, standing.

As she exited the office, she was greeted by an unspoken query from the detective who sat across from her. "Gumm," she mouthed. He chortled.

Ignoring him, she continued to Gumm's desk. When he looked up at her, she said, "Sir, the staff sergeant assigned me to work with you on the Hapless case."

"Glad to have you, Detective Qik. Do you have something for me?"

At least he'd pronounced her name correctly. So many in the department pronounced it *quick* despite her reminders that it rhymed with *pick*. "Yes, sir, the report from Ident Unit."

"Very good. Grab a chair and you can get up to speed while I look this over."

Sied was pleasantly surprised and did as he'd asked. Gumm could be a dick sometimes, but he was already treating her better than half the staff on the floor. And his desk was well organized and clean—she had to give him that. The Hapless case folder was immediately visible.

She was scarcely finished the first page when she chuckled.

"Is something funny, Detective?"

Ignoring her brain's warning signals, Sied said, "A clown gets in the guy's face and he slugs him. Good for him."

There was no response from Gumm. *Uh-oh*, she thought, as she looked up into Gumm's reddening face.

"Do you think that assault is *funny*, Detective? Are you not an officer of the *law*?"

All Sied could do was sit contritely and let Gumm rant at her. It lasted quite a while.

"I'm very sorry, sir," said Sied, after the detective had finished. In her head, she told him to go screw himself. "I forgot myself. It won't happen again." Sied maintained eye contact until Gumm looked down to the forensics report. After shooting daggers with her eyes at the neighbouring officers for their snickering, she began to read again.

The clown, his name was Milton Earle, had been busking without a licence. As he had also admitted to prodding Hapless, he'd declined to press charges. Hapless was released and reported going straight home, where he was knocked unconscious. Someone had called 911 from the home phone, which was a VOIP line. It was likely the assailant, but not definitively. The caller was male, but it was difficult to infer anything else from the brief call. The home had been tossed. Nothing was reported missing, but there was the matter of a room dedicated to clippings about Gumm's previous cases. Hapless claimed he'd never seen them before, and that he'd never even heard of Gumm before that day.

"Sir," Sied said tentatively, noting that Gumm's forehead was furrowed in concentration, "may I ask what the report says?"

"While the prints on the material belong to Hapless, they consist entirely of right thumbprints. Ident Unit thinks it unlikely that he actually handled the material, and more likely that someone made a copy of his thumbprint and placed it there." He glanced at her. "Still, Hapless is hiding something. I'm certain of it."

"Do you think there's a link between his attacker and him?"

"What do you think, Detective?" he asked, his tone sincere.

Sied blinked. *Okay, back to* not *being a dick.* "I think there are two possibilities: either Hapless is up to something, or he's being set up to get your attention. I think we need more information. I would suggest a deep dive into Hapless and Earle. The clown incident must have been a distraction. Something to keep Hapless away from his house while someone else tossed it. Earle has an alibi, but he could be working with someone. I think Hapless is linked in some way to either Earle or the attacker. And the attacker is likely someone who knows you or knows of you."

Gumm eyed her. Had she gone too far? Then he did something completely unexpected. He smiled.

"Good work, Qik. I agree completely." As Sied took that in, Gumm continued. "I'd like you to go through my cases over the past five years, in particular, the cases mentioned in the bulletin board posts. I'm going to go have a chat with the boyfriend."

Sied's eyes glazed over as she picked up yet another case folder. She'd been working her way from oldest to newest. Nothing had struck her as having any connection with Hapless. To give her eyes a break, she looked away and noticed Detective Renfrew gesturing to get her attention.

"Qik. Qik! Check this out."

There was already a small horde surrounding Renfrew's desk, eyes fixed on his monitor. "What am I looking at?" she asked as she approached.

"It's Gumm. He's pulled someone over."

"Turn up the volume," someone said.

Gumm, his face worked up in outrage, was berating the driver. The passenger was apparently live-streaming the whole thing from their phone.

"Do you realize that you changed lanes without *signalling*? Without even a *shoulder check*? Do you know how *dangerous* that is? And now you tell me you're driving without a *licence*?"

"No, that's not what I said," said the driver, a young Caucasian man. "I said that I didn't have my licence *on* me.

It's at home. I took it out of my wallet to show someone and I guess I forgot to put it back."

"You *guess*?"

"That Gumm," said Renfrew. "How does he not just explode from high blood pressure?"

With a sigh, Sied returned to Gumm's desk and the case notes. But as she picked up the next folder in the pile, she paused. Something was niggling at her. But what?

There was a chorus of laughter from Renfrew's desk. Glancing in that direction, Sied rolled her eyes. Then she froze. That was it. Gumm's stopping a vehicle. She'd seen something like that . . . but where? Sied tore through the files again and let out a loud "Aha!" when she found it. Hadn't something happened to the guy Gumm pulled over years ago? She read the file again. *Oh dear.* But was there a connection with Hapless?

She did a quick search, and her face turned suddenly pale. Sied reached for her phone.

He didn't make a lot of money from them, but fantasy illustrations had always been Martin's favourite. He could let his imagination off its leash and create a world that was literally magical. Watercolour seemed particularly suited to fantasy, the way it lent the scene a quality of otherworldliness, and watercolour happened to be his favourite medium. Another plus.

He was putting the finishing touches on an illustration for a book cover when the doorbell rang. Hoping whoever it was would go away, he continued. When it rang again, followed by a loud hammering, Martin set down his brushes with a sigh.

A Question of Judgement

"Important, is it?" said Martin, as he opened the door.

The man had an imposing presence—strong jawline, tall, broad build. He could use this guy as inspiration for some upcoming projects. Martin was picturing him dressed not in a suit but in scarlet wizarding robes.

"Martin Purpurin?"

After Martin nodded, the man pulled out ID and said, "Detective Ridley Gumm. I'd like to speak with you."

"Ah," said Martin. "This would be concerning Vic, then. Please, come in."

Martin started leading Gumm to the living room but paused when the man stopped to examine one of the mounted paintings on the wall—a Frazetta-like scene of a muscular warrior wearing only a loincloth, one arm wrapped about a thin, naked man, his other hand brandishing a sword. In the background, through a mist, was a dragon. With a smile, Martin noted that Gumm was fixed on the signature at the bottom.

"This is your work?" said Gumm.

"Yes, I'm an artist. These are some of my commissions, and the odd one I've done just for my own pleasure."

"Well, you're very talented," Gumm commented.

In the living room, they took seats facing each other. "Mr. Purpurin," said Gumm, "I'm here to ask you about Vic Hapless. In particular, can you confirm that you've visited his house recently?"

"Well, yes, I've been there many times."

"When we searched the house after the attack upon Mr. Hapless, we found a bulletin board with clippings about many of my cases."

"I heard about that from Vic. I can tell you, honestly, that I never saw it whenever he had me over."

"Can you think of any reason why Mr. Hapless would be interested in my cases?"

"No, not at all."

"All right, Mr. Purpurin, thank you. Just for elimination purposes, may I ask where you were between 3:00 p.m. and 4:00 p.m. yesterday?"

"Sure. I was tossing Vic's house, making a total mess, and then I moved the bulletin board and the clippings into one of his rooms. When Vic came home, I knocked him out with a baseball bat."

Eyes wide, Gumm whispered, "What?"

As Gumm absorbed what had just been said, Martin reached behind a throw cushion and retrieved the handgun he'd placed there earlier.

His surprise quickly replaced by anger, Gumm rose to his feet. "You're *admitting* this? That you committed break-and-enter and assault? And now you're threatening an officer of the *law*? How *dare* you!"

"Oh, spare me the moral judgment and just listen for a while," Martin said. "Go on, sit back down. Might as well be comfortable. There, that's better. Now then, four years ago you stopped a car driving at night with one taillight out. That's all, just a taillight. Was that so important? Are you incapable of letting even the most minor infractions go? But I suppose not.

"Don't you remember? Let me jog your memory. The driver's name was Leo Tripp. After you stopped him, and shone a light in his face, you noticed that his pupils were dilated. There hadn't been anything wrong with his driving.

Not a single thing. But you assumed he was high, and, yes, you were right. Not only that, but after searching the car you found a travel bag full of cocaine. Ringing any bells now? Oh, good. But here comes the best part.

"He was convicted of trafficking and sentenced to prison. Six months later, he was dead. The murderer was never found. I imagine they didn't look terribly hard. After all, they'd saved the prison system some money and the world from a bad egg. The thing is, the guy you sent away was my stepbrother. He meant the world to me. And he died for . . . what? Because of your righteousness, your insistence upon following the letter of the law, your outrage at what you might consider a moral deficit. You punish those who don't follow your own personal code.

"That ends today, of course. To get here, I thought I'd have some fun. Get your attention. Poor Vic, I did really like him, but I was going to leave him for Milton anyway. Milton has done some work as a clown, you know, parties and things, so I commissioned him to get in Vic's face. I really didn't expect Vic to have the backbone to punch him. That was quite a delicious twist. I know what you're going to ask, so, no, Milton had no idea what was coming. He thought it was meant to be a practical joke.

"I figured you had an ego, and would love to be the subject of someone's obsession, so I made it look like that someone was Vic. That certainly got your attention. Which brings us to where we are and what's going to happen next. I've something special planned for you. We're going to go for a drive in your car. For you, it will be a one-way trip. Don't even think about refusing. I'd rather not kill you here and now, but I've made a contingency for that.

Now get up. Thanks. First off, we're going to the garage through the kitchen. You'll have noticed that the outside door is already open. You're going to drive your car into the garage so I can get in without being seen. Then we'll be off. Is that clear?"

Gumm seemed to be considering the instructions. "And then you'll kill me."

"Yes, yes, of course, and then I'll kill you. Now, get up and lead the way."

Milton directed Gumm to the garage. Once inside, he prodded the detective with the gun to move to his car. Gumm walked slowly out to the driveway; Milton remained in the garage.

What happened next wasn't quite what Milton had anticipated. After starting the engine, Gumm ducked down, backed the car out of the driveway at breakneck speed, and sped away.

"Well, shit," said Milton.

Sied, driving her own vehicle, followed a couple of uniforms in a patrol car. With sirens blaring and lights flashing, they sped from headquarters along the highway and exited onto one of Alta Vista's suburban streets. They were a kilometre away from Purpurin's address when Sied spotted a car speeding towards them. It screeched to a stop and swerved, blocking their path. Stunned, Sied exited her vehicle and was about to administer a Gumm-worthy tongue-lashing when Gumm himself stepped onto the road.

"Glad to see you, Qik. Very glad. Good work. If things had gone just a bit differently, you'd have saved my life."

Rooted in place, Sied mumbled a "Thank you, sir." She explained that, having read the Tripp file, she'd done some digging and found the connection between Tripp and Purpurin. When she was unable to reach Gumm on his mobile, she'd recruited some officers to provide backup.

After promising to commend her performance in his report, Gumm brought her up to speed.

"So," said Sied, "not the sharpest knife in the drawer, then."

After shaking his head in response, Gumm returned to his vehicle and led the other cars to Purpurin's address, where they took him into custody without incident.

Under interrogation, Purpurin denied confessing to assaulting Hapless and denied threatening Gumm. However, upon searching his house, officers found the gun. It had been hastily sequestered in the kitchen in a bag of flour. They also found a baseball bat, a Louisville Slugger, covered with fingerprints and traces of blood. The prints belonged to Purpurin. DNA tests matched the blood to Hapless. Purpurin was subsequently charged with multiple offences.

Already stunned by the news, Vic was further surprised to see Gumm pull up in his driveway the following morning.

"Detective," said Vic, as he opened the door.

"I thought I might fill you in on the case," said Gumm.

"That'd be great." Vic led Gumm to the living room. "To be honest, I thought for a moment that you might be here to interrogate me again."

Vic was surprised once more when Gumm smiled slightly.

"Who do we have here?" said Gumm, as the black cat approached him.

"This is Tommy."

As Gumm bent to stroke the top of his head, Tommy hissed and, with a swift stroke of his paw, scratched Gumm's hand.

"Oh my goodness, I'm sorry," said Vic. "He's never like that." *Not with, you know, human beings.*

"Well, I suppose I had it coming," said Gumm with another smile, before debriefing Vic and consoling him about his erstwhile boyfriend in an almost humane way.

"Well, I won't take up any more of your time. Have a good day, Mr. Hapless."

"Thanks," said Vic, as Gumm exited the front door. "And thanks for coming over. And for getting to the bottom of this."

"All in a day's work."

A loud crash jolted them both. A car backing out of a driveway had apparently been struck by a car travelling too fast to stop.

Gumm raced towards the collision. Even from the front door, Vic could tell that Gumm's blood pressure was skyrocketing.

"You were *speeding?*" he screamed to one driver. In a *residential neighbourhood?* Are you *trying* to get someone *killed?*"

Then he dashed to the car that had been backing out of the driveway. "You entered the street without a proper check for *traffic*? What if there'd been *children* in that car? I'm going to write up the both of you."

Chuckling, Vic entered the house and closed the door behind him. It didn't look as if anyone had been hurt, thank goodness. And as for Gumm, well, some things clearly never changed.

The phone rang. Vic answered, and after a moment, his face turned red. "Have you nothing *better* to do?" he said. "Do you know how tedious it is getting spam calls all the time? Yes, this *is* a spam call. Good*bye*!"

After slamming the phone down, he paused, wide-eyed. *Oh no*, he thought. *I've got Gumm disease.*

The Knife

I don't often write flash fiction, and welcomed the challenge of telling a story in 1,000 words. In this tale, I've tried to provide a variation on slasher horror. Naturally, the working title of this story was "Slash Flash."

Andrea McKee stands in the kitchen of her fiancé's condo, eyes fixed upon the spot where she found his body. Her hands tremble, and she grips the counter for support.

I can't wait to sell this place, she thinks.

This is her first time back, and now that she's here, it feels like she's living through it again, the shock, the screams, the tears, the anger. The murderer still hasn't been caught. By now she thinks that he never will.

Today is about taking inventory of Ray's possessions, figuring out what she wants to keep and what can be donated to the Salvation Army. Her initial thought was to get rid of everything, all the reminders. But her house is sparsely furnished and equipped, and there's a lot in Ray's condo that she can use. *Besides*, she thinks, *it's not as if getting rid of his things would wipe the slate clean, erase the memories.*

The horror of finding Ray's body will never leave her, of that she is positive.

For a time, she was near paralyzed with grief. Counselling has helped, as has the medication. Mostly. She does feel better but still has trouble sleeping, and has

The Knife

become friends with the stars in the late-night summertime sky. Her counsellor, a middle-aged woman whose face speaks of friendly concern, suggested that she seemed ready to face the memories head-on, rather than hiding from them. And that's what brought her here today.

Andrea decides to begin with the kitchen. Her kitchen is smaller, but there's a bit of room yet. There's definitely room for Ray's high-end cappuccino maker. If there's one thing they had in common, it was a love of good coffee. Selecting a suitable packing box, she wraps the machine, places it in the box, and seals it with packing tape.

What next?

As if in answer, a beam of sun breaks through the grey, overcast sky and illuminates the knife set.

Right, thinks Andrea. *You're coming home with me.*

The knives, nestled within their wooden block, are beautifully balanced with contoured grip and stainless-steel blade. Taking a chef's knife in her hand, Andrea admires the workmanship. But after a moment she nearly drops it in shock. Is she imagining things or is the knife vibrating? No, not vibrating. It's more like a regular beat, faint, but detectable, like a heartbeat.

Wondering whether hallucinations are a side-effect of her meds, she puts the knife down on the counter, takes a deep breath, and picks it up again. There's definitely… something. And she notices that the longer she holds it, the stronger the beat.

Setting it down again, Andrea backs away from the counter, trying to understand. Is this a prank? Did someone, maybe Ray himself, hollow out the handle, insert a pulsing something, and then somehow close it seamlessly?

That didn't seem likely.

Something even less likely happens next. The knife begins to visibly vibrate on the counter, humming like an angry bee. It rises in the air about an inch or two, spins like a top, and stops, blade pointed in Andrea's direction.

Eyes wide and mouth open, Andrea backs further away. She watches, stunned, as the knife hurtles towards her and embeds itself in the left side of her abdomen.

Feeling about to faint, Andrea grabs the handle and tries to pry it loose. It clings to her like a hungry child on its mother's teat, and she watches as the blood seeps out of her abdomen, travels up the blade, and is absorbed into the handle.

Shock is taking hold now. Andrea isn't feeling any pain from the stabbing. Abstractedly, she wonders if this is how Ray died.

Without warning the blade pulls itself free and hovers, trembling, a few feet from her.

A figure becomes faintly visible, six feet tall, a patch of grey, like a faint silhouette. *It's holding the knife, feeding on me*, Andrea realizes.

The knife's trembling increases, perhaps with renewed hunger now that it's tasted her, and Andrea realizes that it's going to stab her again.

The warmth in her wrists rouses her, and anger takes hold. *No you don't, motherfucker*, she thinks. *I didn't fight my way back into the world just to have you take it away*. She taps the bracelet on her left wrist as the knife begins its plunge towards her.

The Knife

Within two one hundredths of a second, her body is sheathed in a nano-polymer fabric, impervious to knives, gun shots, and flame, among other things. A basic self-defence system that is widely available, though not utilized by everyone.

The knife bounces off. It tries again and again, each effort punctuated with a loud clanging.

Andrea feels herself again. The suit is closing the wound and has injected her with adrenaline for the shock, as well as antibiotics and red blood cell growth accelerators.

Laughing, she says, "I don't know what the fuck you are, but the 1980's was a hundred years ago, *bitch!*"

The knife stops in place, and she hears a dim, fading laugh as the figure and the knife dissolve before her eyes.

In a few seconds, when it deems that it is safe to do so, the suit dissolves around her, the nanoparticles once again sequestered within her bracelets.

Ray had eschewed the self-defence system, arguing that it provided incentives for even more violent behaviour. It was the one thing they'd disagreed about. To compromise, Andrea had agreed to turn off the automatic activation feature. She'll have to change that. *The only thing the suit is lacking,* she thinks, *is a mechanism to filter out the damnable virus that's taken more lives even than COVID-19 did generations ago.*

Running her hands through her hair, and feeling calmer, she glances at the knife set.

Nope.

Wrapping it up, she takes the set and tosses it down the garbage chute.

Laura Wilcox

Try to imagine the life of a woman married to a controlling, dominating wizard. That is the life of Laura Wilcox, and this is the story of how she regains her independence. Portions of this story were inspired by, and pay tribute to, the novel Lolly Willowes, *by Sylvia Townsend Warner. A note of caution to the reader: Laura suffers some magical abuse.*

When her father died, Laura Wilcox was bereft. She felt that her world would evermore be solitary and empty. So it was that when the wizard began to woo her, Laura, who'd first treated him with cool indifference, warmed to him, and looked forward to his visits; they began to fill some of the void in her life.

They'd met at a book signing in Toronto following the publication of her debut novel. It was the first day of a cross-country book tour, which, if successful, would be followed by a tour through the United States.

She'd taken the morning train from north of the city, and then the subway. The bookstore was a short, pleasant walk from the nearest station. On arriving, before the store opened, she was shown to a table upon which were set several stacks of her books, a nameplate, and a set of pens. There were two chairs, one for her, and another for a store clerk to assist with purchases.

Taking a seat, Laura picked up a copy of *Never Mind Me* and stroked it fondly, like a favourite pet, wondering if there'd be any interest at all in her or the book. She was roused from her thoughts by a buzz of conversation at the cash register. The staff were looking through the glass of the store entrance. Then they looked at Laura. Peering through a nearby window, Laura placed a hand to her mouth. There was a *lineup*. Not all of these people were here for her, though. Surely not.

She didn't have time to process this as the door opened and the line re-formed in front of her. Her natural shyness proved to be an impediment as she attempted to engage in small talk with each person who approached. After some failed attempts, she decided she wouldn't try, not unless the customer was able to draw her out for a few seconds. Rather, she'd greet them with what she hoped was a friendly smile, autograph the book, and move on to the next in line.

Most in line were women. When the first man approached, she took his book and asked to whom the dedication should be made.

"James Mage Blaise," he said quietly.

Mage. Laura blinked and looked up at him. "Oh, you're a . . ."

"Yes."

She'd never met a wizard, and though she knew not to expect the robes and pointed hat described in fanciful stories, it was surprising how nondescript he was. No, not nondescript. But there was nothing about him that said "Here stands a wizard," dressed as he was in dark slacks, a light-grey jacket, and a black shirt, open at the collar. She imagined passing him on the street and paying him no mind whatsoever. She wondered what had brought him here.

"Well, you're my first," said Laura, handing back the book. "Thanks."

And with that, Laura looked past him to the elderly woman next in line.

The home that Laura had shared with her father, Leonard Wilcox, was a two-storey white-brick affair with a saltbox roof. The longer section faced south and was covered with solar panels. The kitchen, on the south-facing wall of the house, was spacious, with long countertops, an island, and large windows to catch the morning sun. A cozy reading nook at one end included an old overstuffed armchair, a side table, and, opposite the chair, a half-height bookcase jammed with paperbacks, hardcovers, and magazines. This morning, the first morning she'd been home in what seemed ages, the sun streamed into the windows, warming the room sufficiently that Laura removed her cardigan before dropping into the armchair. She cupped the mug of steaming coffee and breathed a sigh of contentment.

The tour had been exhausting but successful beyond the publisher's expectations. Book sales were following a similar trajectory. *Never Mind Me* had appeared on the *Globe and Mail*'s Bestsellers list. Laura felt that current events were completely out of her control, as if she had become the property of the publisher and that her own desires—to simply stay home and read, think, and write, for example—had been waved away as being irrelevant. In a few weeks she would be packaged up and shipped to the United States for an even longer tour.

The phone interrupted her reverie. It was her agent, Grady Nolan. Reluctantly, she answered.

"Laura," Grady said. "How are you doing?"

"All right. Tired."

Ignoring that, Grady continued. "At the signing in Toronto you met a wizard?"

A wizard. Laura had almost forgotten. The memory had been swept aside by the tide of travel, hotels, and hundreds of new faces. "Yes, that's right. How did you know?"

"He contacted me. Wants to meet with you at your convenience. Said he'd be happy to take you out for lunch if that was agreeable."

Laura was silent a moment as she pondered this. "Did he say why?"

"No, he didn't. Maybe he's hoping you'll write about wizards in your next book."

"I doubt that," said Laura. "But I could meet with him once I've had a chance to rest a bit. Do you think I should?"

"Are you kidding? I'll forward you the contact information he left me."

After exchanging a few text messages, Laura and Mr. Blaise agreed on a time and place to meet. Still, Laura was puzzled. For what possible reason would a wizard want to meet with her? That he might be fascinated by or attracted to her hadn't even occurred to her. She certainly hadn't felt that way about him. Though she'd recently turned thirty, she'd never had a serious romantic relationship, just a vague curiosity about men that she'd occasionally, albeit briefly, explored. Her agent's off-hand quip was as good a guess as any, as far as Laura was concerned.

The spell of lazy contentment shattered, Laura went upstairs to the study and sat at her desk, lost in thought. The room had changed little since her father's passing, just over a year ago. The old Underwood 5 typewriter still sat in the centre of an oak writing desk complete with mail cubbies and roll top. Eschewing modern technology, her father had preferred, as he put it, to have as direct a relationship as possible to his writing. He wished to *feel* the words as they took form. The study also included a wall-to-ceiling bookcase (filled with layers of haphazardly stacked books), filing cabinets, and a wall with mounted photos and awards he'd received for his articles. Her father's other love, the MacTier Brewery, which he'd founded, was represented by a wall-mounted shelf with pint glasses embossed with the brewery's logo.

Her father had been a full-time journalist with the *Star* and brewed beer as a hobby. Success led to success, and eventually the brewery's income was sufficient that he could work freelance, covering stories of particular interest.

The small desk where Laura now sat, positioned beside the window, was the one change she had made to the office. Here she kept her laptop computer and peripherals as well as a pad of paper, sticky notes, and a selection of pens. Looking out the window, she smiled at the sight of the dear old swing set and tree house, still in the backyard, beckoning to her as before to come and play.

She thought back to a time when her father had called to her from this very window. He was just back from a trip, and in his absence Auntie Chinara had stayed with her. She'd been engrossed in reading comic books in the tree house, and he'd called to her several times before she floated up and out of her make-believe world. He had something special for her, he said, as she pressed her nose to the tree house's window. After descending the ladder, she hurried into her father's study. His smile widened upon seeing Laura standing before him, ready to burst with impatience. Finally, he opened one of the writing desk's drawers and handed her a small gift-wrapped box.

She tore off the paper, opened the top, and stared wide-eyed at the amulet within. It was oval, and both the chain and the amulet were fashioned from pewter. The amulet's surface was covered in flowing symbols the likes of which she'd never seen.

"Turn it over," said her father.

Doing so, she saw, engraved upon the metal, an inscription: "To Laura, for a magical childhood." As Laura looked quizzically at her father, he said, "It's from one of the members of the North American Wizarding Council, a very important man. That's who I met in New York. He fashioned it for you after learning that I had a daughter."

For weeks afterward, she wore the amulet every day and practised make-believe spells, pretending to turn robins into sparrows and rabbits into chipmunks.

Thinking of it now, she opened the top drawer of her desk and picked it up. She would wear this, she decided, for her meeting with the wizard. It seemed appropriate.

They met at a vegetarian restaurant near the waterfront. The wooden tables and chairs were painted white, the walls with lurid primary colours. Tall green potted plants—she recognized umbrella trees and yuccas—were scattered throughout. Scanning the nearly full restaurant, she saw that Mr. Blaise was already seated and joined him.

He stood when he spotted her and sat again after she did. "Thanks for meeting with me," he said.

Laura, examining his face, saw only friendly openness. "I admit that I was surprised by your invitation, Mr. Blaise. Do you mind if I ask what prompted it?"

He shrugged. "I read your novel and was interested in your choice of words, how they flow together. I became curious about you. That brought me to your book signing, where my curiosity was further piqued, and now here we are."

"I don't recall that we conversed at any length," said Laura.

"My point exactly," said Mr. Blaise. "May I begin by offering my condolences on the recent passing of your father."

"Thank you, Mr. Blaise," Laura said, not looking at him directly. "That is most kind."

"Your mother . . . ?"

"Passed away while I was a toddler."

Mr. Blaise nodded sadly and picked up the menu. Laura did likewise. Uncertain what to order, as she didn't eat vegetarian very often, Laura began with carrot and sweet potato soup followed by a lentil and quinoa spinach salad. Mr. Blaise ordered a Swiss veggie burger with sweet potato fries. They followed their meals with coffees. Laura was surprised not only by how much she enjoyed the meal, but also by the conversation, for it came easily, and Mr. Blaise seemed content to focus on her. But she was curious about the man before her and finally turned the conversation towards him.

"Mr. Blaise, I really know very little about your . . ." To her embarrassment, she was unsure of how to express her question. *His opinion of me as a wordsmith must be diminished*, she thought.

"Vocation?" he offered.

"Yes, thank you. I wonder what you do on a daily basis. It's difficult to imagine you going to work in an office and sitting at a desk."

"The fact is, Ms. Wilcox, we tend to be quite reticent in revealing too much of ourselves. For one thing, it helps discourage fraudsters and the generally curious from wasting our time. That being the case, I'm afraid there's little I can tell you today. But that may change as we come to know each other better."

"Then we are to see each other again?"

"If you wish," he said.

Laura, both curious and flattered, decided that she would like very much to see him again.

Running a finger along the wall of her magical cage, noting its cool temperature and perfect smoothness, Laura thought back to her wedding day, the happiest day of her life. The small civil ceremony was held a year after their first lunch meeting. James was attended by a fellow wizard, Philip Mage Russell, and Laura by Deirdre Marshall, a long-time friend she'd met at the University of Toronto.

Forgoing formal wedding attire, the men dressed in dark suits; Laura wore a knee-length ivory dress with embossed floral patterns and Deirdre a light-blue gown that fell to midcalf.

Following the morning ceremony at City Hall, she and James held a brunch at a nearby hotel and then dashed to the airport, where they boarded a flight to Prince Edward Island. There they vacationed for a week at a waterfront cottage.

It was during their honeymoon that James first spoke about wizards. Their role, he explained, was more about ensuring that magic was *not* used than about using it for any particular purpose. Did Laura know that wizarding began around the same time as the industrial revolution? She did. The arts of magic came into their own during the First World War, during which it was horribly misused by both sides. An attempt to stem magic's inhumane use began with a treaty signed in Versailles, negotiated in parallel with the treaty that ended the war. However, with the onset of the Second World War, the misuse of magic began anew, instigated by the Nazis but perpetrated once again by both sides.

A second treaty, agreed upon by wizards globally, was signed in Paris in 1950. A global body based in London was formed to monitor potential misuses of magic. James belonged to the North American association that formed part of this global body. And that was as much as he was willing to discuss with Laura, at least for the time being. He did answer one question, though.

"One hears about wizards but never witches—do they exist?" Laura asked.

James smiled. But something about the smile left Laura puzzled. For a moment it had seemed condescending, and he had never treated her as anything but equal. Perhaps she'd imagined it.

"We don't use the term *witch*," he said. "All magical persons are wizards. There are some female wizards, but relatively few, and they tend to have more limited skill sets."

Upon their return to Toronto, they agreed that Laura would keep her house, for James travelled a great deal and the old homestead would be a comfort to Laura while he was absent. Otherwise, they would live in his condominium, located on the twentieth floor of a complex near the Toronto waterfront. On her first visit she'd gaped at its understated elegance: gleaming hardwood floors, a marble fireplace, a large video display and expensive-looking sound system, leather furniture, a cherry dining-room set, and a large kitchen with state-of-the-art appliances. It didn't contain a lot of furniture, making the space seem larger and airier. The master bedroom included a four-poster bed, an antique chest of drawers, and a wardrobe. A second bedroom formed James's study. This was kept locked at all times, and Laura was strictly forbidden from entering. The need for this surprised her, but she promised to respect his wishes. They acquired additional bedroom furniture and Laura moved in.

A month later, things started to go wrong.

Laura, having lunched with a fellow writer she'd met through her agent, was full of conversation as she prepared dinner. Dinesh Dhankhar had written several entertaining science books aimed at the general public. They'd met a few months before the wedding and quickly become good friends. She was in the middle of summarizing her conversation when, glancing at her husband, she stopped abruptly. He was frowning severely, and his face was blotched with red.

"James?" she said.

"You are not to see this man again," he said, his voice controlled and level, though the tension in it was unmistakable.

"I beg your pardon?"

"Do not make me repeat myself," said James. "That man is not suitable company for a wizard's wife."

Laura blinked, scarcely able to believe that her husband would say such a thing. "I don't know what you think you've heard, but Dinesh is a good man. He—"

But Laura couldn't finish her sentence; a sudden cramp in her stomach forced her onto a kitchen stool to catch her breath. Had it been a cramp? It had almost felt like a blow to the abdomen.

"He is a *scientist*," James spat out. "Not satisfied with their pathetic efforts to reduce the universe to arithmetic, they attempt to rationalize the beauty of magic. Some have had the temerity to approach us for experimentation. The wife of a wizard may not associate with such people. I'll hear no more about it."

With that, James turned and strode towards his study.

"You surprise me, James," Laura called after him, back on her feet. "Truly. Yes, I'm your wife and love you dearly, but no one will dictate with whom I may or may not associate."

Laura was never able to fully recall what happened next, simply that she found herself stunned and in pain, laid out on the floor. She wasn't able to open her left eye. With her right, she saw that her arms and legs were covered in bruises. Her ankle was sprained, if not broken. Touching her face gingerly, she yelped in pain and withdrew her hand.

James crouched over her, a sad smile on his face. She wanted to ask what had happened but couldn't form the words. Even her tongue seemed swollen. "Shhhh, my dear," he said. "Don't try to speak. I'm sorry. So very sorry. It wasn't deliberate. If I am angered sufficiently, well, you see what can happen. You really must ensure this doesn't happen again. Do you understand?"

All Laura could manage was a grunt and some blinks.

"There now. I'll make it all better. I really do love you, you know. And here's the proof."

For a moment Laura was blinded and felt hot from head to toe. And then it was over. No pain, no bruises. Just a memory. A memory that she already knew would never leave her.

After James helped her to her feet, she looked at him wide-eyed then threw her arms around him and held him tight. Still in shock, Laura decided that, at least for now, she needed to appease him and gain time to think. "Thank you," she said. "Oh, thank you. It's more than I deserve, I know. Of course, I'll never see that man again. I'm so sorry. I promise to be more dutiful from now on."

Grasping her hands, James released her grip from around his neck then put his hands on her shoulders, moving her back to arm's length. "That's better," he said. "Please don't let this happen again."

"It won't, James. I promise."

But it did. Over time, increasingly trivial disagreements triggered James's violent magic. After each such outburst, Laura became more inclined to think that perhaps it *was* her fault, and that, somehow, she was failing her husband. Certainly, for her own safety, there was nothing to do but completely agree with him and submit to him in all things. Early on she considered leaving but soon rejected that plan—his anger might well kill her, and she doubted that even he could bring back the dead.

Laura left home increasingly infrequently. But one day, as she strolled along Young Street, someone called her name. Turning, she saw Chinara Obi, Auntie Chinara, walking towards her. Her heart leaped, and they hugged each other tightly.

"Oh my goodness, Chinara," said Laura. "It's been ages. Much too long."

"Not since the funeral, I think. How are you keeping? Is that a ring I see?"

Laura trembled slightly. "Yes, I've been married a few months now. It was just a small wedding, you see."

"You don't need to explain. I'm just so happy for you. Mind you, you look like you've lost some weight. Everything okay?"

"Oh yes, we're very happy," Laura said quickly, before changing the subject. "And how are you keeping?"

"Oh, same old," said Chinara. "My editor keeps threatening to hire me, but I like working freelance. Just finished an exclusive interview with the prime minister—he was in town recently."

"Well, my father always said you were the best."

"Ha! He only said that because he knew that *he* was the best. I still miss him."

"I know," Laura said with a sigh. "I keep expecting him to be in his study when I get back to the house. It's quite unfathomable that he's actually gone."

Chinara nodded sadly. "We must get together and talk. Lunch sometime? I need to get to an appointment."

"Of course," said Laura. "I'll be in touch." And, after another hug, they went their separate ways.

When Laura returned home, James was waiting.

"You met with a *reporter* today?" he said, his voice thick with disbelief and anger.

Laura stopped and regarded him with surprise and no little amount of fear. Still, keeping her voice matter-of-fact, she said, "I was going to tell you about running into Chinara. She used to work closely with my father. We're good friends. More, she's like family. James, are you having me followed?"

She immediately regretted her words and trembled at what was to come. However, to her shock and relief, James's anger turned to sadness. His shoulders slumped.

"I can no longer trust you to go out, I'm afraid. You just don't understand what it is to be a wizard's wife. What happens next is for your own protection."

Fear overtaking her, she backed away. But after just a couple of steps, the apartment they shared turned to mist, swirling around her in pale, pastel colours. When the mist cleared, Laura was somewhere else. A long rectangular room, its walls pulsating with the same pastel colours.

James was behind her, and the sound of his voice caused her to whirl about.

"This is where you will stay from now on. It is safe. Everything you need you will find here, and you need no longer fear meeting the wrong people or doing the wrong thing. It's for the best. As for me, I will visit occasionally, though, as you know, my work takes me far afield for extended periods. Goodbye, my love."

And with that, James was gone.

Laura had a lot of time to think. How much time, she had no way of knowing, though she'd taken to counting how many times she'd slept—as of "today," forty-three. There were no visible light fixtures in the cage, but the illumination brightened when she woke and dimmed when she was tired, as if prompting her to sleep. The cage included a well-stocked kitchen, sofas and chairs, a bed, and amenities. But she had no way of communicating with the outside world, and there were no writing implements. Not so much as a sheet of paper and a pencil. And of course, there was no way out. Sometimes the walls showed her views of the world, but only landscapes, mountains, forests, oceans, prairies. Never people.

Laura didn't have many friends and preferred one-on-one meetings to larger groups. Nevertheless, she was lonely. She missed people, and missed her father all the more. Her father. Thank goodness he wasn't here to see how she'd been mistreated. For she knew now that she *had* been mistreated, that something in James was broken. She realized that no rational person would think the fault hers.

She needed to get out of here. She needed help. Finally, she called out, "Is there *no one* who can help me?"

A moment later, the floor vibrated, and she felt a slight gust of wind. Blinking, she looked around and gaped. Books. Many books, jammed into a tall ebony bookcase that hadn't been there moments before. Curiously, the book bindings and covers were all as deep a black as the bookcase; the titles and author names were embossed in silver.

Fascinated, she approached and scanned the titles. *Pride and Prejudice*, *Anne of Green Gables*, *Little Women*, *The Fortunes and Misfortunes of the Famous Moll Flanders*, and many others. The books were all about women. While curious as to where they had come from and why, she had been so long without a book to read that she set aside her questions and gazed at the collection hungrily, wondering where to start. A mild tremor, and one of the books fell from its shelf. Catching it, she looked at the front cover. *Lolly Willowes; or The Loving Huntsman*, by Sylvia Townsend Warner. Clearly, this was where she was meant to start. Clutching it to her breast, she made some coffee. Then she sprawled into a chair and began to read.

She stopped and stretched twice.

First, after reading the sentence *Nothing is impracticable for a single, middle-aged woman with an income of her own.*

A deceptively simple sentence that provided much food for thought. She need not be dependent upon James, of course not. Her novel had sold very well, after all. That achievement was hers and hers alone. And then there was the income from the brewery. That, in itself, was more than sufficient for her needs. Her sense of self-worth began to reassert itself.

The second time she stopped was after reading this passage: *"No!" she cried out, wildly clapping her hands together. "No! You shan't get me. I won't go back. I won't . . . Oh! Is there no help?"*

After this call, the protagonist was aided by magic.

Looking at the bookcase, Laura noted that it was magic that had brought it here. But what magic? From whom?

After she'd finished the book, Laura paced and thought. She remembered something James had said at their first lunch. Finally, her eyes widening, she gleaned the truth and, as she did so, felt a warmth on her chest. It was the wizard's amulet—the one she'd worn every day since that first lunch with James. Pulling it out from under her top, she gazed at it and smiled. As before, the symbols on the face shifted slowly, forming many different patterns. What was different was that the symbols now glowed. Not just glowed, but pulsed, brighter and weaker. Laura let the amulet rest outside of her top and knew what had to happen next.

"It was dark in the woman's cage," she said, and it was.

In a few minutes, the cage brightened again, and there stood James, staring stupidly at the bookcase. He turned to Laura. "What is this?"

"My freedom," Laura replied simply, standing with her hands folded behind her back. "I'm leaving you, James."

"Really?" Now there was a glint of amusement in his eyes. "And if you could leave, if I permitted it, what would you do?"

"I'm going home. I'm going to write. And I'm going to tell the world about you."

She looked closely at her husband's eyes as the amusement faded, replaced by uncertainty—he'd finally noticed the glowing amulet.

Smiling, Laura glanced down for a moment before looking James in the eye. "This is why you're here, isn't it? The amulet alerted you. But I'm afraid it's too late."

His eyes changed again, turning into narrow slits of anger. She noted the tensed muscles of his shoulders and arms, the downturn of his mouth, the reddening of his face. Rather than hate, all she felt was pity. Turning her back to him, she began to narrate as she walked away.

"And in the end, she realized that the cage was his, not hers. It meant nothing to her, and so, with no further purpose, it ceased to be."

There followed a deafening noise as the walls shattered into myriad gleaming pieces. Laura continued to walk while her husband protected his head with his arms.

"In his anger," she said, "his magic lashed out at her. But she said, 'No.' Just no. And with that, the magic rebounded, striking him as it should have struck her."

The screams behind her told her that this had happened. Glancing back, she saw a mass of broken flesh and bone shivering on the floor, and the sound of weeping. She started forward again and stopped.

"She could have walked away and left him to his pain, a just retribution, perhaps, for the suffering he had inflicted upon her. But she realized that she was better than that. Better than him. And so, she made him physically whole. Yet there was no healing his confusion, his fear, his disbelief that her magic was stronger, and that he was beaten."

As James stood and stared at her wide-eyed, she said, "I know now why you married me, James. Perhaps there was some affection, but it was all about control. Your people have been aware of me since I was a child. That is why my father was permitted an interview with the council in New York, and why I received this amulet as a gift. You wanted to make sure I never realized my potential. You disgust me."

Turning her back upon him, she moved forward again, uncertain what life would bring. What she did know was it would be a life of radiance—one in which no man could blot out the light.

Truth to Power

"Truth to power" is a phrase that became all too familiar in the midst of a recent Canadian political scandal. In this follow-on to "Laura Wilcox," a reporter uncovers a major scandal in the wizarding world. Again, as in "Laura Wilcox", please note that the story includes some magical abuse perpetrated upon women.

As Laura Wilcox bustled in the kitchen, the wizarding amulet that hung from her neck reflected the morning sun, casting odd, shifting patterns upon the cupboards and countertop.

Chinara Obi shivered. To distract herself, she cast her eyes about, looking at the familiar furniture and objects that seemed oddly different now. As did Laura. The change both scared and fascinated her.

Laura placed a teapot on the table, covered it with a floral cozy, and retrieved two saucers and cups from the cupboard.

"What?" Chinara said, noting Laura's smile and the twinkle in her eyes.

"You're looking around as if you've misplaced something," said Laura as she took a seat.

"Oh. It's just that it's been—what?—well over two years since I was last here. Before your father passed."

Chinara had known Leonard Wilcox since before Laura was born. They'd both worked as Toronto-based journalists. After his wife died, they'd become closer, with an unspoken understanding that, while neither needed a permanent relationship, they could be close friends and more as situation and need demanded. Did Laura know how close they'd been? she wondered.

"Now that I'm here," Chinara continued, "it's hard to believe he's not upstairs, banging away on that old typewriter."

Laura nodded. "I know, and I'm sorry I haven't been in touch. I withdrew from everything and everyone, focused on my own pain. At least, until . . ."

"Until that son of a bitch came along," said Chinara. "Blaise."

"Yes," said Laura, her cheeks colouring as she removed the cozy and poured the tea. She touched the amulet at the mention of her husband. "Until him."

"I remember when your father gave you that," she said, gesturing to the amulet. "You were maybe ten? A gift from the wizards through him. But there was more to it, wasn't there?"

The face of the pewter amulet displayed intricate, flowing symbols, perhaps forming an alphabet with which Chinara was unfamiliar. The symbols pulsed slowly and emitted a dull glow that was just visible in the morning light.

"It was a way of keeping track of me. It began to glow as I became aware of my magical abilities."

"May I ask—why do you still wear it?"

A tired smile. "It's a connection with my father," said Laura, "who gave it to me with love. And a reminder that, try as they might, the wizarding community has no hold upon me."

"So they've contacted you? Since?"

"They've tried. I want nothing to do with them. Or, at this point, with the rest of the world, if I'm honest. I need time to let myself heal."

"Of course. Still, you've had an impact. The wizards have a new, young leader, and the world is watching them now. Maybe their days of having free rein are coming to an end."

"Perhaps," Laura said with a shrug. It's nothing to do with me. I'm focused on my next novel."

"The first one was certainly a big success. And that was before the world heard about . . . well, heard about what happened to you. Do you feel any pressure as a result?"

Setting down her teacup and smiling broadly, Laura said, "Chinara, are you interviewing me?"

"Oh my God. Sorry, sometimes these things just come out. It's the journalist in me."

"No, I'm sorry," said Laura. "I couldn't resist teasing. And no, I'm not feeling any pressure at all. I'm writing this book for me. Obviously, I won't be doing a promotional tour this time. That would be difficult."

"And there's probably no need, considering how well known you are now." Chinara took a sip of her tea and changed the subject. "I'm going to meet with the new leader of the wizards in a few days. Any advice? I'm a bit worried that he might cast a spell upon me, to be honest."

Laura reached across the table and patted Chinara's hand. "Don't worry. He won't."

"How do you know?"

"Because I said so," said Laura.

Taking a tentative sip of her steaming jasmine green tea, Chinara spotted Maggie Gott, a deputy editor at the *Globe and Mail*, as she entered the crowded cafe. As their gazes locked, Maggie smiled, and then she approached Chinara's table.

"I'll just grab a latte and join you," said Maggie, pulling off her leather shoulder bag and resting it on a chair. Upon her return moments later, she said, "I do have an office, you know. We even have a coffee maker."

"No, thanks," Chinara said with a chuckle. "I've tasted the coffee there. Besides, if I go to your office, I'll have to spend ages catching up on gossip."

"Heaven forbid that a journalist should enjoy talking to people."

"You know what I mean. I enjoy it, I just don't always have the time."

"Gossip can lead to some great stories. Speaking of which, you're following up on the Wilcox story."

Chinara nodded. After taking a sip of her tea, she said, "I contacted the wizarding council. I have to say, I was surprised when they agreed to an interview. With the new leader, no less."

"And why do you think that happened?" Maggie rested her head on her hand and regarded Chinara quizzically. "This is an organization that provides the odd press release, but I can't think of when they last granted an interview. Not since—"

"Leonard." Chinara looked down for a moment then regarded Maggie. "I don't know why. An attempt to seem more transparent? I can't imagine they'll actually tell me anything substantive. Maybe they're just curious to meet the journalist who broke the Laura Wilcox story."

"You exposed a senior member of their community as a wife beater. At best," said Maggie. She sipped her latte and continued. "If he were anyone else, he'd be in jail for physical abuse, emotional abuse, assault, unlawful confinement, and Lord knows what. So, you know, it concerns me that they may be after some kind of payback. This is a group that's not exactly used to the spotlight."

"You think they're going to come after me?"

"At the very least, they may try to discredit you."

Chinara considered this. "Well, I can't say I'm not nervous, but how do we know there aren't a lot more Laura Wilcoxes out there? If there are, someone has to tell their story. I mean, wizards live in the same world as we do, right? People have a right to know what they're up to."

Maggie pursed her lips as she looked at Chinara. "Which raises a good point. There are things we know but prefer not to know. As a society. Do you agree? For example, wizards are rarely mentioned in the media. At least, up until Laura Wilcox. I can think of two reasons. Maybe, and I'm just speculating here, maybe that's because they've extended their tendrils to the media powers that be, to make sure they don't receive unwanted attention. If this should happen to be true, and I do mean *if*, I don't think you'll find the public complaining. On the whole, people seem to prefer *not* thinking about wizards, as long as whatever they do doesn't impact the rest of us."

Setting down her mug, Chinara narrowed her eyes. "What exactly are you telling me, Maggie? Are you warning me off?"

"Not at all. If you get a story, we'll print it. Probably." She sighed and took a drink before adding, "Anyway, if we didn't, you'd probably just post it on your blog. How many followers do you have now?"

"About 500,000 on Twitter, so yes. But I'd rather publish it through you, of course."

Placing her hand over Chinara's forearm, Maggie nodded. "Do me a favour, though. Ask yourself why you're doing this. Is it just pride?"

Chinara narrowed her eyes, but Maggie continued. "No, hear me out. Is it that you feel a need to top the previous story, to prove that you've still got it?"

"Look," said Chinara, "since Leonard, my career is just about all I have. So, forgive me if I value it."

Maggie nodded and squeezed her arm gently. "Just be careful, okay? A lot of people consider you a national treasure. And since Leonard Wilcox passed, you may be one of a kind. No one wants to lose you, too. Least of all me."

The North America Wizarding Council occupied an office building in Manhattan, near 10th Avenue and 30th. Stepping out of the cab, Chinara gazed up at the building, shivered in the pouring rain, and dashed to the revolving door. The ground floor was an expansive open space with a receptionist, security guards, a metal detector, and an airport-like conveyor belt and X-ray machine. After identifying herself to the receptionist, Chinara placed her raincoat, umbrella, and shoulder bag on the conveyor belt and walked beneath the metal detector at the guard's prompt. While Chinara collected her belongings, the guard called for the elevator and then escorted her to the twentieth floor. William Mage Pearson was waiting for her when she arrived.

He was young, perhaps early forties, with curly dark hair and pleasingly proportioned features. Dressed in a blue suit, white shirt, and pale blue tie, he was a walking photo op. Perhaps this was why he'd been selected as leader at a time when wizards, for the first time in living memory, were under the microscope. Relatively speaking.

"Chinara Obi," he said as they shook hands. "William Mage Pearson. What a pleasure to meet you."

"Thank you," Chinara said. "Thanks for agreeing to meet."

"Not at all," he said. After a similarly dressed assistant took Chinara's coat and umbrella, Pearson led her to a nearby meeting room, where an array of large windows looked out over the grey, bleak Manhattan skyline.

Pearson and Chinara sat in opposite-facing armchairs. The assistant, who had a Québécois accent, popped his head in and offered food and beverages. Chinara declined and the assistant left, closing the door behind him.

Chinara, always interested in body language, noted that Pearson was slouched slightly with legs crossed and arms bent upon the armrests. He seemed completely at ease and welcoming. She'd known that he was good-looking; she'd seen photos. What she hadn't expected was his disarming nature. Charming, even. Still, there had to be more. There were dark, still waters under the surface, most certainly. No one could tell her that an international, secretive organization like the wizarding community wouldn't be political as hell. Not one to form negative feelings unduly, she nevertheless had the feeling that there would be more theatre than truth in this room.

Pulling her phone out of her bag, Chinara asked, "Do you mind if I record our conversation?"

"It would be preferable if you didn't. You may, of course, take whatever notes you please."

"Of course." Chinara placed the phone back in her bag and withdrew a notepad and pen instead.

"Thank you," said Pearson, acknowledging her acquiescence with a nod. "I don't know if you'll be surprised by this, but the wizarding community owes you a great debt. We were deeply shocked by the Laura Wilcox story."

"You consider this an unusual situation, then?"

"Very much so."

"Can you tell me where James Mage Blaise is?"

"That I'm afraid I cannot reveal."

"Can you confirm whether or not he'll be facing charges for his actions? As would anyone else who battered and illegally confined their spouse."

"He will not. As you know, since the 1950 Paris accord, the wizarding world has operated independently of previously established systems of law and government. This has been deemed for the best by all parties, and has been shown to work very well. Our primary occupation as a community, after all, is to ensure that the practice of magic does not impact those who do not practice magic. You're aware, of course, of the atrocities committed on both sides during the two world wars. An extreme example, but it shows what can happen when governments are directly involved with the wizarding community."

"Laura Wilcox might disagree that your independence is for the best."

"I can't imagine what Ms. Wilcox suffered as a result of this tragic affair. Naturally, we have invited her to join us so that she may benefit from our experience and counselling. We hope that, in time, she will see that this, also, is for the best."

"Best for her or best for the wizarding community?"

"The best for all concerned."

"Are you aware of any other instances of spousal abuse at the hands of wizards?"

"Not at all. To abuse another human being goes against everything we believe in."

"If you're agreeable, I'd like to interview some of the wizards and their spouses."

"I understand why you would want to do that, but no, I'm afraid we cannot permit it."

"If you have nothing to hide, then why not?"

"We live in the world, Ms. Obi, not in some ivory tower. Anonymity is one of the things that makes this possible. Frankly, it's one of the things that keeps us safe."

"Safe? You mean from ordinary people?"

"Sadly, yes. As you must be aware, there are small segments of the population for whom the practice of magic is heresy—who would be happy to literally burn us at the stake."

"You've recently taken over the leadership of the wizarding community from Wen Mage Cheng."

"Yes. In light of recent events, and considering that he had overseen the community for some time, he felt it best to bring in some fresh leadership."

"Can you discuss how wizarding leaders are selected?"

Pearson sighed. "I know this must be frustrating for you, but I'm afraid that I cannot."

Setting down her notepad, Chinara regarded the leader for a moment. "I'm not sure why I'm here, Mr. Pearson."

The hotel was a three-star, a short walk from the wizarding headquarters. In the lobby, Chinara called the elevator, her fingers trembling as she hit the button repeatedly. Upon reaching her room, she slammed the door behind her and exhaled as if she'd been holding her breath for ages.

Perhaps she had.

"That complete and total *bastard*!" Chinara muttered. He'd tried to magic her. Pearson. She was sure of it. And she was pretty sure he'd just tried to have her killed.

Knowing full well that she was being stonewalled, Chinara had asked Pearson why she'd been invited to speak with him. He'd gazed at her for a moment, before his face took on a pained expression and he rubbed his forehead. Looking at her again, he said, "I simply wished to assure you and your readers that the Wilcox incident is being treated very seriously by the wizarding community and that you have our assurance it will not happen again. I hope that you will consider the matter closed. Now, if you'll excuse me, there are other matters to which I must attend."

They shook hands and he left. He seemed to be in a hurry. The assistant, bearing her raincoat and umbrella, escorted her to the elevator and wished her a good day.

Chinara was on her way back to the hotel, lost in thought, when the light turned red at thirtieth and ninth. The rain was finally letting up. Glancing around, she noted that there was only a smattering of pedestrians about, and none on the north side of the street going in the same direction that she was. The light turned green, but before stepping onto the street, she had the oddest feeling, and a shiver ran down her spine. Blinking, she was about to cross when a white cargo van blasted through the red light. It would have struck her if she hadn't hesitated. The van took a sharp right, and its tires screeched as it sped away.

"Laura," she whispered now. "Was that you? Were you warning me?"

After a hot shower—she'd felt hopelessly dirty since her meeting—she dressed in jeans and a sweatshirt and looked for her notebook. Not finding it in her bag, she panicked for a moment then remembered. It was in her coat pocket. But that wasn't the only thing in her pocket.

She stared at the crumpled scrap of paper. She hadn't put it there. Chinara opened it and read the brief text in Courier font.

```
LW not the only one. Meet 5th Ave. NY Library,
rare books. 4.
```

Chinara looked again at her watch. It was 4:20. She was aware that the room was gorgeous: gleaming tabletops, buffed floors, and walls lined with glass cabinets full of books. But the beauty barely registered. With her notebook and pen at the ready, Chinara fixed her eyes straight ahead, unfocused, as she processed the events of the day.

She'd been the only one in the room since arriving at 3:45. It was disappointing that her contact was late, but not unexpected. Sometimes her sources took risks in meeting with her. Risks to their careers or even their lives. Today, that would be true in spades.

It was after 4:30 when Chinara heard footsteps behind her. Despite her curiosity, she resisted turning.

The woman who appeared across the table from her was youngish, no older than thirty. Wearing no makeup or jewellery, she was dressed in jeans and a hoodie, as if trying to appear as anonymous as possible. She remained standing, regarding Chinara as if working out whether to sit or flee.

"You were never here," Chinara said, hoping to put her at ease. "We never spoke."

With a sigh, the woman pulled back her hood and sat. "You're friends with Laura Wilcox?"

"I've known her all her life. She's more like family."

"And you believed her when she came to you. I mean, after . . ."

Chinara blinked. "It didn't occur to me to do anything else."

"Will you believe me? Will you believe what I have to tell you?"

"We've just met. All I can promise is that I will listen and take you seriously."

The woman nodded. "So, you're sensible. That's good. That's what I need." She took a breath and began. "Laura is not the only woman to have suffered at the hands of her wizarding husband. There are others. The ones that I know personally are here in New York. But there are more. Lots more."

"Suffered how?"

"It depends. Most every wizard practices a different sort of magic. Some of their wives suffer physically, some wake to find gaps in their memories. They take to writing detailed diaries, kept secret from their husbands, and later read entries they have no memory of writing. They have no way of knowing what else might have happened during those intervals. Some are imprisoned until they learn a lesson their husband thinks they need to learn. Some are compelled to do things they would never have done. It goes on."

"And what about you?"

The woman smiled slightly. "A bit of all of that, to be honest. Not as bad as what Laura went through, but bad enough at times. I think Laura was a tipping point. The straw that may have broken the camel's back. But you don't have the whole story yet, and it's worse than you know."

"What do you mean?"

Shaking her head, the woman said, "You might not believe me if I told you. You need to speak to some of the others. There are three other wives who are willing to meet with you. Will you do it?"

"Will I? Of course. That's why I came to New York."

"We think that no more than three of us can meet you without being noticed. They'll be in Central Park tomorrow, at 1:00 p.m.. Meet them at Umpire Rock.

There's something special about the mica in the rock that inhibits the transmission of magic, at least a little. It will help. Enter the park from the east. The others will enter from the north, south, and west."

The woman got to her feet.

"Wait," said Chinara. Unable to contain the disbelief in her voice, she continued. "Is that all? Is that all you're going to tell me?"

"We're all taking terrible risks," the woman said as she raised her hood. "My role is to simply set up the meet. The others will give you the details you need."

Of course, Chinara thought, as the woman departed. *There's more at stake here than just my story. Patience, Chinara. Patience.*

The next morning, Chinara sipped coffee in her hotel room while scrolling through news sites on her laptop. Opening the *New York Times* online, she scanned the usual headlines and opinion pieces about Washington politics until a piece near the bottom of the page caught her attention. The headline read "NY Wizarding Community in Mourning." As Chinara read the piece, her eyes widened with shock. The accompanying photo was of the very woman she'd met with yesterday. Her name was Edith Mage Taggart, wife of Ian Mage Taggart. She'd apparently suffered a massive heart attack overnight and was pronounced dead at Mount Sinai West.

Chinara stood and looked out at Eighth Avenue but could see only the face of young Edith Taggart, who'd risked everything by meeting her. Sorrow was soon replaced by guilt. Was Maggie right? Was she responsible for this because of her unwillingness to rest on her laurels? Had this poor woman paid the ultimate price for the sake of Chinara's pride? No. Maybe. But there was more to it than that. And the more she thought about it, the more she felt guilt gave way to anger. Fury, if she was being honest.

"I'm coming for you, Pearson," said Chinara, clenching her fists. "I'm going to take you down. You and your entire, anachronistic, misogynistic society."

She hailed a cab at noon, gave the driver a twenty, and sent him on his way. Who knew if he was working for the wizards? She hailed a second cab and got in, exiting at Fifth Avenue and Sixty-Fifth Street. Taking her time, she strolled leisurely through the park, stopping to gaze at the carousel with its beautiful painted horses, before making her way to Umpire Rock. It was 1:05 by the time she arrived. She was late but didn't care. If her sources had any sense, they'd stay the hell away.

So, when she saw three women sitting upon the rock's north face, Chinara was stunned.

"Chinara Obi?" one of them said.

"Yes," said Chinara, blinking. "To be honest, I didn't think you'd show. Not after—"

"We all knew the risks. But it's time. Now more than ever. Something needs to be done."

"It certainly does." It was a man's voice. She knew that voice. Chinara swung around and was suddenly very afraid.

"I saw you yesterday," said Chinara.

"Yes." The man smiled. "I took your coat and offered you refreshments. That's my world for the time being."

"It's okay," said one of the women. "We asked him to come. He's tried to help us from within, at great cost to his position in the community."

"Also," said another woman, "his gifts might come in useful today. We need all the help we can get."

Chinara, feeling a combination of fear and hope, glanced from the man to the women and back again. The third woman said, "Why don't we all sit, make introductions, and talk."

"Sounds perfect," said Chinara, taking a deep breath and sitting so that she could see all three of the women. The man sat beside them, to Chinara's left. "Before we start, can I record this?" she asked, lifting her phone.

The women regarded each other and nodded. So did the man. "Sure," one of the women said. "At this point, we might as well go all in."

Chinara began recording and set her phone down. "I'm Leslie Connor," said the woman to Chinara's right. "This is Wendy Schmidt, and Aoife Usnech. And last but not least, Jean-François Legault. Each of us has Mage as a middle name, all wizards do, but that gets boring. Why don't we start with you, Jeff?"

"Sure. Previously, I was fairly senior in the North American Wizarding Council. My position was that of monitor. My chief magical gift is that I can detect the use of magic over long distances. Months ago, I felt a dramatic spike in the aether, the medium that acts as a carrier for magical waves. You see, the aether's relationship with magic is similar to space-time's relationship with gravity." Aoife gave him a gentle nudge with her elbow.

"Yes, well," said Jean-François. "Moving right along. This spike was from a powerful wizard, one I'd never detected before. Of course, this turned out to be Laura Wilcox. I gave the council a heads-up. To say that Ms. Wilcox ruffled some feathers would be an understatement. Some of the council members were near apoplectic, unable to accept what had happened or agree upon a response. You see, from two perspectives, this was an entirely unprecedented event in wizarding history. First, magical strength, once it appears, normally increases in small increments, and always under the guidance of a more senior wizard. Secondly, and far worse as far as the council was concerned, this wizard was a woman."

Nodding, Chinara said, "Blaise told Laura that, normally, female wizards aren't as strong as their male counterparts."

Jean-François cleared his throat as he shared a glance with the others. "Yes, well, we'll come to that. The thing you need to understand is that the wizarding community, in its current form, came into being in 1950. Given how insular we are, social changes in society as a whole have not been realized within the community. Women are still considered subservient, and so on."

After receiving a nod from Aoife, Jean-François continued. "What happened to Laura Wilcox is not unusual. In fact, it is very common. Women in the wizarding community, wives and others, are subject to all manner of magical punishments. Any physical signs of abuse are conveniently removed."

"Edith spoke to me about this yesterday, about the ways in which they control and punish you," Chinara said, nodding towards the women. "But there's something else. Something even worse. Something, she said, that I wouldn't believe if I didn't hear it from more than one source."

Wendy spoke next. "You said something about female wizards being weaker. That's both true and not true. Innately, it's not true. In practice, it is. But that's because male wizards feed upon our magic, strengthening themselves and reducing the magic that we can call upon. In the wizarding community, women are basically a magical food source."

Chinara, too stunned to speak, looked at the women, all of whom nodded. So did Jean-François.

"When the Wilcox story broke," said Jean-François, "I took it as a sign that we needed to make some changes in the community, to bring us into modern times. I was warned not to pursue this, but I thought of my mother. She wasn't a wizard; neither was my father. My mother often said to me, 'Never be afraid to speak truth to power, for if you don't, you are as complicit as anyone else.' So that's what I did. After Pearson's appointment as leader, I approached him and put my case forward. I was immediately rebuffed. I tried speaking to the cabinet members, but in short order I was warned to cease or suffer the consequences. I continued to try to drum up support amongst some of the wizards, but eventually they had enough. They drained me of much of my magical ability, as they typically do to the women, and demoted me from a senior position to that of assistant."

All were silent.

Finally, Chinara spoke. "Shakespeare said it best in *The Merchant of Venice*: 'At the length truth will out.' I promise you, today, that the truth will out. And those bastards in that tower will find their walls crumbling around them."

Jean-François stood just then, a look of panic on his face. "Someone is coming," he said. "A very powerful wizard. Even in my weakened state I can detect them." He looked at Chinara. "You should go. Perhaps you'll be spared."

"Not bloody likely," said Chinara, getting to her feet. As the others peered around anxiously, Chinara uploaded the interview to the *Globe*'s server and sent Maggie a message.

Jean-François pointed to a path to the west of them. Moments later, a woman emerged from the trees.

"Laura!" Chinara blurted, scrambling down to meet her. Taking Laura in a big hug, she said, "Oh, thank you. Thank you so much for coming."

"Dearest Chinara," said Laura. "I should be the one thanking you. You've brought me out of my shell, back into the world. How could I have left you to face this alone?"

By now the others had stepped down from the rock. Chinara made the introductions.

"I've been listening from afar," said Laura. "And I've a gift for you all—a gift I expect you to share with any who need it. No longer can you be harmed by magic. Furthermore, I sever the bond that allows others to feed upon your power."

Chinara was fascinated. She was witnessing magic performed for the first time. Well, not counting Pearson's thwarted attempt. There were no grand gestures, no wands, just words. Wonderful words.

"Oh my goodness," said Aoife. Her eyes were wide with amazement, as were the others'. The four hugged each other and then gathered around Laura. "I'd no idea it would feel like this. Being able to realize my potential."

"We promise to pass this gift along," said Wendy. "And nothing will be the same."

"And to that end," said Laura, tugging on Chinara's sleeve, "we have a meeting to go to."

"Are you sure?" said Chinara. "Will that be safe? For you I mean."

"I'll be fine, and so will you. After all, my magic stems from Story. What could be more potent?"

The coffee shop was on thirtieth, across the street from the wizarding tower. Laura and Chinara had been there for twenty minutes when Leonard Mage Pearson entered.

Looking at him, with his perfect hair and boyish smile, Chinara shook her head. She wondered whether his apparent charisma was the result of magic. Perhaps charisma in all its forms was a *form* of magic.

"Ms. Obi, delighted to see you again," he said, as he took a seat at their table. "And Laura Wilcox, what an honour to finally meet you. I promise you that the wizarding community will welcome you with open arms."

"Stop talking," said Laura. Pearson, looking nonplussed, did so. Again Chinara wondered: Magic, or just the force of Laura's presence?

"I might have stayed out of this if you hadn't tried to harm my dear friend," Laura said evenly. "But you did, so this is what's going to happen: Your female wizards, other women, and any sympathetic men in your community are going to be liberated. You will not be able to harm them with magic, nor will you be able to draw upon their power. What these people do with their newfound freedom is up to them, though I wouldn't be surprised if they leave your community en masse. The repercussions are upon your own head. If you attempt to harm them in any way, as you tried to do with Chinara—and don't waste our time trying to deny it—you will be very displeased with the consequences. Are we clear?"

By this point, Pearson was perspiring. He was also, Chinara noted, trembling, though whether with fear or anger she couldn't discern. Perhaps it was both. "I do understand, Ms. Wilcox, that you have been through a terrible ordeal—"

"Stop," said Laura. "I asked you a yes-or-no question. You will answer yes or no."

Pearson's face twitched, his mouth formed a snarl, but finally he said yes.

"Good," said Laura. "You may go." When the wizard didn't move right away, Laura narrowed her eyes. "Now."

"Are you sure?" Laura asked.

They were back in Laura's kitchen. It was late afternoon, but even without sunlight, the room seemed bright and warm. Chinara now felt as comfortable here as at home. In some ways, more so. At home she was alone. But Laura was here. Dear Laura, who had not only saved her life, but also given her two stories that would cement Chinara's reputation in journalism for a lifetime. And that, she found, was quite enough. There was nothing to prove anymore.

Chinara smiled. "Pretty sure. I've quite had my fill of investigative reporting, of putting people at risk, including me. Going forward, I'll be happy to focus on analysis and commentary." After taking a sip of the delicious jasmine tea Laura had made, Chinara gazed at her friend across the kitchen table. "And what about you? Will you be joining the new magical community?"

Laura shook her head. "No. But I'll be keeping an eye on them. Besides, they don't need me at this point. And I don't need them. I've got all the family I need right here." With that, Laura reached across the table and took Chinara's hand.

Family. More than the next big story, more than renown—Chinara knew now that family was what mattered. It was all that mattered. Her eyes tearing up, Chinara gripped Laura's hand. "Same."

Too Close

I had a lot of fun with this story, in which a horror writer discovers the cost of getting too close to the Truth. It came about as I thought about the World Fantasy Award trophy no longer being modelled upon H.P. Lovecraft, whose personal views on topics such as race were quite distasteful. I recalled that an author, someone of whom Lovecraft would not have approved, had written about how uncomfortable it would be to have Lovecraft glaring at him from the mantle. As my thoughts meandered, they led me to this story.

On a good night, when Charles Mitchell sat down to write, the characters from his stories spoke to him, their voices so clear that all he needed was to take dictation. Tonight, they were distant and indistinct. Less so than yesterday, perhaps, but they weren't ready. He needed to wait. With a sigh, Charles closed his laptop, wandered from the study to the living room, and looked out the window to the street below.

Dusk was coming on, and only a handful of people were about, most walking towards the city centre. It was a short walk to Princess Street, where one could find anything, even an old single-screen movie theatre.

Hmmm, he thought. Tonight, *Get Out* was playing. Just the distraction he needed.

Arriving late, Charles found few empty seats, and so he sat closer to the screen than he would have liked. That thought evaporated as soon as the lights dimmed. Charles was enthralled, to the extent that he was startled when the credits rolled and the lights came on. Rubbing his neck, he stood and slipped into his jacket. He couldn't exit the aisle, however. The woman next to him was still seated, staring wide-eyed at the screen.

Glancing towards Charles and noting his bemused expression, she said, "Oh my God, that movie was—"

"Awesome?"

"Disturbing as hell," she said.

Interested in her opinion and noting that the woman was attractive and roughly his age, Charles invited her to have coffee with him, suggesting a locally owned coffee and dessert place at the end of the same block. She accepted, and they chatted for a long while, until near closing time.

"I'm a writer," said Charles in answer to the inevitable question. "I write horror stories."

"You're kidding me," said Anita Jackson.

"Nope. Well, I don't write full time. I work on software contracts during the day, horror at night."

"Horror at night," Anita repeated. "As it should be."

"Exactly. How could you get into the right headspace if you're at a beach on a sunny day?"

Anita considered this. "Unless some ancient cosmic horror is lying dormant under the sand, waiting to give you something special when you come back from the bar after too much to drink."

Charles eyes widened. "I like the way you think!"

"I've been reading horror forever," said Anita. "Not *just* horror, but I've read a lot of it. Have you published anything?"

"A couple of short stories. I'm working on a novel now. It's called *Promises, Promises*. It's about a bunch of people who, well, die horrible deaths."

"And no fairy godmother to look after them, I suppose."

Anita was a cardiac surgeon. Charles learned this when she was called away to an emergency.

"Before you go, maybe you could be *my* fairy godmother and grant a wish," said Charles with a smile. When Anita gave him a quizzical look, he continued. "Let me see you again."

Regarding him thoughtfully, Anita rose. Then she dropped a business card on the table and hurried out of the coffee shop.

"Yes!" Charles beamed.

Taking a breath, Stephany Hill patted her mouth with a napkin, rose from the table, and climbed the steps to the stage. Acknowledging the applause, she stepped in front of the podium. Most of the audience had finished dinner and were gulping down the last of their wine or sipping coffee.

She knew many of them. You didn't become president, even of a writers' association, without at least some schmoozing. Still, good fortune had had a lot to do with it. Several of her friends, though not the best-known writers, were influential among their peers. Their support had made her election fairly painless.

Stephany cast her eyes over the audience and sighed. *Which of you unlucky bastards will it be this year?* Sensing that her smile was becoming strained, Stephany moved a bit closer to the mic and began. "Welcome to the seventeenth Big Chill Awards." Some hoots and cheers, then she continued. "Tonight, we honour the achievements of today's finest spinners of tales of horror." Here she paused. She'd been advised—warned in fact—not to say what she wanted to say. Gripping the edges of the podium more tightly, she made up her mind. Screw it.

"Whether celebration or sympathy is due the award winners, well, that's for you to decide."

Anita glanced around, noting the audience's spotty, nervous laughter. "What does she mean?" she whispered to Charles.

They were seated at a round table near the back of the salon. Theirs was one of thirty identical tables, each with place settings for six, and it seemed every chair was occupied. The serving staff were still removing dinner plates and pouring coffee and tea.

In answer, Charles ran his forefinger horizontally along his throat.

"Seriously?" Anita said.

Charles nodded solemnly.

"So tell me."

Charles mouthed, "After."

Felix Boyd sat in a high-backed red-leather armchair, his face warm from the fire blazing in the hearth before him. It was evening, and the flames composed the sole source of light in the small living room. The crackles from the burning logs reminded him of the beats of a story, a few quiet pops punctuated by the odd loud burst that made you jump.

Turning his gaze from the faded Turkish carpet, Felix cast his eyes to the wall shelves holding the figurines and statuettes he'd collected from his travels to Turkey, India, China, and Africa.

On the mantle, his new acquisition, the Big Chill statuette, glared at him with more than a hint of disapproval. Fashioned from brushed metal, the statuette had the shape of a jagged ice dagger, thick at the top and tapering until it disappeared into a two inch-thick base. A bronze plate attached to the front of the base was labelled with the year, his name, and "Best Novel". Carved into the top of the statuette were a pair of narrow eyes that glared straight ahead, and had the peculiar property that, in certain lighting conditions, they seemed to follow you.

That's right, Felix thought. *You hate that I won this award, don't you? Well, you're not the only one. But honestly, I don't care.* In Felix's opinion, people were overrated. He rarely ventured into town. The solitude suited him and was the best inspiration for his writing. His characters were the only close friends he needed. Shame he had to keep killing them off.

His old stone cottage could be found by travelling east from Ottawa to Old Highway 17 and then turning left onto a meandering, cracked, and pitted lane almost entirely hidden by the trees and shrubs that dotted the road. The cottage was nestled in a clearing surrounded by a jumble of birch, maple, and oak. A footpath from the rear led through the trees to the Ottawa River.

Gazing at the statuette, Felix reflected on his career. All it had taken was twenty years of writing and starving to get this far. The good news was, the winning book was the first of a planned trilogy. Maybe not so much starving in the future. He'd never written a sequel before, but this time he'd saved a couple of characters from the grim reaper. At least, for the time being. His expression took on the malevolent grin of a grisly fiend as he contemplated what lay in store for his surviving protagonists.

Unsure how long he'd been lost in thought, Felix blinked and noticed that the fire was getting low. He picked up the poker and adjusted some of the logs. Better. But before he could step back, a spark leaped from the hearth and landed on his sleeve. In short order, a small flame erupted. As he stared stupidly at the sight, the flame began to grow. Finally, as the pain registered, he shook off his daze, dropped to the floor, and wrapped a corner of the carpet around his sleeve.

With the fire extinguished, he took off his shirt, ran some cold water from the kitchen tap over his arm, and went to fetch a gauze bandage. The burn didn't seem too bad. Mostly, he realized, it had scared the dickens out of him. He put on an old shirt that he'd picked up from the bedroom floor and buttoned it.

In the kitchen, he set a wine glass on the counter and opened the oddly shaped bottle of Châteauneuf-du-Pape—his gift to himself. After letting the bottle breathe for a couple of minutes, he poured a glass and returned to the living room. "Here's to you," said Felix, raising his glass to the statuette and taking a sip. He paused. Was it his imagination or was the statuette glowing? Setting his glass down on the side table, he moved closer, all the while keeping a leery eye on the statuette. Yes, heaven help him, it *was* glowing. He touched it gingerly with the back of his forefinger. It was warm to the touch. From the fire? He tried to pick it up, but as it was uncomfortably warm, he immediately set it down again, fumbling and almost dropping it.

Looking back at the wine glass, he wondered whether it had been spiked.

A loud thud outside prompted him to swivel his head towards the back door. Had the garbage blown over? That didn't seem likely. The bin was heavy and sturdy.

With a sigh, he grabbed a jacket, slipped on some shoes, and went out the back door. Yes, there was the bin, lying on its side. This was puzzling. There was scarcely a breeze. Even if there were, he'd never encountered a wind that could topple this thing over. It was also unlikely that any animal in these parts could have done it. A big dog maybe? Or maybe someone was here, snooping.

"Hello?" he called. There was no answer and no other sound.

Shrugging, Felix approached the bin and bent over to set it upright.

He froze at the snap of a twig.

Straightening, he strained his eyes but could see little in the dark, overcast night. The only light bled from his shaded windows.

Then he saw it. Began to see it. A blackness set against the black of the trees before him. Large and shapeless, it was moving slowly towards him accompanied by a wet, dragging sound and an odour that made him gag, as if he'd stumbled upon the open graveyard of a thousand decomposing animals.

It didn't occur to him to be afraid. Not at first. When it did, and he became conscious of the nausea in his stomach and the tightness in his chest, he was out of time. His last words were ". . . the fuck?"

During the next scheduled break, Charles turned to Anita. "Felix Boyd won Best Novel five years ago. He's no longer with us."

"What happened?"

"Mauled to death by a bear, they figure, though some investigators were doubtful. There weren't supposed to be any bears in those parts. The following year, the writer of the Best Graphic Novel was dead within a year. Shall I go on? Pretty much every year for the past few years, something horrible has happened to an award winner."

Anita put her hand to her mouth and stared wide-eyed at Charles. "Oh. My. God. So can you tell me what we're doing here?"

"Not to worry," Charles said with a wry smile. "It's not very likely that I'll win."

Seeing that most people were standing and milling about, Charles was about to suggest to Anita that they do the same when he spotted Gheeta. She was sitting alone at a table. He watched as she downed a glass of white wine, refilled the glass, and downed it again.

"I need to speak to someone for a minute," he said. "Do you mind?"

"Schmooze away," Anita said, rising. "I'm going to check out the dessert bar."

"Hey," said Charles, as he sat near Gheeta Sadana.

After glancing at him from the corner of her eye, Gheeta took another drink and then said, "Not now. I'm not exactly in the mood."

"Gheeta," Charles said quietly. When this didn't produce a reply, he repeated her name more forcefully.

"What?" she said sharply.

"Look, no kidding around. Just tell me, what's happened?"

"Not now," Gheeta repeated. Then she looked at him. "Maybe tomorrow, while I'm nursing the hangover that I'm going to have."

Surprised at being so readily dismissed, and with no snark on her part, Charles rose and walked slowly back to his table. Upon taking his seat, Anita asked, "Who was that?" She put down her fork, her slice of chocolate mousse gateau half eaten.

"My archrival," said Charles, abstractedly.

"You have an archrival? Is that like an archenemy?"

"Sort of, but friendlier. Mostly friendlier."

"Do go on," said Anita. "I'm listening." Picking up her fork, she speared some cake, placed it in her mouth, and nearly groaned with delight.

"A few years ago, we both had short stories up for a Hugo. She was favoured to win but didn't. I won instead. The following year, we were both up for a Nebula. That time she won. Since then, we've been teasing each other on Twitter, and the odd time when we're in public together. And now here we are, both up for First Novel."

Reflecting on this, Charles realized that this made him happy. His writing career was taking off. So was hers. It was some comfort to know that someone else was going through the same thing at the same time, outward shows of rivalry aside.

Hours earlier, Gheeta Sadana had been sober and happy. Hair still wet from the shower, she hadn't quite finished dressing when she heard the text-message alert on her phone. "You've got to be kidding me," she said.

"What is it?" said Kate Longchamps. Kate was exiting the bathroom, white hotel towel wrapped around her.

Under normal circumstances, the sight of Kate in a towel would have arrested Gheeta. Now, she simply glanced wide-eyed at Kate then immediately looked back at her phone, staring at it as though the world might shift on its axis at any moment.

"Gheeta?"

Tearing her eyes from the phone, Gheeta said, "It's from my agent. He says David Dewer wants to meet. Apparently, he read *Am I Wrong?* and loved it."

"David Dewer," Kate repeated slowly. "You mean *that* David Dewer?"

"That's the one. My favourite author. Well, second favourite, but I won't tell him that. He's receiving the Grand Master award tonight. He wants to meet for lunch today at his Airbnb. Which is, well, it's an estate, an hour north of the city, near Deep Lake."

"Hmmm," said Kate. "Lunch. Perfect, that gives us time to . . ."

"To?"

Kate loosened her towel and allowed it to fall to the floor. "To celebrate," she said, a glint in her eye.

The Uber stopped at a wrought-iron gate at the end of a crumbling paved road. Beyond the gate, a weathered brick path, from which grass and weeds erupted in patches, led past empty, cracked fountains and dry trees and shrubs. The building, more lodge than home, was two storeys, with east and west wings set back from the central area.

It was in a state of considerable disrepair. Shutters dangled at odd angles from the windows; some windows were boarded up; the roof was a patchwork of ancient curled shingles and exposed underlayment membrane; and vines were growing in odd twisting patterns along the faded brickwork. Overhead, dark-grey clouds moved briskly across the sky, driven by a strong wind that puffed at Kate's and Gheeta's hair.

They stared at the house and then glanced at each other.

"Seriously?" said Kate.

Gheeta shrugged. "I guess he likes to get inspiration from his surroundings."

"I thought writers were supposed to have, you know, imagination."

"Let's just go in and find him."

A knock at the door went unanswered. They tried the rusted brass door knocker with no better success. As there was no bell that they could see, Gheeta turned the knob and pushed the door slightly.

"Hello?" she called. "Mr. Dewer? It's Gheeta Sadana."

After she'd slowly opened the door, she and Kate found themselves in a cavernous, dimly lit entranceway with faded rose-coloured wallpaper. The sole furnishings were a battered oaken bench and an enormous chandelier. Kate found a wall switch and flipped it without effect.

"We should leave," said Kate, her voice trembling slightly. "Really, we should leave."

"Are you kidding me?" said Gheeta. "This is David *Dewer* we're talking about."

"Who's obviously not here."

"For all we know, he's in an alcove somewhere lost in his writing. It happens."

To their right and left were narrow entranceways leading to the east and west wings of the building. "Let's go look for him. I'll take the right," said Gheeta. "You can take the left."

Seeing the uncertainty on Kate's face, Gheeta squeezed her hand, smiled, then set off.

The first room in the east wing was . . . actually, Gheeta wasn't sure what it was. Dimly lit, with thick curtains covering the windows, she noted a fireplace, sofas and chairs with torn and faded upholstery, and a few tables. Approaching the wall to her left, she made out oil paintings, with dim figures set against seemingly black backgrounds.

The next room was a library with books stacked floor to ceiling, accessible by rolling ladders, and armchairs nestled close to window alcoves. As the windows were unobstructed, there was actually enough light to see. *Now this is more like it*, Gheeta thought.

She picked up a book and had started to leaf through it when she heard the scream.

Gheeta froze. She wasn't sure for how long. But all the while, the scream continued unabated, actually increasing in volume, and for longer than should have been possible. Dropping the book, she ran towards the sound. Past the reception room. Past the entranceway. Past a dining area. Then she came to a screeching halt. There was Kate, wide-eyed and slack-jawed, lying in a pool of blood, convulsing, her torso and limbs flailing, splashing blood all around her. The scream had faded, but her mouth was fully open as if she would have continued her scream but for lack of breath.

Then the smell hit Gheeta, something strong and foul, and she nearly vomited on the spot.

Fumbling for her phone, she called 911.

"Turns out it was David Dewer's blood she was swimming in, not her own."

It was the morning after the awards banquet. Gheeta, seated in an armchair in her hotel room, took a sip of coffee.

Charles and Anita were seated on her bed, faces pale. "Jesus," Charles whispered.

"They found Dewer's body in the next room. It had been dragged there. I heard them say it looked like he'd been mauled. Practically torn to pieces. They didn't say by who. Or what. Kate had no external injuries. All they can figure is that she witnessed something. The murder, most likely. And that this was what sent her over the edge.

Thing is, Kate's a paramedic. She's seen plenty of dead bodies before—things that would turn you or me to mush.

"At any rate, they had to sedate her. Once the police were finished with me, I figured I might as well attend the banquet. I mean, what the hell. At least I'd be able to get drunk. Which I did." With her free hand, Gheeta rubbed her eyes, then added, "Sorry about walking out."

"That's okay," said Charles. "At any rate, you didn't walk so much as stumble out. But no one was paying attention to that. I think we were all still stunned by the announcement after the break."

"Fair enough," said Gheeta. "I guess I should congratulate you for winning First Novel, you prick."

Charles couldn't help but laugh. Anita seemed shocked but then, she didn't know Gheeta.

"What will you do now?" Charles said.

"I'll go back to the hospital. They told me she was still unconscious but that they'd start to ease up on the medications this morning and see what happens. So, I should go over there. I've already cancelled our return flight. I'll stay here until she's back on her feet."

Charles and Anita exchanged a glance and rose from the bed. "We'll leave you to get ready," Charles said. "Thanks for calling. And let me know if I can do anything at all."

"Yeah, you just want me out of the picture so you can get a head start on your next crummy book."

"Seriously," said Charles, "let me know. I'll be in touch once we're back home."

Gheeta nodded absently. Charles took a deep breath then gestured Anita out and closed the door quietly behind them.

"You guys have a weird relationship," said Anita, while they waited for the elevator.

"Tell me about it."

There was a pause. "So, shall I say it?"

"Say what?"

"That David Dewer was to receive the Grandmaster award. Now he's dead. If there is some kind of curse on horror-award winners, this means you're in the clear."

"Maybe," said Charles.

"It doesn't look very happy."

Charles and Anita were in his apartment, which was comprised of several large rooms on the top floor of an old home on King Street.

Anita, holding a wine bottle and two glasses, sat beside him on the sofa and followed his gaze. "You do realize that a statuette can't change its expression."

"I'd almost swear this one has," Charles said. "Those eyes look angrier now than when we first brought it home."

"Well," Anita said, pouring the Pinot Noir, "I'm sure that your fans love you to pieces. I mean, what's not to love?" She punctuated the comment with a peck on his cheek.

Raising his glass, Charles proffered a toast. "To love."

"To love," Anita repeated, as they clinked their glasses and drank. "So what's next? What will you write about next?"

After pondering this for a moment, Charles said, "I've been wanting to do something Lovecraftian for a while."

"Really?" Anita said. Her face looked oddly sad.

"You don't approve?"

"It's just that . . . don't you think it's been done?"

Charles grinned. "Not the way I'm going to do it."

Anita drained her glass and set it down, her eyes sparkling with mischief. Then she took Charles's hand and stood. "You were saying something about love?"

As they sped to the bedroom, Charles's eyes fell upon the statuette. *Is it . . . glowing?*

Sometime later, wrapped in each other's arms, Charles was near exhausted from their particularly vigorous bout of lovemaking. They kissed again, then Charles fell back on his pillow, Anita's head resting on his left arm.

Propping herself up on her elbows, Anita whispered, "Ready for round two?"

"Oh please," Charles said with a chuckle. "I think I need just a few minutes yet."

"Oh, I think I can get you pretty excited sooner than that."

With one swift movement, Anita swung herself over his midsection and retrieved something from under her pillow. While her thighs gripped his ribcage, she brandished a gleaming chef's knife.

Charles blinked. "Anita?"

In reply, Anita moved the knife so that Charles felt it kiss his neck.

"What. The. Hell?"

"It's a shame, really. I quite liked you. But you've gotten too close to the Truth, and now you're getting too popular. We can't take any chances."

Charles began to struggle, but Anita's thighs clamped down on his ribs so he could scarcely breathe, and the knife made a superficial cut. A trickle of blood ran down his neck. He stopped.

"What. Is. Going. On?"

Anita sighed. "There are two things about horror writers: how close to the Truth they are, and how popular. If no one reads them, then it doesn't matter. Otherwise, we have to step in, so they don't spoil everything. I'm afraid, Charles, that you're very close, and now that you've won the Big Chill, you're getting too popular."

Charles, as he sought a way to gently question Anita's sanity, shuddered. He suddenly felt he had double vision. There was the Anita he knew, straddling him, but there was also . . . *something*, with a bulbous head, tentacles, and long claws that looked even sharper than the chef's knife.

Then he got it. "Oh, come *on*. Are you telling me I've been dating Cthulu?"

Anita, the Anita thing, barked a laugh that was both human and otherwise, wet and hoarse and rumbling. An odour, which Charles hadn't noticed before, was getting stronger—an odour of rotten, fetid meat. He'd have puked if he wasn't about to die.

"Lovecraft was the worst, of course. He was far too close, and the first one we had to take care of."

"Lovecraft died of cancer."

The Anita thing, the human part, gave him a pitying look. "We've had to get rid of others over the years. We've only failed once. We kind of gave up on him and went on taking out other threats. Now it's your turn."

"You know," said Charles, grasping at straws in his panic, "I could write something else. It doesn't have to be horror. I've also got a thing for cozy mysteries."

"I really am sorry, Charles, but it doesn't work that way. Goodbye."

He witnessed the human part of the creature raise the knife for the death stroke, while—in some other reality?—the monster part lifted a sharp claw. But just then, a thought bubbled to the surface of Charles's consciousness. It was something the Anita thing had said. If Lovecraft actually *had* been close to the Truth, then he still had a chance.

It was colder than he expected. He was sure he'd see his breath were it not for the damp mists that surrounded him. The dim light was diffuse, its source hidden, but he could make out the dark patches that were the walls beside him and the next few steps leading downwards. The stairs were slippery. He edged over to the wall, pressing against its rough, damp surface for support. It was going to take a while to descend all seven hundred steps.

Charles contemplated his situation. To start with, he was alive. For now. As if to punctuate this thought, howls of rage from the Anita thing reverberated all around him. Yes, for now, at least, he was alive. And for all he knew, the space between heartbeats in the waking world amounted to ages in the Dreamlands. Time would tell.

He would confer with the cats of Ulthar. After that, he wasn't sure what would happen. But they'd think of something.

Under the Sand

The inspiration for "Under the Sand" comes from a line uttered by Anita in "Too Close": "Unless some ancient cosmic horror is lying dormant under the sand, waiting to give you something special when you come back from the bar after too much to drink." It occurred to me that perhaps Anita was aware of a horror that actually was lurking under the sand somewhere. Say, La Jolla Shores Beach.

"Why don't we start at the beginning?"

"The beginning." Nathan Carter looked wistful for a moment, smiled slightly, and said "A man walks into a bar and meets a woman in a dinosaur dress."

The bar in question was at a hotel near the beach in La Jolla. Yes, *that* beach. It was a clear night with a slight chill in the air, and I'd just watched the sunset over the ocean. I could scarcely turn away, despite feeling that the light was scorching my retina. The thing that surprised me most was how *fast* it was over. And that gave me my only melancholy thought of the day, that, like the sun, a life can burn brightly one moment only to be snuffed out the next.

On the way back to my car, I heard music and voices coming from behind a hotel fence. Stepping closer, I saw an outdoor, poolside bar where the chill air was kept at bay by gas-powered fire pits.

I entered the hotel, the door held open for me by a tanned valet with blond hair and white golf shirt, and took the entrance off the lobby to the bar. After ordering a beer, I milled around. It was crowded but I soon spotted an empty table and made for it. I'd done a lot of walking and my feet felt like they'd welcome a bit of rest.

Turns out, someone else had the same idea, and we almost collided.

She was dressed in a close-fitting, light cotton dress and was very easy on the eyes. I backed up and gestured for her to take the table. But after looking at me for a moment, sizing me up, I think, she said, "Look, why don't we both sit down? Unless you're here with someone?"

I hadn't expected this. "No, actually, I'm not. Thanks. And my feet thank you too." So, we both sat and set our drinks on the table.

"I'm not here to meet anyone," she said. "I just wanted to chill a bit."

I couldn't help but smile. "Same," I said. "My name's Nathan."

"Briana," she said, and extended her hand. We shook.

The thing is, as I leaned across the table a bit, I noticed the pattern on her dress. I hadn't quite been able to make it out before.

"Are those ... dinosaurs?"

Briana shrugged. "I like dinosaurs."

"Well, there's only one thing to say to a woman wearing that dress."

She raised an eyebrow.

I leaned across the table as far as I could. She looked puzzled at first, but did the same. Then I whispered into her ear, "Curse your sudden but inevitable betrayal."

Her reaction surprised me. I expected her to look at me like I was insane. Instead she snorted a loud laugh and giggled.

"Oh. My. God." After wiping her eyes, she added, "That is the best thing anyone could have said."

My eyes must have popped out of my head, or near enough. "Browncoat?"

"Are you kidding? I've only watched Firefly, like, a hundred times."

From there the conversation seemed to take on a life of its own. She was vacationing from Portland where she was a project manager for FLIR. I mentioned my work in marketing at VMWare in Austin, and that I was in San Diego for a conference, though I'd added a few vacation days.

We ordered drinks and talked about everything, friends, family, relationships, and yes, geek culture. We clicked immediately, like we were meant to have run into each other. Now, of course, I wish we hadn't. At any rate, she was staying at that hotel, and when the bar closed, invited me upstairs.

This next part I'm not telling you to be salacious. It's just that its important if you're going to understand how all this came about. We undressed in a flurry, clothes flying helter-skelter, and we laughed and kissed each other all the while. It was after we found ourselves in bed, and I'd entered her, that the furniture began to shake. A lamp fell onto the floor, and what started as a dull roar became near deafening. It was almost like the amplified, subterranean drawl of speech dramatically slowed down. Finally, it stopped. I was still inside her, too stupefied to move, and we looked at each other wide-eyed. Then Briana smiled and stroked my face and said, "I think I felt the earth move."

I laughed out loud, and so did she, and we clutched each other, laughing until our eyes were streaming tears.

It had been a great day. I mean, obviously, but even aside from meeting Briana. The conference had finished in the early afternoon and I took the opportunity to drive up to La Jolla and stroll the village, sampling coffee and pastry shops, browsing a book store, and getting a beer on the sidewalk in the late afternoon. When I got hungry, I drove to the Shores and ate Italian while I watched families and friends stroll past in their swimsuits and wetsuits, or in their summer T's and shorts. After finishing my meal, I took my shoes and socks off and walked along the hot sand of the beach, cooling my feet occasionally in the ocean. Pretty much my idea of an ideal afternoon.

So, it was pretty weird that I had the worst dream of my life that night.

I found myself in a square, the ground covered by interlocking stone slabs. Surrounding the square were windowless buildings of every shape and size. The slabs and buildings were fashioned from a sickly green polished onyx with odd, marble-like veins darting hither and thither in outlandish patterns. There was something about the buildings, something wrong. I couldn't put my finger on what it was at first. Then I noticed that they changed with each new perspective, with protuberances and extensions visible at one angle, but disappearing altogether at another. They were tall, and then they weren't. They were straight up and down, and then they had a significant tilt. The rooftops were many-pointed, then they were flat.

I don't know what time of day it was. There was little enough light, so perhaps it was dusk. The air was still and carried the faint scents of ozone and sulfur and something else, as if there was a pile of rotting meat just around the corner.

I came to a building whose surface was covered with glyphs, oddly shaped representations that seemed to combine various living creatures into one. I looked closer and realized that the glyphs hadn't been carved *into* the wall, they protruded *from* it. They were reliefs, not glyphs. Monstrous things, completely alien. Tentacled creatures with claws and ravenous maw, for instance. I stopped and realized that, very slowly, the damned things were moving.

Part of me wanted to back away, but I felt compelled to look more closely. What came next happened so quickly that I was caught completely unawares. The tentacles of one of the carved creatures leapt out, enveloping me, pulling me towards the wall. I screamed and struggled. Then I couldn't breathe as the tentacles covered my mouth and nose.

It was Briana, bless her heart, who roused me. I'd been screaming right into her ear. I must have given her a fright as bad as my nightmare.

There was no way we were going to go right back to sleep, so we made some tea, sat at the end of the bed, and talked. Briana asked about my dream. I really wasn't ready to think about it, much less talk about it, so she told me about hers instead. Turns out, it was also horrible, but in a different way.

"It was like I was right there. I mean, invisible, but there. I guess all dreams seem real while you're dreaming, but I can remember every detail. Usually my dreams just melt away, until I can only remember something vague, like I was getting chased by dragons or some such silly thing.

"I was in a mansion in Providence, owned by an old-money family. White, of course. This young black woman, couldn't have been much more than 18 or 19, a housemaid, I think, was carrying a heavy tray of drinks and food to the top floor.

"She set the tray down on a side table and knocked. As the door opened, she picked up the tray and brought it inside. Then she stopped dead in her tracks and looked around her.

"The floor was covered with plush maroon carpeting. Heavy curtains of the same colour, hid the windows. The walls were covered in tiled mahogany paneling. Overstuffed leather chairs were placed in a semicircle around the fireplace. A polished mahogany buffet held a decanter and crystal glasses. Small tables were scattered throughout. The only light was from candles, lots of them, set throughout the room.

"I think what actually made her stop dead was the group of men. There were a dozen of them, old white guys, some bald, some with beards, all wearing dark robes and arranged around a thin pedestal which held a gold chalice. I peeked in the chalice and saw red liquid. Something told me it wasn't wine.

"Then I noticed something, or maybe the lack of something. A black smudge in a far corner of the room. I walked towards it and realized it was a man, tall, thin, also enveloped in dark robes. He was bald and had the blackest skin I've ever seen. And I don't mean dark brown. I mean *black*. I'm not sure I'll ever call myself black again after that, except it was a dream, of course. I got closer, then things started to get creepy. He had been looking at the maid, but then he turned and looked directly at me. His wide eyes were full of amber, just like a cat's, complete with black vertical slit.

"Basically, the guy freaked me out. I backed away and walked towards the door, starting to wish I could wake up. So, yeah, I must have known that I was dreaming.

"Meanwhile, one of the men took the tray from the maid, set it down, and said, 'Now, Ida, you're about to become greater than yourself. Greater even than me. You're going to become something special.' He waved his arm towards the other men, who bowed their heads slightly in acknowledgment. 'Greater than any of us.'

"Do you think he had a big enough ego? Anyway, he continued. 'All it will take is a drop of your blood. Perhaps a few drops. We've already done the same. Come and have a look.'

"Poor Ida, she was wordless with fright and tried to back away, shaking her head. The man who'd spoken gestured to the group and two men came forward and grabbed Ida, shoving her towards the chalice. She put up quite a fight. It took four of them to hold her still enough for one to take a knife and cut her palm. He gripped her hand so that that drops of blood fell into the chalice.

"Howling in pain and fear, Ida continued to struggle. The group holding her found themselves moving towards one of the walls as they tried to keep her in check. Then someone picked up the chalice and, while a fifth man held open her mouth, began to pour the liquid down her throat.

"They didn't get far before Ida really began to raise hell. She managed to knock over a candle, igniting the cloak of one of the men holding her. He released her, and so did another as he tried to help him. Ida stamped another on the foot, and kicked the last man on the shin. Then she ran across the room, screaming, knocking down and hurling many of the candles. Flames erupted from several of the mens' robes and the curtains and finally the carpeting. Ida took the chalice and ran, smashing the forehead of the sole man trying to block her exit.

"Flying down the stairs, Ida stopped on the ground floor, opened the fireplace screen, and used a fire iron to toss the burning wood into chairs and carpeting. Grabbing a coat, she left by the front door and dashed across the street. She paused long enough to see that the top floor was engulfed in flames, and licks of fire were shooting from the ground floor windows.

"I think she'd forgotten that she still had the chalice in her hand. She looked at it, wide-eyed, then stuffed it into her coat pocket and walked away without looking back.

"And that's when I realized that this woman, Ida, was my Nana Ida, who founded my family tree. We can trace our ancestry to her, but no further back. She must have melted down the gold to buy the farm that was our homestead. Some dream, huh?"

I said nothing, but I think I turned pale and my hands were trembling. With a puzzled look, Briana took my hands in hers and said, "Nathan?"

"Nana Ida," I mumbled. "From Rhode Island. And she established her homestead when? In the late 1800's?"

"Yes …"

"The thing is, I'm descended from her too."

Releasing my hands, Briana got to her feet and looked at me closely. "You're not messing with me, are you?"

"I swear. I can recite the whole family tree from her to me if you like. Which means we …"

"Are not exactly first cousins. Nathan, don't sweat it. This is a crazy coincidence, that's all."

I must have still looked upset. Cupping my face with her hands, she said, "Look, let's get back under the covers. No more talking. We'll just let sleep come to us. Tomorrow will be another day."

So that's what we did, and though I didn't expect to sleep any more that night, I did. In fact, we didn't get up until near noon. We showered and dressed and ordered in brunch. After eating our fill, we sipped on the remaining coffee and shared a copy of USA Today.

"Oh my God," said Briana. I looked up from the section I'd been reading and said, "What?"

"It says here that Felix Boyd has passed away. Well, not passed away, he was brutally murdered, actually."

"And who's Felix Boyd?"

"Are you kidding me?" said Briana. My face was a complete blank, so she continued. "He's a well-known horror writer. He won an award, I think, for his latest book. It was creepy as hell. I loved it. The thing is, it was supposed to be the first in a trilogy. Oh well."

Setting down the section I was reading, I said, "You know what? I think I've had quite enough of horrible things for just now. Why don't we come up with a plan for the day?"

We did. First, at Briana's suggestion, we checked me out of my downtown hotel and moved my things in with her. Afterwards, we drove to the village and visited the shop with the stairs to the sea cave.

We descended the 145 steps, walked to the end of the boardwalk, and gazed out at the ocean as it splashed at the cave opening and filled the space with its smell. Kayakers off in the near distance paddled in our direction.

After a few minutes, I heard Briana grunt, "Huh." I turned and she pointed back to where the boardwalk met the cave floor. It was hard to see in the gloom, but off to the side there was another stone staircase leading further down. We'd walked right past it.

We were already at the point in our relationship when words weren't always necessary. By unspoken agreement we took the stairs. While the first set of stairs had been lit with electric lights, these were illuminated by torches, the flames crackling and the heat warming our skin as we passed.

The sounds of the ocean receded as we descended. I'm not sure how many steps there were. Lots. They weren't as slippery as the first staircase, and just as well because there was no railing. Our hands trailed along the cold stone walls for support.

I think we were about ready to give up and climb back when we realized we were at the bottom. Ahead of us was pitch blackness, but a slight breeze was blowing towards us, and it seemed we must be at the mouth of a large cavern. I went back to the staircase, grabbed a torch, and rejoined Briana. Together, we stepped gingerly forward.

It did occur to me that perhaps we shouldn't be there. There'd been no mention of a lower cavern in what we'd seen online. But then, there'd been no signs warning us to keep out, either. We glanced at each other, and continued.

After a hundred yards or so, we could make out objects standing erect in front of us. They were round pillars, some twenty feet tall, arranged in a rough circle, and spread about three feet apart from one another.

"What the hell?" I said.

"What do you think? Maybe they were carved from a natural formation of stalagmites."

"They're certainly not natural," I said. "Way too regular. Mind you, there's this freaky rock formation in Northern Ireland …"

Just then, I noticed carvings on one of the pillars. We stepped up closer to get a good look. The symbols were arranged vertically. At the top was a cup. Underneath the cup, a diamond shape, and underneath that, something resembling an octopus, with big eyes and lots of tentacles.

"Not so natural, then," said Briana. "I wonder what the point is? Maybe some other tourist did this? But … oh no."

Glancing at her, I saw Briana's mouth gape open. "What?" I said.

Turning to me, her eyes wide, Briana said, "I can think of one interpretation. You won't like it."

"Well now you have to tell me."

Pointing to the cup, she said, "This could be the chalice that Nana Ida stole. The top of the diamond represents the family line diverging. The bottom is the convergence, and the point where they meet is …"

"You and me?"

Briana shrugged. "Too far-fetched?"

"I don't know," I said, then added, "Yeah, actually, quite far-fetched." Moving around the pillar I noted something else.

"There's another carving on this side," I said. "No, not a carving, a relief, and it's… Oh no. No way."

I suddenly was unable to breathe, and felt my heart was going to burst through my chest. Backing away from the sight, I tripped over something. Then I screamed. Twice. Once for the pain, and once for what I landed beside.

I had tried to break my fall with my hands, but now they were covered in blood and they hurt, like I'd been stung by a dozen wasps. I didn't know which way to turn and for a moment was completely confused. For one thing, why was I lying right next to a skeleton, the empty eye sockets inches away from my face?

For another, why was I bleeding? I ran my forefinger gingerly over the ground and realized that it wasn't flat, but serrated. It was as if I'd fallen atop of a fine grater.

Briana must have been tougher than me because she didn't scream at all. However, before I could stop her, she knelt down and placed one hand on the ground to brace herself and offered me the other. She withdrew her hand immediately and shook it vigorously. It was bleeding as well.

"What the hell is this place?" she said.

I reached for the hand she offered and started to pull myself up. It was just as our blood mingled that the earthquake started. It didn't last long, not as long as the previous night, but it seemed even louder, almost as if it were trying to speak to us in some forgotten, guttural language. And it felt stronger than before, certainly strong enough to give us a good jolt.

When it subsided, we got to our feet. I shook the blood off my hands, picked up the torch, and said, "No objections, I'm sure, if we just get out of here?"

I don't actually remember our flight up the stairs from the lower cavern. Having attained the upper cavern, we trudged up to the shop. By then the cuts on our hands had already begun to heal. The punctures had been tiny, tinier than I'd realized.

We tried to tell the guy in the shop that he had a skeleton in the lower cavern and that he might want to call the police. He looked at us like he had no idea what we were talking about. Finally, he said that there *was* no lower cavern and suggested that we might not want to smoke whatever it was we'd been smoking.

I was set to argue the point, but Briana just tugged at my sleeve and said it was best to just leave it.

Driving back to the hotel, I couldn't get the image of the relief out of my mind. It had been the same one as in my dream. Which was possible how? I couldn't see a way in which it made any sense. And, of course, if the relief from *my* dream was on one side of that column, perhaps

Briana was right, and the cup on the other side *was* Nana Ida's. Which meant what?

We stopped at the hotel bar for a beer, then went up to change and had dinner in the rooftop restaurant, where we had a great view of the ocean. We ate mostly in silence. I think we were both thinking of the same things, the fact that the images from our dreams had appeared in that cavern, and that our time together in La Jolla would come to an end in a couple of days.

By the time we finished our meal it was getting dark. Briana was all for taking a walk along the beach. As for me, I felt the need to take a shower and somehow wash this day off of me. After teasing me for being a wuss, she went down on her own, taking a flashlight with her. I waited for her, standing out on the balcony until I saw her shine the flashlight on herself. Then she pointed up at me and I waved.

That's when the light went out and I heard the scream. Frozen, I just listened as the scream dragged on for seconds. I don't know how many. Finally, I came to my senses and bounded down the stairs, two or three at a time, until I exited the hotel and ran to the beach where she'd been standing.

Except … Well, you know what I found. I stumbled upon the flashlight, turned it on, and that's when I must have screamed myself, because there was Briana, or what was left of her, in a hundred bloody pieces. Guts, organs, limbs, scattered about, and blood everywhere. Of course, I was covered in her blood by the time the police arrived.

And … I think that's everything.

What do I think happened? I think that when Briana and I got together, we woke something up. Something that's been dormant a long time. Something that can get into your dreams. Basically, we're its parents. And like some organisms, this thing eats its parents. Sacrifices them, maybe. Briana was first. Maybe I'm next.

Detective Rick Spence exited the interview room shaking his head, then noticed Captain Billy Pérez, leaning against the wall, hands in his pockets, waiting for him.

"What do you make of him?" the captain asked.

"Well the story is ridiculous, of course. The thing is, *he* believes it."

"Psych eval?"

Nodding, Spence said, "I think so. I'll get on that in the morning. Meanwhile, we've no physical evidence he did this, or is even capable of doing this. And we don't have a murder weapon. The uniforms will pick up the search at daybreak."

"Well," said the Captain, "we'll hold him as long as possible and find out everything we can about him." Noting Spence's sagging form, he added, "You look done in. Best call it a night."

"Yeah," Spence answered gratefully. "See you in the morning."

Spence arrived home half an hour later, kissed his sleeping wife on the cheek, and climbed into bed, grateful for her comforting warmth. Still, his sleep was anything but comforting, as it was full of images from the tale that his suspect had spun. He found himself descending a dark, stone staircase where the walls began to close in on either side, and tentacles carved from the stone began to wriggle and reach out for him. In a panic, as he wondered if he should run up the stairs or down, he was jolted awake by the phone.

"Spence," he growled when he managed to grasp the thing.

"D-Detective." The man on the other end gulped. "Officer Baker here. You need to come back to headquarters. Now. Captain's orders."

Spence blinked. "What's happened?"

"J-just come. Now," he repeated. And with that, the officer disconnected the call.

Spence stared at the phone in wonder, then leapt out of bed and dressed, urging his wife to go back to sleep.

The unkempt, bedraggled detective rushed to the officer on duty. The officer's face was pale, even considering it was the middle of the night. Something had scared the crap out of her.

He didn't need to ask. "The detention area," she whispered.

Jogging to the detention area, he nearly collided with Captain Pérez. The captain turned and, wordlessly, led Spence to Nathan Carter's cell.

The first thing Spence noted was the pool of vomit outside the cell. Then there was the smell. Not just the vomit, but the vestiges of another pungent, putrid stench. Standing in front of the cell, he gazed at the scene wordlessly. Blood was everywhere, on the cell walls, the floor, and the ceiling. Severed body parts and internal organs were scattered about. After bending down to look more closely at the floor, he turned to the captain and asked, "Is that …?"

"Sand," the captain confirmed.

The two men looked at each other, their faces ashen.

Spence felt the floor beneath him sway, undulate, as he remembered something Carter had said.

I think that when Briana and I got together, we woke something up. Something that's been dormant a long time. Something that can get into your dreams.

Sinking to the floor with the cold enveloping him and blackness descending, feeling tentacles writhe out of that blackness and brush against him, he clutched the captain's shirt and uttered in a hoarse whisper, "It was in my dream."

Unfinished Business: A White Rose Mystery

I love noirish detective stories. In this one, I wanted to avoid writing from the point of view of the detective. Throw in hints of maybe-it-is-maybe-it-isn't fantasy, and that's where the story came from. There may be more White Rose mysteries in the future. We'll see.

Dr. Nikki Meadows entered Ruth's Wine & Spirits Bar and took a stool at the bar.

The atmosphere suited her: dimly lit pseudo gas lanterns, panelled walls, hardwood floors, brown-mahogany-stained bar, and some Diana Krall playing quietly in the background. The clientele seemed mostly upscale; lots of little black dresses and sport coats. She didn't care about that, as long as they left her alone.

The bartender nodded in her direction and approached after pouring a Johnnie Walker Black Label neat for a man a couple of stools to her left. Healthy-looking and fit, he was dressed in black slacks, a grey plaid wool sport coat, and a white shirt open at the collar. His hair was short, dark, and neatly combed.

"Evening," the bartender said. "I'm Ruth. What can I get for you?"

"Nikki. Dry martini, please."

"Sure thing." Ruth mixed the drink and handed it to Nikki, who raised the glass and downed it in one gulp.

"Another."

"Bad day?" said Ruth, as she picked up the glass.

"You could say that. Got left at the altar today."

"Ouch. Sorry to hear that. Tell you what, first drink's on me."

"Thanks," said Nikki. "Appreciate it. Mind you, it wasn't his fault. He was murdered an hour before the wedding."

Ruth blinked. "You're kidding."

"Nope. God's honest truth. The police just finished questioning me." A silence-filled minute later, Ruth passed the fresh martini to Nikki. "Thanks." Nikki sipped it more slowly.

Glancing around, Ruth whispered, "And you're here by yourself?"

Nikki nodded. "My maid of honour wanted to come, of course. But she would only have reminded me . . ." Blinking back tears, she continued. "And just for a while, I'd like to try to not think about it."

"Of course," said Ruth, and went to serve another customer.

Nikki was starting her third drink when a man took the stool to her right and ordered an IPA. He regarded her unselfconsciously.

"What?" said Nikki, keeping her eyes fixed in front of her.

"I couldn't help but overhear," said the man. "Wondered if I could help."

"Help."

"Sure. Take your mind off your troubles, you know?" With that, the back of his hand brushed her skirt.

Nikki made a point of not responding. The man, taking that as a sign of acquiescence, rested his hand lightly upon her thigh.

"Seriously?" said Nikki, finally turning towards him. His BMI was unhealthily high, she decided. His hair was light brown and close cropped. Dressed in a dark blue suit, he smelled of aftershave, perspiration, and beer. The expression on his face, part grin, part leer, made her want to cringe. She didn't. "My fiancé was murdered and you want to help by feeling me up?"

He shrugged. "By making you feel better."

He was now toying with the hem of her skirt and touching her bare knee.

The man to Nikki's left cleared his throat. "Pardon me, miss, might I be of some help?"

"Nah," said Nikki, not taking her eyes off her accoster. "Let's all just feel sorry for this lowlife," she said, in a louder voice. "After all, the only thing smaller than his dick is his IQ."

Picking up her drink, she moved to the stool to her left. The well-dressed man chuckled quietly.

"Bitch," the lowlife muttered.

Ruth leaned across the bar. "I think it's time you were leaving, don't you?"

After taking another gulp of beer, the lowlife slammed the glass on the counter. "Crummy bar, anyway," he said, and left.

Nikki raised her glass in his direction, finished her drink, and ordered another. "Last one," she promised.

"Not a problem," said Ruth. "If anyone deserves a good buzz tonight, you do."

"I'll drink to that." After a moment, Nikki said, to no one in particular, "Before today, my biggest problem was the old boys' club. And now, it's entirely possible that the only decent man in this city was murdered this afternoon." Turning to the man beside her, she added, "No offence."

"None taken," the man replied with a wry smile. "I don't live here. Allow me to say, though, that I'm very sorry for your loss." After sliding a business card towards her, he continued. "I'm here on a vacation of sorts, but if I can be of any assistance, please don't hesitate to call."

Picking up the card, Nikki mentally cut through the fog of alcohol and read out loud: "Bill Moore. Private Investigator." Below was the phone number for an answering service.

"You use an answering service? That's going back a bit, isn't it?"

Moore shrugged. "It's useful."

"Well," said Nikki, "the police are all over this, trust me. But I'll keep this just in case. Thanks."

Moore stood, placed a fedora on his head with practised ease, and nodded to Nikki on his way out.

Jake Haskell stumbled out of a bar. Not the fanciest, but at least he hadn't come across any more frigid bitches. Standing and breathing deeply of the night air, he decided to walk rather than order an Uber. The exercise might sober him up before he got home to the missus. And another self-righteous lecture.

Muttering to himself, he looked up after a few paces and saw a familiar figure walking towards him.

"You," Jake said, standing in his way.

The man stopped. "You got a problem?"

There was something about the man's tone that gave Jake pause. But he blustered on. "How'd you get on with that bitch? Fuck her in the bathroom after getting some drinks in her?"

The man stepped up to him, grabbed him by the lapels, and nearly lifted him off his feet.

"Listen, pal. You want to watch your mouth. And you want to make sure you never go near that young lady again. If I catch you pulling that sort of stunt, you'll have me to answer to. I'll have something special just for you. Got it?"

Letting him go, the man backed up, cast Jake a dismissive glance, and continued past him. Nate, perspiring now despite the slight chill in the air, turned, but the man had already melted into the crowd.

"Moore Investigations." The voice on the phone was cool, even, and gentle—just what Nikki needed to hear right now.

"May I speak with Bill Moore, please?"

"I'm afraid Mr. Moore isn't available at the moment. May I take a message?"

"Yes. This is Nikki Meadows. Mr. Moore left me his card a couple of weeks ago and it turns out I think I need his help."

"I'm sure he'll be happy to do everything he can, Dr. Meadows. If you can suggest a time and place for a meeting, I'll let him know."

As she disconnected the call, Nikki wondered, *How did she know I was a doctor?*

It was a sunny, warm day in early June, though Nikki was oblivious to the good weather. Lately, when she didn't feel numb, she felt cold. Paying scant attention to her surroundings, she navigated the ByWard Market with its bright colours, floral scents, noisy buskers, and bustling fruit and vegetable stands. Throughout the market's outdoor stalls, tourists picked at souvenirs.

She almost missed the coffee shop. After backtracking a few steps and looking in the window, she saw that Moore was seated at a corner table taking sips from a mug. Sighing and straightening her shoulders, Nikki entered and approached the table.

"Dr. Meadows," said Moore, standing as she approached him. He was dressed in a light-grey suit, a white shirt, and a patterned dark-grey tie. A white rose adorned his lapel.

"Thanks for meeting with me," said Nikki. "I'll just get something to drink and join you."

When her cappuccino was ready, she took a seat and found herself looking down at her drink, trying to slow her rapid breathing.

"Take your time, Dr. Meadows," said Moore. "I know this isn't easy."

"Nikki, please," she said, looking up at Moore finally. "And you're right. None of this is easy. I feel like my whole world has been turned upside down."

"That's a fair description, and completely understandable," said Moore. "I've read the papers, but I'd like to hear about it in your own words. You can start by telling me about yourself, what happened on your wedding day, and why you need my help."

Nodding, Nikki took a breath and began. "Okay. I'm thirty-four years old. I'm an ER doctor at the Ottawa Hospital. I started dating Brian about three years ago. Brian Whittaker. He's . . . he was an accountant. We met through a mutual friend, Derek Summers, Brian's best man. Two years ago we moved in together. Last year we got engaged. We wanted a small civil wedding, just a couple of close friends and family.

"I was at City Hall with my parents and my best friend, Alyssa, all ready for the ceremony, when I got the phone call. Brian had been at Derek's apartment getting ready for the wedding. Derek told me that Brian had gone ahead to the parking garage. He'd wanted to decorate the car a bit. When Derek came down, he found Brian face up on the ground, blood pooling around him. He says he froze for a moment then approached Brian while calling 911. Brian was still alive for a few seconds, but he passed before the ambulance and police arrived.

"A knife had penetrated his heart. There's nothing anyone could have done. The police haven't been able to find it, so the killer must have taken it with him."

"And they've arrested Mr. Summers for the murder," said Moore.

"Yes, despite not having found the murder weapon. They haven't found anyone else with motive or opportunity."

"What motive?"

"Brian and Derek work—worked—at the same accounting firm. They were both eligible for a promotion.

Brian got it. So at first the police thought Derek might have done it to get the job. I asked the detectives whether they really thought he'd kill someone just for a promotion. They said I'd be surprised what people kill for."

Moore nodded. "In this case, they have a fair point."

"Well, after going through his email history, they began wondering if he and I weren't both involved in the murder."

"And why would they think that?"

"Derek and I dated for a few months. It didn't work out. I'd already met Brian, through him. Derek seemed okay with it all when Brian and I started seeing each other, and we've stayed friends. Anyway, the police are inclined to think that Derek and I were plotting to get back together and that first, we wanted to get Brian out of the way."

"And were you?" said Moore. "Planning to get back together?"

Nikki barked a laugh. "God no. Been there, done that. Besides, if I had the slightest inclination, all I'd have had to do was call off the wedding, right?"

Moore regarded her for a moment. "Are you the executor of Mr. Whittaker's will?"

"No, Brian's father is dealing with that."

"I see. I take it that you're not aware of your fiancé's life-insurance policy?"

"What? No, he didn't discuss it with me and I haven't had a chance to think about it."

"He changed his policy shortly after your engagement," Moore continued. "In the event of his death, you are to receive $500,000. So, you and Derek might have planned to kill Brian and split the insurance."

Nikki's eyes widened. Her mouth opened and closed. Casting her eyes upwards, she muttered, "Oh for God's sake, Brian." She glanced out the window. "And here I am, still in debt to the tune of $100,000. No wonder the police suspect me." She shook her head then looked Moore in the eye. "And what about you? What do you think?"

Moore gave her a thin smile. "I've learned to trust my instincts over the years. No, I don't think you were involved."

Nikki exhaled. "Thank you. I really needed to hear that. So, what do we do now?"

After taking a sip of his coffee, Moore said, "The police are assuming that your fiancé was the target of this attack. I'd like to look at it from another angle. I think that *you* were the intended target and that he was collateral damage."

Nikki blinked. "Me? You think someone did this to hurt me?"

Moore withdrew a small notebook and a pen from his jacket pocket. "It's a definite possibility. Now, you may want to get another coffee. This could take a while. I need you to tell me about your friends, family, work, and daily routine in great detail."

When she'd finished, Nikki sipped the dregs of her second cappuccino and said, "Well, I really appreciate your help. I remember you said you were on vacation."

"More like a working vacation," said Moore. "I've some unfinished business to attend to. Now there's one more thing. We need to close this quickly, before the police decide they've got a solid case against you. We can do that if you agree to take a risk and do exactly as I say. I promise that I'll do everything I can to keep you safe, but there *will* be a risk."

She knew that Moore expected her to be getting nervous right about now. But through the course of their conversation, her anxiety had fled. Her breathing and heart rate felt normal. She was alert and fully attuned to the sights and sounds and smells around her. She was back. For the first time in, well, since *that* day. Maybe it was the prospect of finally doing something.

"I'm an ER doctor," she said, leaning forward. "I eat risk for breakfast. What do I have to do?"

Nikki was chopping up vegetables for a salad when she heard her phone buzz. It was her maid of honour.

"Alyssa."

"Hey, Nikki. Holding up?"

"Well, you know. About as well as can be expected. How are you doing?"

"Interesting. I mean, I just had a visit from a Bill Moore. Says you hired him as an investigator?"

"Oh, that *is* interesting," said Nikki. "Yes, I hired him. I had no idea he'd be visiting you."

"I've never been interrogated before, so it was actually pretty cool. Tell me, does he seem . . . old to you? No, that's not the right word. I know he *isn't* old, but . . . I don't know."

"Old? No. He did strike me as being very professional. Certainly, he doesn't give much away."

"Never mind, don't listen to me," said Alyssa. "The thing is, he's under the impression the police will soon be dropping the charges against Brian. And that you'll be in the clear yourself. As if that were ever an issue."

"Yes, he mentioned that to me as well. I think he's hoping to hand over evidence to the police that identifies the real killer. Fingers crossed."

"Yes, definitely. As if you needed any of this on top of … well, you know."

To her annoyance, Nikki found herself tearing up again. "Sorry, Alyssa, but I think I need a moment. Is that all right?"

"Of course. I'm here if you need me, babe. Later."

"Later," said Nikki, and disconnected the call. Staring at the phone, she whispered, "Please don't let it be you."

Dr. Lester Michaels poked his head through the reception door. "Mr. Moore?" he called. He tried not to smile as Moore got to his feet. Of *course* that was him—the only guy in the waiting room wearing a suit.

After gesturing Moore into his office, Lester closed the door and took a seat at his workstation. Moore sat in a chair next to the examining table.

"You've been hired by Nikki," said Lester, glancing at Moore's card. His receptionist had passed it to him after Moore's request for a meeting.

"Yes, as I told your receptionist. I appreciate your seeing me. I noticed that your waiting area is full so I won't keep you long."

"We are busy, of course, but I'll be happy to help Nikki any way I can." Lester kept his face neutral while puzzling over what the investigator could possibly want with him.

"How long have you known Dr. Meadows?"

"How long? Well, since med school, so, I don't know, at least a dozen years."

"The Ottawa Hospital informed me that you'd both applied for the position of ER physician. Is that correct?"

Lester blinked. "Yes, that's certainly true. But that was Nikki's idea, not mine. I only applied, quite honestly, to get her off my back. Nikki can be very insistent. It was my childhood GP who inspired my going into med school. All I've ever really wanted was to become a GP like him. To make a difference to families the way he did."

Moore nodded and continued. "You're aware, of course, that Derek Summers has been charged with the murder of Brian Whittaker."

"Yes, though it's hard to believe. I've met Derek a few times. I never would have thought that he had it in him to kill anyone, let alone his best friend."

"The police have been building a case against Dr. Meadows also."

"That's just ridiculous."

"Then you'll be pleased to learn," Moore added smoothly, "just between us, that they'll soon be dropping the investigation into my client and releasing Mr. Summers."

"Well, that's wonderful news, of course," Lester said with a broad smile. "Absolutely wonderful. Glad to hear that the police have finally seen reason."

"Well, I won't take up any more of your time, Dr. Michaels. Thank you. I can see myself out."

Upon hearing the doorbell, Farida Anand took a deep breath, as she'd been instructed. It didn't help. Her anxiety didn't retreat, though it didn't worsen.

After flipping the deadbolt, she opened the door a crack and peered out.

"Mrs. Anand?" said a tall, well-dressed man. "Bill Moore. We spoke on the phone." His voice, even and reassuring, as well as his general appearance, made Farida feel comfortable enough to invite him inside.

"Have a seat and I'll bring out some tea."

"That's very kind of you," said Moore, taking off his hat. "Thanks."

In short order, Farida entered the living room carrying a tray laden with a teapot, cups and saucers, spoons, and milk and sugar. "You have some questions concerning the death of my husband?" she said, pouring the tea.

"Thank you, yes," said Moore, taking a cup and saucer. "First, let me say how sorry I am for your loss. It can't be easy to talk about this."

"It's *not* easy," said Farida. "But this, my husband's death, is something I must face. And the more I talk about it, the more real it becomes. Does that make sense to you?"

Moore smiled. "Perfect sense. As I mentioned on the phone, I've been hired to investigate a case related to your husband's death, and the events that followed."

"And those events have to do with my having accused the doctor of killing my husband."

"In part, yes," said Moore. "I understand you felt that your husband died unnecessarily."

"That's certainly a polite way of putting it. I was incensed, and in retrospect I regret what I said at the time. Unfortunately, my anger took a long time to subside. And when it did, I came to realize that there was nothing anyone could have done."

"If you don't mind my asking," said Moore, "what brought you to that conclusion?"

"My husband was a construction foreman, you see. On the day of his death, a load of lumber fell upon him and crushed him. He was still alive when he got to hospital but died in emergency. I lodged a formal complaint. It was dismissed.

"Some time later, Dr. Meadows came to my home. I nearly slammed the door in her face. But she showed me how I could access my husband's medical records online, and she walked me through them and answered my questions about the jargon. The end result was that I finally understood how broken my husband's body had been. Not just outside, but inside. And I saw that the staff, including Dr. Meadows, must have done everything they could to save him. Sometimes your time on Earth is simply over. Do you agree, Mr. Moore?"

Moore nodded. "You say that you nearly slammed the door on Dr. Meadows. How did you feel by the time she left?"

"We hugged. We cried. And I apologized for adding to the stress of what must already be a very stressful, and at times thankless, job."

Moore wrote down some notes, then asked, "Have you had any contact with Dr. Meadows since?"

Farida shook her head.

"Or her family members or friends?"

Puzzled, Farida frowned. "No. Of course not. Why would I?"

"Just putting together the last few pieces of a puzzle, Mrs. Anand," said Moore, standing. "Thank you for your time. You've been very helpful."

Also standing, Farida smiled. "I'm glad. Perhaps in some small way this helps make amends for my previous behaviour."

"I'm sure Dr. Meadows would say you've nothing to apologize for. Goodbye, Mrs. Anand."

Moore had just stepped outside when he turned back. "You've heard, of course, of the murder of her fiancé. It's been reported in the newspapers."

"Yes," said Farida. "It's horrible."

"Well the good news is that the police will soon be dropping charges against the best man, and Dr. Meadows will no longer be a person of interest."

"I'm glad," said Farida. "She must be most relieved."

"Goodbye again, Mrs. Anand."

Farida closed the door. She paused. Then her eyes widened, and she opened the door again. She *had* seen Dr. Meadows on one other occasion. But as she looked up and down the street, there was no sign of Mr. Moore.

Putting away the last of the previous night's dishes, Nikki nearly jumped at the sound of the phone. After drying her hands with a dish towel, she took the call.

"Hello?"

"Nikki, it's Lester. I'm downstairs. Thought I'd pop by and see how you're doing."

"That's sweet of you," she said. "I could use a friend right about now. I'll buzz you in."

When the doorbell rang, Nikki walked the short corridor from the kitchen to the living room, turned the deadbolt, and opened the door. "Hi Lester," she said. "Come in."

Lester, whose hands had been behind his back, smiled and revealed a large bouquet of flowers wrapped in gift paper.

"These are for you," he said. "I've been worried about you."

"Well thank you. Let's put these in some water."

He followed her into the kitchen after wiping his feet on the mat.

"Would you like some coffee?" said Nikki. "I've just started a pot."

"That would be great, thanks," said Lester. "Mind you, I'm also here to celebrate."

"Celebrate?" Nikki frowned. "Not sure I feel much like celebrating, to be honest."

"Of course," said Lester. "It's just that a Mr. Moore came to see me yesterday. Your investigator? He said the police were about to drop charges against poor Derek. And that you were no longer going to be a person of interest."

"Mr. Moore's been busy," said Nikki with a nod. "He's seen at least a half-dozen people—that I know of—over the past while. All he told me was that he needed to 'clear up some details.' What that means exactly I've no idea."

Leading her friend into the kitchen, Nikki gestured to a stool by the island. Just then the coffee maker pinged, and Nikki fetched two mugs, which she filled. "You take yours black, don't you?" said Nikki.

"You still remember! Yes, that's fine, thanks." He took the proffered mug.

"Well," said Nikki, glancing at the bundle of flowers, "let's see what we can do with you." After retrieving a pair of scissors from a nearby drawer, Nikki cut the tape and opened the wrapping.

And stopped in her tracks.

The flowers were dead.

After staring stupidly at them for, well, she wasn't sure how long, she glanced at Lester. He was smiling.

"Lester, what …?" She picked up the flowers, and something clattered to the counter—a chef's knife, caked with blood. Nikki's mouth dropped open, and she looked wide-eyed at Lester.

Reaching forward, Lester picked up the knife. "Yes. This is the knife I used to kill poor, poor Brian. And no, I didn't clean the knife afterwards. Makes for a better souvenir that way."

Nikki, on the opposite side of the island, backed away. "Lester? No. It was *you*?"

Without a word, Lester got up and walked slowly around the island.

"But why?" Nikki backed into the kitchen counter and stopped.

Lester continued his approach. "Why? Because you've always been so stuck-up. So superior. So much better than everyone else. You just had to have the ER job, didn't you? Who did you sleep with to get it, I wonder?"

"What? Are you serious? Lester, where's this coming from?"

"Where's it coming from? You took everything from me. So I pretended you were still my friend. I've pretended for a long time. And then, when you got engaged, it occurred to me that I could do something about it. You'd get hurt by losing your fiancé, and then, the icing on the cake, you might be charged as an accomplice in his murder. Too bad that part didn't work out. But I couldn't just let you off the hook. No, that wouldn't do at all. So, this is me, taking the direct approach."

At that moment, Nikki saw Moore step quietly into the kitchen behind Lester. Shaking her head slightly, she said, "Lester, you don't have to do this. You need help. I can help you. But you have to put down the knife."

"No, I don't think so. I think it's time to end this."

While they talked, Nikki felt behind her and grabbed the coffee pot handle.

Lester rushed forward, closing the gap between them. Nikki shot the steaming contents of the pot into his face.

Screaming, Lester dropped the knife and clutched his face. "You bitch!" Then he charged at her again. "You bloody—"

But he didn't get a chance to finish before Nikki delivered a swift kick to his groin. Lester grunted and fell to the floor, whimpering and curling into the fetal position.

"You know what?" said Nikki, standing over him. "I've had about enough of horrible men calling me a bitch."

Moore, chuckling, turned off the video recorder. "Somehow I had a feeling that anyone on your bad side would come to regret it. You know what to do now?"

"Oh yes," said Nikki, dialling 911.

Lester tried to get up. A kick in the ribs convinced him to lie still.

The police took Lester into custody, and Nikki accompanied them to the station. Seated in an interrogation room with two detectives, she explained that she'd hired Moore. He'd reasoned that Brian might have been killed to make Nikki suffer, and to incriminate her in the process. If the culprit was told that Nikki was in the clear, they might try a more direct approach. Basically, his plan had been to use her as bait, and she had readily agreed. It was Moore who'd suggested that she mount motion-triggered video cameras in her unit. After making her statement, she left, promising to return for a follow-up the next day.

By the time Nikki returned the following morning, the detectives had reviewed the video footage from her unit and had interviewed Alyssa and some of the other friends and acquaintances on Moore's list. Lester, meanwhile, had fully confessed to the murder of Brian and the attempted murder of Nikki.

The detectives questioned her in more detail. To Nikki's surprise, most of their questions concerned Moore. They wanted to interview him, but his answering service was discontinued. With a shrug, Nikki told them she had no other way of reaching him. The detectives, in unspoken response, looked at her oddly, as if she wasn't mentally altogether.

"Well, I didn't just make him up," she said.

With seeming reluctance, they agreed that she hadn't. Lester had mentioned him in his statement, and Alyssa and others had also confirmed meeting him.

"Still, we've no record of a PI named Moore," one of the detectives said.

All Nikki could do was shrug again.

Moving on, one of the detectives asked, "How did he get into your condo?"

"I gave him guest keys to the outside door and my door."

"Does he still have them?"

"No, he left them behind. That's the funny thing. Because after I called 911, he was gone. But the door to my condo was locked and bolted."

"So, he had duplicates made," the detective suggested.

"Perhaps," said Nikki.

"Moore didn't appear on the video. Do you know why that is?"

"No, I don't."

"How were you going to pay him?"

"I gave him a retainer cheque. Maybe that covered everything?"

"Has he deposited it?"

"Not yet, to the best of my knowledge. Look, why do you even care? You've got the killer. Isn't that the important thing? Which reminds me—you were right about one thing, at least."

One detective did not react; the other raised a querying eyebrow.

"Not getting a job *is* motive for murder," said Nikki.

The deadpan detective remained so. The other's face darkened for a moment before saying, "Let's start at the beginning, shall we?"

And so it went. In the end, however, they had to admit that Moore was a mystery that would remain unsolved. For now. With that, they informed her that she was free to go and that Derek would be released the following morning, as soon as the paperwork was complete.

It was odd to be back home. Nikki had stayed with Alyssa overnight while the forensics team did their thing. She felt as if the attack had happened days ago, and that her wedding day had been a lifetime ago.

Locking the door behind her, Nikki put her keys in a bowl on the side table and went to the kitchen. She stared, puzzled, at the brown stain on the floor, then remembered. The coffee.

After retrieving the open bottle of Chardonnay in the fridge, she poured a glass, took a couple of sips, and stopped short.

On the kitchen island were two things that didn't belong: the retainer cheque she'd written for Moore, and beside it, a long-stemmed white rose.

The Right Time

I completed this story back in 2015. I once lived in the rooming house described herein, and always wanted to write a story about it. It was such an odd place, housing fascinating and nice people. They weren't however, quite as extraordinary as the characters in this story. At least, not as far as I know.

Michael Rousseau danced under the full moon. Tall grasses scratched his naked thighs. The wildflowers smelled sweet. All the while, the flute's irresistible song urged him on. Raising his arms, he near howled at the moon, so complete was his joy.

Upon awakening, Michael wished it hadn't been a dream. He could still hear the flute and the tune to which he'd danced, just faintly. It faded until there was nothing left but the tick of a clock.

Fully awake now, Michael considered his surroundings in the dim light of early morning. The night had been his first in the new apartment, though that was a generous use of the word. It consisted of one small room with a bed, a fridge, a table, two chairs, a closet, and a sink.

Last week, the landlady, no more than middle-aged but who tottered about as if she were much older, had met him at the front entrance, led him slowly upstairs, and unlocked the door to unit 207.

"The other tenants are, well, to be honest, they're a bit eccentric, but they're harmless," she'd said. "Gentle creatures, really. Nice to everyone."

Each unit in the rooming house was the same, and, like a university dorm, they lacked a private washroom. There was one shared washroom per floor, with three toilets and one shower stall.

The building seemed clean enough. The dull-yellow walls in the corridor had been painted recently. So had unit 207, judging from the faint odour. The fridge was clean and the bed didn't sag when he sat down. No oven, but as the landlady had pointed out, Michael could purchase an electric hotplate. You could do a lot with a hotplate and perhaps a slow cooker or microwave.

The room was small by off-campus standards, but then beggars couldn't be choosers. Classes started in just a few days. He'd been accepted at the last minute, so living in student residence was out of the question. It would be a long walk to campus, but he liked walking. Gave him a chance to empty his head, let things percolate.

He'd take it, he'd said.

The landlady gave him an appraising look. "I don't normally rent to students. Too noisy, usually. But I like to think I'm a good judge of character and you seem all right." With that, her guarded expression relaxed into a smile. "So, let's go to my office and we'll see to the paperwork, shall we?"

He'd taken occupancy yesterday. A local friend, Daniel, owned a car and took him shopping for his immediate essentials: kitchenware and the like. Later, they'd gone to a nearby pub for some supper and stayed for the band, a local folk/jazz-fusion quartet. They were surprisingly rousing and had the whole place dancing and singing along.

He'd come back here just after midnight and fallen into bed exhausted.

Michael rose, stretched, and froze. There it was again, the flute, its song gently building from silence to a shimmering, almost-living thing.

Wearing a T-shirt and pyjama bottoms, he opened the door, peered to the right, and saw the musician. He sat cross-legged on the floor at the end of the corridor, in front of the window, the morning sun streaming upon him like a spotlight.

Remembering that the doors closed and locked automatically, Michael scooped up his key and then approached the man.

"Good morning," Michael said. The man played on. "It's a bit early, isn't it?"

The man paused for a moment. "Sunrise," he said, without taking his eyes off the window, then continued.

A door opened. And then another.

"Oh, you'll get used to him," said the man walking out of the first door. He was tall, moustached, and had short, black, curly hair.

"Always starts the morning like this," said the other. He was a bit shorter than the first, and heavier, but his hair was also curly and black, though a bit longer. He scratched his head and yawned. "Kind of gets us started on the day."

"Well, that would do it," Michael said. "I don't suppose he could play in his room, perhaps, or maybe outside?"

Both men shook their heads. "It's been suggested, but here he is. Like I said, you'll get used to it."

Michael sighed and reached out his hand. "On with the day, then. I'm Michael."

"Hugo," said the taller man, shaking his hand. "This here's my brother, Martin."

"Glad to meet you, Michael," said Martin, shaking his hand in turn. "What brings you here?"

"Oh, I'm a student. Starting classes next week. How about you two?"

The two men glanced at each other. "We're in the news business," said Martin.

"News. You mean, journalism?"

"Something like that," Hugo said. "Not much going on just now, though, so we're lying low here for a bit."

"I see." *They must be unemployed*, Michael thought.

Another door opened and a tall, thin man with snow-white hair and goatee sauntered into the hallway. He stretched as he yawned. "That time then, is it?"

"This here's Cornelius," Hugo said. "Cornelius, Michael." Addressing Michael, Hugo continued. "Cornelius is a good man to know. He can take care of pretty much any ailment you might have."

"Really? I'll have to remember that."

Cornelius winked at him. "And if you find you've trouble with your memory, I can fix that as well," he said with a smile.

Just then the flute player finished his tune and stood up. He was also quite tall, well over six feet, and thin. He had curly, sandy hair, blue eyes, a goatee and . . . Michael had seen him before.

"Of course," Michael said. "You were in the band last night."

The man's eyes widened a bit. "Ah, you were over at the pub, were you? It was a great crowd. I'm Satria. People hereabouts just call me Sat."

"Michael. I didn't recognize that music just now. It was beautiful."

"You liked it?" Sat beamed. "It's my own composition. More of an improvisation, actually. I always play at sunrise, and I play whatever pops into my head that particular day."

Michael couldn't help but smile. Although not an early riser by nature, there was something deliciously romantic in the notion of waking up at sunrise to the sound of a flute. All things considered, if this was the worst of Sat's faults, it wouldn't be so bad. Nodding to all three before returning to his room, he wondered what other surprises his house-mates had in store.

Monday morning, the first day of classes, and it was unseasonably hot. More like July than September. But the sky was clear and the air was fresh, and Michael was invigorated and looking forward to the day.

He'd awakened early, courtesy of Sat, so he had lots of time. After showering, shaving, and putting on a T-shirt, jeans, and running shoes, Michael decided to take the scenic walk rather than the most direct route. His knapsack packed with notebooks and textbooks, he took the sidewalks until he came to a footpath that would lead him around the lake and through the arboretum. He'd be able to cross the canal by walking over the locks and would end up right on campus.

Although a fast walker, Michael slowed his pace as he entered the arboretum proper. The path meandered past deep green grass and all manner of trees. A plaque staked to the ground next to each tree provided its common and Latin names. Wooden bridges took him across streams, and further along he came to several large ponds. The greenish waters were dotted with toadstools and bordered by tall grasses.

A large willow tree stood next to one of the ponds, and at its base, lying on her back with her eyes closed, was a young woman. She had thick, shoulder-length red hair, a short nose, many freckles, and full lips. She was wearing a pale-green short-sleeved top and a yellow floral skirt that brushed her knees.

Michael stopped, uncertain whether to continue or to ask if she was all right.

After a moment, without opening her eyes, the woman said, "Well, are you going to just stare at me all day?"

"Actually, I was wondering whether you were okay."

"I'm communing," she said.

"Communing. With . . . ?"

"The willow tree, of course. I think it's talking to me. Or trying to." She opened one eye and squinted at him. "Maybe you can help. Come beside me and see if you can make it out."

"Beside you?"

"You don't *have* to, of course. But it might help."

Bewildered but curious, Michael set down his knapsack. Unsure how close to get, he lay down a couple of metres away from her.

"No," she said. "Over here. Closer. Take my hand." She stretched her arm in his direction. He hesitated. "Look, it's alright. I don't bite."

He chuckled, shuffling over a bit, and took her hand. It was smooth and cool. Then he closed his eyes.

After a minute or so, he asked, "Anything?"

"No. You're not concentrating, are you?"

"Well, not on the tree, no," he admitted, opening his eyes.

The girl sighed, let go of Michael's hand, and sat up. "Well, we're going to have to get to know one another then, aren't we? Then *this* won't seem like a big deal. My name's Alse Flouret."

Michael sat up as well. "Michael Rousseau. I'm just on my way to class, actually."

"So am I," said Alse. "Biology, of course. At least, that's going to be my major. I've always loved living things."

"And you can talk to trees?"

She gave him a look. "Don't be silly. Still," she said, resting a hand on the tree's trunk, "this one seemed ... different. I wanted to listen, that's all."

"Fair enough," said Michael.

They got up and started walking together. "So," said Alse, "what about you?"

"Biochemistry, I think. I'm interested in living things as well, but more at the cellular level."

When they reached the locks the gates were open, and they watched as a large cabin cruiser lumbered through.

"What a shame," said Alse. "We'll have to wait in this beautiful place."

Michael grinned, and they took seats at a nearby picnic bench. Resuming their conversation, they were oblivious to the fact that, half an hour later, the boat had cleared the locks and the path across the canal was open again.

Michael and Alse clinked their glasses together. It was Friday and they were at the White Hart, seated at a small table close to the stage.

"To the end of the beginning," said Michael.

Alse swallowed a last mouthful of ale. "You know," she said, still gripping the empty mug, "I've an almost irresistible urge to smash this on the floor and call out for another."

Michael's face fell a bit. "Please don't."

Her eyes glinting, Alse raised her mug.

"Oh, look," Michael said with relief, looking past her. "The band is setting up."

Alse turned her head. "Saved by the band. You know though, if I'd broken the mug, they'd need someone to sweep it up. Maybe they'd have offered me a job."

"That'd be doing it the hard way," said Michael. "Are you looking for a job?"

"I have a grant and a scholarship," she said, "but it's not enough. I need something part time to make up the difference."

"Your parents didn't leave you much, then."

Alse shook her head. "They died young. So young they hadn't even got around to life insurance. My foster parents are great, but they don't have a lot of extra money, and they have two kids of their own to see to."

On the stage—a small area raised about six inches from the floor—Sat began his soundcheck. He winked at Michael as he tapped the microphone.

"You know him?" Alse asked.

"Sat? He lives on my floor. Plays the flute here and, just for good measure, outside my door every morning at sunrise."

"Does he?" Alse said, brightening. "What a lovely way to wake up."

"If you say so," Michael said, just as Sat approached the table and sat down.

"Hey, Michael. Glad you could make it."

"You guys were a blast the last time I saw you. Sat, this is my friend Alse."

Sat nodded. "Glad to know you, Alse."

Michael regarded Sat as he fidgeted in his chair, his eyes darting everywhere but towards him and Alse. "Nervous about the show, Sat? You seem a bit on edge."

Sat blinked then smiled. "Well, you know, there's always jitters before a show. They go away soon enough, once we get going."

Alse leaned forward. "I don't suppose they're hiring here, are they?"

Michael's eyes widened a bit in surprise, and he mouthed "Sorry" to Sat.

Sat didn't take his eyes off Alse. "Nothing wrong with a bit of forthrightness. Actually, they're looking for someone to wait tables, part time. You interested?"

Alse's grinned broadly and said, "Yes, absolutely."

"Consider it done. Just speak to James—he's the manager here. Come in tomorrow, tell him I said so, and you'll be all set."

"I can't believe it!" Alse leaned over and kissed Sat on the cheek.

Blushing, Sat rose to join his band for a last-minute warm-up.

Michael, recovering from his surprise, grinned. "Well, I think that calls for another round. On you, of course, as you're now gainfully employed."

Michael and Alse welcomed the cool air outside when they left the pub at midnight. Alse lived just a few blocks away, so they walked together, Alse linking her arm with Michael's.

When they reached her apartment, Alse stepped back and regarded Michael for a moment.

"What?" he asked.

"I'm not going to invite you up. Not tonight. Will you be upset?"

Michael smiled. She truly was like no one he'd met before. "Why yes," he said. "Yes, I will. I'll likely go home and pout and stamp the floor in frustration. But that's okay. Don't worry about me."

"You're silly," Alse said, and kissed him lightly on the lips. "I think I love you. But, I don't know. Something tells me the time just isn't right."

Michael put his hand lightly on her shoulder. "It's right when it's right for both of us. See you soon."

Alse beamed brightly and then dashed through the door of her apartment building.

Michael stood, lost in thought for a time, before going home. Not that he would get much sleep. He thought he might be falling in love as well.

One month later, Michael asked, "Is the time right?"

"Sorry, it just isn't," Alse said. "Are you okay?"

November. Michael was coughing.

"Quite a cough you've got there," Cornelius said. "I can fix that."

And he did.

After fall-term exams were over, Michael whispered to Alse, "What about now?"

Alse shook her head sadly.

It was near the end of the winter term. Wearing slippers and a dressing gown, with a towel thrown over his shoulder, Michael crossed the hallway to the washroom and realized he'd forgotten the key to his room. He turned around just in time to see the door shut and lock.

"Oh, great," he said with a sigh. "Now I'll have to go see Daphne."

After showering, he dried himself, put on the dressing gown, and thought of the first time he'd run into Daphne.

It was a few days after he'd moved in. As he trudged up the stairs after an exhausting day of classes and labs, he found her in front of him on the landing, blocking the way. She was washing the floor with a bucket and mop.

Not much older than Michael, she regarded him with mild curiosity. She had a long but attractive face, large eyes, and fair hair pulled back into a ponytail. Her checkered shirt was tied in front, revealing a few inches of flat belly, and was open quite low. Michael willed himself to maintain eye contact.

"So, who are you?" she asked.

"Um, I'm Michael. I live in 207."

She nodded, unimpressed. "I heard about you. The student."

"That's right. And you are . . . ?"

"Daphne," she said. "I do the maintenance around here. Keep an eye on things."

Michael removed his heavy backpack and set it on the stairs. "Nice to meet you, Daphne. Do you think I could get up to my room?"

She shook her head. "Not just now. Floor's wet. You'll have to talk to me till it dries. Unless there's anything else you'd like to do?"

Michael blinked. He couldn't quite read her face, but he wasn't completely comfortable with what he saw there.

"Oh, give him a break, Daphne," came a voice from down the hall.

"Give *me* a break, Dunmore," Daphne called back. "Just being friendly. Is that a crime?"

There was a pause. "That depends."

Daphne laughed sharply then looked at Michael again. "Well, the floor seems dry enough. See you around, Michael. Need anything, just let me know. My apartment is downstairs, 107. You're right on top of me." She grinned.

Michael tried to smile back as he picked up his backpack and moved past Daphne to his room. Daphne happened to back up as he passed, causing her breasts to gently brush against him.

"Sorry," she mumbled.

Taking a breath, Michael noted the man a few doors down leaning against the wall. He was short, just over five feet, and rotund. His hair was thick and black, as were his beard and moustache.

"Dunmore?" Michael asked.

"Dunny, as my friends call me," he answered with a Scottish accent. "You'll have to not mind Daphne. She chases after everyone. Half the time she's teasing, half the time not. Girls, too, I should think. So don't take it personally."

"There are some interesting characters here, aren't there?"

Dunny smiled. "You've no idea."

Now, his dressing gown tightly knotted, Michael swallowed his embarrassment and knocked on Daphne's door. She opened it then looked him up and down.

"Well," she said, smiling broadly, "this is a nice surprise. Come in."

"I, um, locked myself out. Could you let me back in?"

She stepped closer and took hold of one end of his dressing gown's belt. "Don't you want to come in first?"

She gave the belt a light tug. "I'm sure we'll find something to talk about."

Michael sighed and stepped back slightly, gripping the belt. "Thanks, but no. I really need to get back in my room."

"Shame," said Daphne, retreating into her apartment before returning with a set of keys. "Some other time maybe. No need to dress up for me."

Michael smiled uncomfortably and let her lead the way to his room.

Such an odd space, Michael thought, as he and Alse wormed their way through the crowd at the White Hart. When it was empty, it didn't look particularly large. Yet somehow, no matter how many people showed up on a given night, there was room for everyone. Well, standing room if nothing else.

They'd finished the last of their winter-term exams that afternoon and were at the pub to celebrate. To Michael's surprise, it had been Alse's idea. He'd said he was really tired, but then she'd whispered in his ear, "I have a feeling. This might be the right time."

Michael's fatigue had melted away.

It was hot. The faces of most in the crowd glistened as their bodies moved in rhythm with the music. The band was playing a slow number now, and Michael was very conscious of Alse as her body pressed into his. He put his arm around her, and she dropped her head onto his shoulder. After a while, she lifted her head up, brushed her lips to his ear, and whispered, "I'm thirsty."

Michael grinned and kissed her. "I love the way you whisper sweet nothings," he said. "I'll see if I can't get us a couple."

After worming his way through the crowd, Michael squeezed into a spot in front of the bar. A minute or two later, he managed to catch the bartender's eye.

"Michael!" Dunny said with a broad grin. "Had a feeling you'd be here tonight."

"How's life as a bartender?" Michael asked, struggling to speak loudly enough over the music.

"Grand, really. It's a great gig—all thanks to Sat. Almost makes up for the early morning wake-ups," he added with a wink. "Now, what can I get you?"

"Two lagers, I think."

"Ah. So you'll be here with Alse then," Dunny said, as he collected two glasses and started running the tap. "And how is she?"

"Great, thanks. We just finished exams."

"Well, she's quite a girl, isn't she?" said Dunny, setting the beers down in front of Michael. Then his eyes drifted towards the stage. "Quite the girl indeed."

Michael took a sip from one of the glasses and turned to see what Dunny was looking at. He nearly dropped the drink. The band was playing a lively Irish jig featuring Sat's flute. Alse had found her way onto the stage and was dancing with Sat as he played. Her face was flushed, her green eyes wide and bright, her mouth set in a bright smile that made Michael's heart melt, her skirt flying about her bare legs.

The Right Time

Michael took a long draft of beer. He looked back at Dunny, who gave him a wink then went to serve his other patrons.

It was after midnight. Tipsy and giddy, Michael and Alse lurched and laughed and hushed each other until they reached Michael's building. Then they crept stealthily to his room. It wasn't unusual for tenants to pop in and out of each other's rooms or have conversations in the hallway. Michael had dreaded the teasing comments and looks they'd get. But he needn't have worried. The floor was quiet. He'd hardly ever seen it so quiet. Tonight, though, that suited him just fine.

No sooner was the door closed behind them than they shed their coats and then their clothes and set about exploring each other's bodies with their hands, mouths, and tongues. They found their way onto the bed, and Michael could feel her wetness on his thigh.

But just as Michael started to reach for the protection he kept close by, Alse stiffened and sat up, swinging her legs over the side of the bed.

"What?" Michael asked. "Are you all right?"

Alse took a moment to answer. "I'm fine. But something's . . . changed."

Groaning inwardly, Michael hardly dared say anything. *Please come back to bed*, he thought at her for a time, before giving up. "What is it?" he asked.

After grabbing Michael's shirt and putting it on, Alse stood and approached the door.

"I'm not sure," she said. She paused and turned to Michael. "Do you hear it?"

"Hear what?" Michael said, getting up and putting on his jeans.

Alse opened the door a crack, peered through, then stepped back and threw it open wide.

Michael, standing next to Alse, was transfixed. Outside the door, where the hallway should have been, was a meadow with grasses and flowers lit by a full moon and myriad stars. Fireflies darted about, leaving silver streaks in their wake. The meadow was bordered by a forest ahead and to the left, and a stream to the right.

Alse stepped out of the room. Michael tried to stop her, but she turned, smiled gently, and, taking his hand, led him forward.

"This can't be real," Michael said, as he bent over and brushed his hand against the grass. "I must be dreaming."

"Really," said Alse. "So, you were about to make love to me and just nodded off—is that what you're suggesting?"

"Doesn't seem likely, does it?" Michael admitted. "Still, this place seems dreamlike. And familiar. Ah! I know," he said. "My first night in the apartment, I had a dream and saw this very place—"

Michael stopped short as, at that moment, a unicorn sauntered out of the woods.

It was pure white and had a long, snowy mane and a horn that gleamed like polished ivory. Michael and Alse, transfixed, approached the unicorn slowly, until finally they were just a couple of feet away.

Whenever Michael had imagined unicorns, he'd thought of them as large and majestic. The unicorn in front of him was surprisingly small, more like the size of a large pony. It looked at Michael and Alse with large, unselfconscious eyes, and then it spoke. "Hey, Michael. And you must be Alse. Great to see you here."

Michael took a step back and blinked. "You know our names?" he asked stupidly.

"Well, yeah," said the unicorn. "But you've never seen me in this form. I'm Cornelius."

Michael frowned. "Cornelius? Cornelius who lives on my floor?"

"The one and only. I helped you get over that cough in November. Hugo and Martin introduced us right after you moved in. Isn't that right, guys?" said Cornelius, turning his head to the left.

A pair of ravens approached and landed on Cornelius's back.

"Indeed we did," said one of the ravens, whose voice was identical to Hugo's.

"I think I'm just going to sit down for a minute," said Michael, "before I fall down."

"Feeling light-headed?" said Cornelius. "I can fix that."

"Just shut up, will you?" said Michael.

Alse crouched beside him and put an arm around his shoulder. Michael rubbed his face with his hands and looked up at Cornelius, who hadn't vanished. Then he turned to Alse. "You seem pretty okay with this."

"I can't explain it," Alse said, with that gentle smile of hers, "but somehow I feel quite at home here. While all this is strange on the one hand, on the other it feels perfectly natural."

Michael stood again. "So," he said, "are all you guys magical creatures of some sort? Is that what you're telling me?"

"Not just the guys," said a woman's voice.

Glancing towards the stream, Michael groaned. There was Daphne, emerging from the water, naked as the day she was born. She moved towards them, a mischievous smile on her face, with a slow, seductive strut. He gulped. Daphne pulled her wet hair back, highlighting her chiselled face. Water was still dripping off her. Michael's eyes were particularly drawn to the drops falling from her breasts.

Reaching Michael, she walked around him in a close circle, touching him all the while with her index finger. When she came up behind him, she pressed her body to his and wrapped her arms around his waist.

"Something tells me you're happy to see me," she murmured, as her right hand started to descend.

Alse interceded. "If you don't mind," she said, unwrapping Daphne's arms from her boyfriend, "he's with me."

"Hmmm," Daphne murmured, as she stepped away and moved beside the unicorn. "Shame."

"Behave yourself, Daphne," said another voice.

The speaker was a man, or male, some two feet tall. On his head was a long, pointed hat, and he was dressed in earth-toned colours.

"Dunny," said Daphne, "you never let me have any fun."

"Well then," said Michael. "The only one missing is Sat. Or is he here as well?"

The words were just out of his mouth when Michael heard a flute. It was playing a tune he could just barely catch, something soft and gentle, in a rhythm that was calming, beautiful, and at the same time as old as nature herself.

All heads turned to the woods. A faun emerged, half man, half goat. A satyr, Michael realized. *Of course.*

When Sat was a few feet away, he said, "How are you feeling, Michael?"

Sat looked remarkably like himself, though the hair and beard were a bit different, longer and wilder somehow. His legs, covered in thick brown fur, ended in hooves.

"At the moment? Wonderful," Michael said. The music had calmed him. He was smiling and relaxed, despite the strangeness.

"That's great," said Sat. Then turning to Alse, he got down on one knee and lowered his head. The others did likewise.

Alse and Michael looked at each other, puzzled.

"Why are you doing this?" Alse said.

As they all rose again, Hugo, the black raven, said, "We've been looking for you. For a long time. Until we finally realized we would never find you. What we *could* do, though, was find the one who would discover you for us."

At that, Hugo flew onto Michael's shoulder.

"Me?" Michael said. "You didn't find me. I moved in with you."

"And how did you come to do that?" asked Cornelius.

Michael thought back. Daniel had driven him around town to look at several apartments. None were suitable, being either too expensive or too dilapidated.

They'd gone to get some coffee after a while and sat on a bench outside. Daniel was trying to be encouraging, but Michael had a feeling he was sunk. That was when he noticed a newspaper lying on the end of the bench, folded in such a way as to reveal a few advertisements in the classifieds. Michael picked up the paper and noticed an ad for the apartment in the rooming house, the apartment he was living in now.

"I found an ad," Michael said. The unicorn seemed to grin. ". . . And one of you left it for me to find."

The creatures about him nodded. Hugo flew back to Cornelius.

"But how? How did you know?"

"We did," said Sat, "and for now, let's just leave it at that."

Michael shook his head and blinked. "Just hang on a minute. I'm still trying to come to grips with all of this. First question: how is it you were just like everyone else when I saw you before?"

"That would be the magical part of being a magical creature," Daphne said.

"Not helpful, Daphne," said Dunny. "We don't actually change, you see, Michael. When we're in your world, what you see is a projection of what we actually are. It's kind of like holding up a ball to the light. What you see on the wall is a flat circle, not a three-dimensional object. We exist, well, not in a higher dimension, necessarily, but certainly a different one."

"Which brings me to the next question," Michael said. "Where are we, exactly?"

Dunny took off his hat and looked up at Cornelius, who nodded.

"We're in the Someplace Else," said Cornelius, "which kind of goes without saying. Let's put it this way: After the Earth was formed, and life took hold, in a very real sense the Earth came to life in its own right; and this place, and all of us who live here, came to exist. It's just as real as your world. They exist side by side is the best way I can put it. There are doorways joining the worlds sometimes, in this case quite literally." Cornelius nodded towards something behind Michael and Alse. They turned and saw that the door to Michael's room was still there, and still open.

"The door didn't close," Michael said. "It always closes."

"Well, that might be because what you're seeing here is a representation of your door more than the actual thing," said Cornelius.

Michael ran his hand through his hair. "Okay. So let's talk about why. Why are we here?"

"You read the news," Hugo answered. "You know what's going on around you every day. The Earth, the living Earth, is none too healthy these days. There's a lot of checks and balances in nature, but this time it's really flummoxed and doesn't know how to find a balance between its needs and human needs anymore. It knows it's going to take something special to fix this but can't do it alone. It needs someone who's human, or was at least raised as a human, to help. This is where Alse comes in."

Alse, who'd been calmly listening up until now, widened her eyes. "What do you mean *raised* as a human? What are you saying?"

"What he's saying," Sat replied, "is that, from a human's perspective, you're as much a so-called magical creature as we are. Just in a different way."

Without saying a word, Michael and Alse took each other's hands and backed away a step.

Sat continued. "When you were conceived, Alse, a part of the Earth, call it the Earth Spirit if you like, became part of you." He paused.

"Go on," she said.

"The Earth needs someone, a human, to join with it. Someone who understands your world and can kind of act as a go-between."

"And that's . . . me?" She looked at the magical creatures before her. There was no need for them to answer. "Of course it's me," Alse said. "At some level, I think I've always known." Turning to Michael, she said, "This is why I was drawn to that willow tree. It was a kind of communication channel. I knew I could feel it, almost understand it."

"What are you saying, exactly?" Michael said, turning to the creatures. "That you want Alse to stay here? That's not going to happen."

"Michael!" Alse said, her tone admonishing. "It's not your decision to make, is it?"

Michael dropped his head. "No, of course not. It's just that I don't want to lose you. I couldn't bear it. We've just found each other."

"I don't think you will lose me," Alse said, pulling Michael into a close hug. "I'll always be with you. Just in a different way, I expect." Releasing Michael, she turned to the others. "What do I have to do?"

At this, the creatures cast their heads down and shuffled their feet, or paws. All except Daphne.

"You have to make love to your boyfriend," Daphne said. "Here. Now. After that joining, you'll be ready to join with the Earth completely."

"What will happen to me?" Alse asked.

"You'll change," said Cornelius. "You'll still be you in a sense, but you'll also be part of the living Earth."

Alse beamed. "That sounds wonderful."

"But, Alse—"

Alse put a finger on Michael's lips. "Hush," she said. "This has to happen. You know it does. This is why I knew that tonight, the time was finally right."

Alse took Michael's hand and lowered herself, and him, down to the ground.

"With all of them watching?" said Michael. "Seriously?"

"Come along, everyone," said Sat. "They need privacy. Michael, we won't be seeing you again. At least, not any time soon. So we wish you well. And thank you."

With that, the creatures dispersed. Daphne stooped to pick up Dunny and then nestled the tiny creature between her breasts.

Michael's jaw dropped. "Daphne and Dunny? Who'd have thought."

"Shut up and kiss me," said Alse.

Michael woke up alone. The moon was no longer visible, but the sky was full of stars—more stars than he'd ever seen. There was no sound other than the bubbling of the stream and the occasional splash.

"Alse," he called. He looked all around. He was alone. "Alse!"

As he sat up, he realized that he was no longer lying on a bed of grass but one of poppies. Each had red petals and, in its centre, what looked like a green eye. The colour of Alse's hair and eyes.

"Alse?" he said, as he began to tear up. He brushed the poppies gently with his fingers. "Oh, Alse, what will I do without you?"

Just then a breeze came up, and as the grasses brushed together, he heard a faint voice. "Live," it said.

With a sigh, Michael gathered his jeans and shirt and walked back through the door into his room. The door closed behind him. When he turned and opened it again, the meadow was gone. There was just the dimly lit hallway. Turning away, he collapsed onto his bed and fell into a dreamless sleep.

Michael was awakened by a loud knock at his door. He opened it to find the landlady.

"Morning," Michael said with a yawn. Then the events of the previous night came back to him, and he staggered for a moment.

"Oh, are you all right dear?" she asked.

"Um, yeah, I guess so. What can I do for you?"

"Well, I don't know. I'm glad you're here, though, because all the other tenants have gone. Like they've disappeared off the face of the earth with all their possessions. Even Daphne's gone, and that's not like her, she's not missed a day since she started here." She looked up at him with sad eyes. "You wouldn't know where they are, would you?"

"I really wouldn't," said Michael as he rubbed the sleep from his eyes. "Sorry I can't be more help."

"Never mind, then. It's not your fault." As she shuffled off, even more stooped than before, she muttered to herself, "Don't know what I'm going to do now."

Michael closed the door, turned, and saw Alse's clothes lying on the floor. Sitting on the bed, he picked them up and buried his face in them.

Fifty-five years later, Michael set down the cloth bag of groceries he'd been carrying, took out his key, and entered room 207, the same room he'd lived in all those years ago. Despite his successes, Michael had eschewed financial gain, preferring to live as simply as possible. When it came time to downsize, he'd thought, *Well, might as well do it properly.* And so he'd come full circle, moving into the single room he'd rented during his first year of university.

He still owned little furniture, though his walls were covered with plaques and photos. One wall featured a mounted copy of his doctorate in environmental science, awards for popularizing science, newspaper clippings of interviews, and a couple of magazine covers featuring him and his works. The opposite wall displayed his AAAS awards and mounted reprints of his major papers. The awards were for a series of review articles that laid out the case for global climate change in such a way that, even for the most diehard deniers, the evidence was insurmountable. Real policy changes had followed, and were making a measurable difference. It wasn't yet clear whether this was too little too late.

One reprint in particular caught Michael's eye: the now classic *Science* article in which he'd identified a new form of algae—one that was entirely airborne, and that absorbed sufficient carbon as to help tilt the scales towards environmental recovery. Its origins remained unknown. As the algae multiplied, it had added a greenish tinge to the sky, so that it would forevermore be closer to turquoise than blue. He'd coined the name *Alseid aerium*, after Alse, of course. *We did it together*, he thought with a smile.

He approached the table, where he kept the only picture of Alse that he had in a small frame. He touched his finger to his lips then touched the photo, gazing at it with a sad smile.

Carrying the groceries had tired him out. After putting the perishable items in the fridge, he lay down on the bed to nap. But no sooner had he dozed off than he awoke. There was an odd sound coming from the corridor. Was someone calling him? He shuffled to the door, opened it, and stood stock-still.

There was the meadow. At times he wondered if he'd dreamt it. Maybe he was dreaming now. But he didn't care. He stepped forward, feeling better than he had in ages. It was broad daylight. Birds were singing, a gentle wind blew the grasses, and he relished the clean scent and deep greens all around him.

Then he saw her, coming out of the forest.

"Alse?" he said.

There was no mistaking her. After all these years, she hadn't changed an iota. In fact, she was wearing the same skirt and top she'd had on the day they met.

He started to run then stopped, surprised that he *could* run. He looked at his arms and hands. The wrinkles and age spots had vanished, and he felt strong—as strong as he'd felt in his twenties.

Alse had nearly reached him by this time. He stepped forward and they embraced, long and hard.

"Alse," said Michael, running his hands through her hair. "How can this be?"

"Hush," said Alse, putting a finger to his lips. Then, as she had done before, she lay down in the grass, taking Michael with her, and they made love.

Night came, and then morning. Alse and Michael were gone. Where they had lain, amid the dew-covered grasses and wildflowers, was a bed of poppies.

Where the Dragons Sleep

This is the first story I completed, which was back in 2002. It's a children's story, but I remain fond of it, so here it is to close out this collection. The inspiration came from noting, while walking in a typically cold Ottawa winter, how steam rose from the sewers, twisting and curling into the sky…

I love the sounds of winter. I especially like the crunch your boots make when it's very cold. I go for walks with my daddy on the weekend, even on the coldest days. He makes sure I'm wrapped up in the warmest clothes—long underwear, thick pants, snow pants, a turtleneck, a thick sweater, a parka, and a toque. Then he helps me put on bright red mittens and a scarf.

When we go outside, I run and grab handfuls of snow. On very cold days, the snow looks like sugar and I toss it up and let it land in my face. Daddy tells me I'm being very silly, but sometimes he does it too. Then we look at each other, laugh, and go for our walk. As we walk, I hear the crunch, crunch my boots make on the snow. Daddy's boots make that noise too.

Sometimes I stretch the sound out—c-r-u-n-c-h—by setting the heel of my boot down and slowly shifting my weight to my toes. Then I spring up and do the same with my other boot. If I do that too many times, though, Daddy stops and gives me that look which means I'd better cut it out. I guess he gets bored waiting. Sometimes Daddy gets bored faster than I do.

I've noticed that on these very cold winter days you can see steam coming up from the sewers. One day I asked Daddy where the steam came from.

"It's from the water in the sewer," he said.

"But why does it make steam?"

"Well, it's like when we boil water on the stove. When the water boils, you see the steam coming up from the pot."

I thought about that. "There's a stove in the sewer?"

"No, silly," Daddy said. "I didn't mean that."

"Then what makes the steam?"

Daddy gave me one of his looks. The one where his eyebrows get lower, his forehead gets wrinkly, and his eyes get smaller. That's when I know it's time to be quiet.

"So, Alice Draco, do you want to go skating tomorrow?"

I guessed he didn't want to talk about the steam anymore.

At bedtime, Daddy gets me my toothbrush, which is high up in the cupboard. One day, I'll be able to brush my teeth without any help—that's what he said. *First*, I think, *you'll have to leave my toothbrush where I can reach it.*

But I *can* get dressed without any help. When I'm getting ready for bed, I take off all my clothes and put them in my hamper. Then I open the top drawer of my dresser and pick out the pyjamas I want to wear. I like pyjamas with bears. It's easy to find pyjamas I like because they almost all have bears.

Sometimes I go upstairs by myself to read. I sit in my chair and read *The Cat in the Hat*, or *Curious George*, or *Winnie-the-Pooh*. I know some of the words but not all of them. But you can tell the story from the pictures. *Winnie-the-Pooh* is my favourite. It doesn't have many pictures, but the story is funny. Bump, bump, bump goes Edward Bear's head down the stairs.

I finish putting on my pyjamas, get into bed, and cover myself with my comforter. Then Daddy reads my story. Yesterday we finished a story about another girl called Alice. There were hard words that Daddy had trouble saying. Tonight, the story is about a woman called Meribel. There aren't very many pictures, but I can imagine her house by the forest and her long walks into the village. I use my mind's eye, like Meribel.

Meribel had never seen a dragon. But she had heard stories about them.

Once a month, Meribel made the half-day-long journey on foot to the village for supplies. When she stopped by the village fountain to rest, she listened to the men who gathered around it to talk. The talk always turned to dragons.

And Meribel would smile. Her smile, with her full lips and prominent cheekbones, was contagious. When Meribel smiled, the village men found themselves smiling as well, and would really look at her, as if just then realizing how beautiful she was—deep brown eyes, tall and muscular, with a full figure that was pleasing to the eye, and light-brown hair that fell halfway to her waist.

Thinking that she must admire their bravery, her admirers felt encouraged to tell more stories. The dragons got bigger, their hides scalier, their fires hotter. And the men got braver. But in her mind's eye, Meribel pictured how they would run if they ever really saw a dragon, and that's what made her smile.

There was one man, Taar, who did not brag to Meribel about dragons. Taar was not a handsome man, nor was he ugly. He was over six feet tall, thin, and muscular. Wiry. His hair, what he had left, was blond with a touch of grey. Most of the top of his head was bald, but his hair was long and tied into a ponytail. His forehead was lined, and his blue eyes crinkled on the rare occasion when he smiled. But it was equally rare to see him angry. His nose was large and flat, his beard closely trimmed and flecked with grey around his chin.

A clever woodworker, he built and sold tools, hunting weapons, and musical instruments from a shop near the centre of the village. His musical instruments, which included recorders, small drums, and stringed instruments such as mandolins and fiddles, fascinated Meribel. They would talk about many things—his shop, her father, the weather, and jokes they had heard. Taar loved the sound of her laughter. Sometimes, but not often, he talked about his life before the village, when he was a sailor.

Taar came to know Meribel well. Well enough to know that she might drift off during a quiet moment, even during a conversation, to some place in her mind's eye. Where it was he didn't know and didn't ask. After all, everyone had secret places inside themselves. If it happened—when it happened—he would wait patiently, carving a new instrument or cleaning the shop, until she came back, and then they would continue their conversation from where they'd left off.

Meribel saw many places in her mind's eye, but most often she was with her mother, who had died when Meribel was a child. Alecia's face had been warm; crinkles around her eyes and lines on her forehead told you if she was happy or sad. Her lips were thin, her smile forgiving, and her voice full and confident. Meribel remembered her mother's apron almost as well as her face: the red-and-white-checkered apron with the magic pockets that seemed to have just the thing to fix what was broken or to mend what was rent.

What triggered Meribel's daydreams? Often it was a thing she was doing. While kneeling to weed the garden, Meribel might find herself sitting on the grass beside Alecia learning how to grind herbs into medicine. While cooking dinner, staring into the boiling water, she would turn to see her mother smiling at her, adding meat and vegetables to the broth. Sitting by the fire in the evening, Meribel was once again a little girl seated on a stool by that same fire, knitting her first pair of socks while Alecia patiently explained how to hold the needles and yarn, and to twist her wrist just so.

But now Meribel and her father, Turlough, lived alone in the small wood-frame house Turlough had built years before. As Turlough got older, he was able to do less and less to help. But Meribel didn't mind. When Turlough was tired, she helped him into his chair and made him tea and stroked his hair. Meribel would speak to him about the garden, the birds she had seen, and the songs she had heard. She would ask what kind of pie to bake for their dessert; what type of bread for their breakfast the next day. Then Turlough would close his eyes and doze until it was time for their meal.

Turlough's greatest love, other than Meribel, was his garden. Set at the back of their house, it was the home of every sort of vegetable, including potatoes, onions, cabbages, leeks, peas, lettuce, beans, and garlic. The air was scented with herbs such as basil, thyme, sage, and rosemary. A well in the centre of the garden provided their fresh water. In the woods, fruit trees were plentiful and game likewise. To obtain the few other things they needed, Meribel walked to the village once a month.

On returning from the village, Meribel would call to her father and he would come from the garden to greet her. Meribel would take him by the arm and lead him inside. Then she would sit by him as he sipped his tea and tell him all that she had learned that day.

One evening, Meribel returned from her daylong trip and called out to Turlough. There was no answer. Worried, Meribel set down her parcels and looked for her father. He was not in the garden, nor at the front of the house, so Meribel looked inside.

She found Turlough lying on the floor near his chair. Hot, feverish, weak, he didn't seem to know his own daughter. Meribel was grateful she had her mother's strength. Lifting him onto his bed, she wrapped him in blankets and added extra wood to the fire.

A fever could be treated with a soup of certain herbs. Alecia had taught her that. But they didn't have the herbs she needed, and it was dark outside. Shivering, Meribel crept to the door, took another look at her poor father, and then stepped outside, closing the door softly behind her.

It was a clear night and the moon was full. For that, at least, Meribel was grateful. But there were many dangers in the woods, and she faced a long walk.

Most of what happened this day and night was etched in Meribel's memory for the rest of her life. Yet she was never able to remember clearly what happened during that one fateful hour. She had been walking for some time and had managed to keep to the path.

Then there was noise, pain, shouts, and she was lying on the ground, looking up at the full moon, unable to move. There were voices. A bulky shape passed high above, between her and the moon. The shape passed in the opposite direction, bigger now. Then it passed again, and was bigger still. Then screams, confusion, and she felt herself lifted by large, clumsy hands. Finally, she slept.

Meribel woke on a bed of dry leaves in a dark place she didn't know. There was an odd, wet smell in the air. Drifting up from the darkness before her was a column of smoke. Following the smoke with her eyes, Meribel watched the smoke rise, curling and dancing, up a wide shaft into the night sky.

Daddy puts the book away and bends over to give me a kiss. When he tries to get back up, I hug him and won't let him go. Not until he tickles me. Then he puts out my light, closes the door, and goes down the stairs.

That's when I get out of bed. My bedroom window looks out over the street. Sometimes I like to get out of bed, climb on my chair, and put my head under the pull-down blind. When it's cold, I can blow on the window and make steam. *Just like the sewer*, I think. Then I look down at the sewer in the dark.

The streetlights are on and there's light in the windows of the houses. I can see little bits of steam coming from the sewer, curling and dancing, climbing into the sky. Then a car drives past, over the sewer. Its red taillights look like the eyes of someone behind Alice's mirror. Not my mirror, but Alice who goes through a mirror to a place that's all mixed up.

The car reaches the end of the street and turns right. *Bye-bye, car.* Then I look at the sewer again.

Is more steam coming up than before? Maybe, but I can't pay attention to the sewer. My nose is cold from pressing against the window so long. I go back to bed and bury my head in my comforter to warm up my nose.

In the morning I am all warm, but my head isn't under the comforter anymore. That happens sometimes—my sheets and comforter change after I go to sleep. Once, after Mommy put me to bed, I took my comforter and threw it on the floor. I was too hot. When I woke up in the morning it was back on my bed. I think that I might ask Daddy how that happens, but sometimes he doesn't like questions. Mommy likes questions but doesn't answer sometimes. Like when I asked Mommy about the steam from the sewers. She didn't answer. She just smiled.

It's Saturday, and on Saturdays I go downstairs by myself while Mommy and Daddy sleep. They need more sleep than I do. I sit on the living room floor just in front of the TV, closer than Mommy and Daddy like. When I hear them, I move back and lean against the sofa and say "Good morning" when they come downstairs. Daddy sits on the sofa and then I get up and sit on his lap while I watch TV and he tries to read the newspaper.

"You don't want to read that newspaper," I say, during the commercial. "You want to spend some quality time with your sweet daughter." Then I show Daddy my sweet face. He just looks up at the ceiling and reads his newspaper some more.

But soon Mommy calls and my blueberry pancakes are ready. They're my favourite, with lots of maple syrup. I have two big ones and Mommy wonders how I can eat so much. Daddy eats only one, she says. I can't answer because my mouth is full and it's not polite, so I shrug. Then I remember it's not polite to shrug. Oh well.

When we are all dressed, Daddy and I walk to the bus stop and take the bus to go skating. When we get there, cross the bridge, take the stairs down to the ice, and enter the wooden shack. Here, Daddy helps me tie my skates and then ties his own. We go back out the door and onto the ice. It's slippery, but Daddy holds my hand and this time I don't fall too many times. Daddy falls down once, where the snow has covered a hole in the ice, and I laugh as he lies there on his back. I pull on his arm to help him up but he's too heavy. Then he jumps up and lifts me up and gives me a bear hug for laughing at him.

We reach the end of the ice in front of the castle and we eat BeaverTails. I think it's a funny name for something to eat, but they taste good, even better than blueberry pancakes. Maybe that's because we get to eat them outside, and you can see the steam rising from them in the cold air.

"Who lives in the castle?" I ask. "The Queen?"

"No, that's not the Queen's castle," Daddy says, as he swallows his BeaverTail. "That's where visitors stay when they come to the city. They stay for a while then leave again, then more visitors come. It's a hotel, not a castle."

I look at the castle. "It looks like a castle."

"Yes, it does, doesn't it? But it's really a hotel."

"Can we stay in the castle?"

Daddy smiles. "We live here, we're not visitors, so we can't stay there. It's just for visitors."

We finish our BeaverTails and skate back to the shack where we left our boots. I'm cold by the time we get back, but it was fun to skate. I still wish we could stay in the castle.

Mommy gives us fresh bread and baked beans for lunch, then she takes me to the library. They have a circle group on Saturday afternoons, and today they talk about animals that hibernate. "They sleep all winter," says the storyteller lady. "Their bodies get colder and they live off the fat they have from all the food they eat during the summer."

I don't think I could hibernate.

At bedtime I brush my teeth and put on my Pooh pyjamas.

Then Daddy reaches for my book. "Let's read your Mommy's book some more. I bet we finish tonight."

"It's not Mommy's book, it's mine."

"Is it?" Daddy replies, looking like he knows better.

"Of course," I say, taking the book. I open it to one of the front pages. "Look here, near the start. It says, 'To

Alice.'" I close the book and hand it back to Daddy. "See?"

In the village, a man walked unsteadily down the main street and entered the tavern, where a hot fire crackled and sparked in a large stone fireplace. Small round tables were set with tankards of ale and bottles of wine. Men crowded the tables, talking, laughing, drinking, and spitting. Some who were seated near the door turned and sniffed as the man entered, for he was followed closely by a strong, unpleasant smell.

"Phew, spare us would you, and go back where you came from!"

"Oh, it's Verdallin," said another customer, who had turned in the direction of the smell. "Well done, Verd, you've outdone even your regular stench."

"Very funny," said the man sullenly, his face, hands, and clothes nearly black with soot. "Wine!" he called to the owner, as he sat at a table in the corner by himself. His neighbours glared at him and tried to shift their tables away but couldn't move far in the crowded room.

As the tavern owner set the wine bottle and glass on the table, he suggested quietly that perhaps Verdallin should go clean up a bit then return to his wine. He was, after all, disturbing the other customers.

"Disturbing!" Verdallin thumped the small table with his fist. "Well I was a little disturbed myself when I had to fight off the dragon!"

The tavern didn't become quiet all at once. The quiet spread like ripples of water in a pond in which a stone has been thrown. Finally, someone broke the silence, calling out, "Meribel's not here, dimwit. Your empty bragging won't get you anywhere tonight."

Someone else followed up with, "It doesn't get him anywhere even when she is!"

This was greeted with laughter all around, which broke some of the tension in the air.

Then Verdallin said something that made everyone go silent again. After taking a draft of his wine, he wiped his lips with his sleeve and said in a hoarse, loud voice, "No, Meribel's not here, and won't be coming back, neither. Not now that the dragon's got her."

The silence seemed to last a long time. Finally, a tall figure pushed a chair away from one of the tables, stood, and walked slowly to Verdallin. Grabbing him by the shirt and yanking him rudely to his feet, Taar asked him, in a calm but deadly voice, "Tell me exactly what happened to Meribel."

"So you're awake."

Meribel felt that the voice, while deep and gravelly, was not unfriendly. Startled only for an instant, she replied, "Who are you, and where am I? Why can't I see you?"

"It is not my wish to frighten you, and that is why I have placed myself out of your sight. For now."

"I am not frightened," said Meribel, and she realized that she was not. "I don't believe you intend to harm me. But why have you brought me here? My father is sick and I must attend him."

"What do you last remember?"

Meribel paused. She wasn't sure. Then she became aware of the soreness of her face and arms. "I don't know.

I was in the woods. Searching for herbs to heal my father. Then something happened. Noise, hurt. I'm not sure what . . ." Meribel sat up on her bed of leaves, trying to clear her head.

"Your father is sick?" the voice asked gently.

Meribel stood. "Yes. I need to find the herbs and return to him immediately."

"You haven't far to look for what you need. Ten paces behind you will do."

Meribel turned and found a sack. Picking it up, she saw that it contained all that she required for her father.

"How did you . . . ?"

"You spoke in your sleep. You were asleep for some time. You must return to your father now. You will be safe. The villains who hurt you have been scattered away."

"Will you let me see you?" she asked, as she attached the sack to her belt.

"No. It is better that you don't. Go now, you can climb up the vine to the outside."

"I cannot thank you enough. Now I must return home."

However, just as Meribel had started to climb up, the voice called out, "Wait!"

Meribel froze, puzzled. But then she heard it—the sound of men's voices in the distance. From the darkness ahead of her, Meribel detected a new smell, sharper than the dull wet scent. More distinct.

"They have returned, and have found us," the voice rumbled.

"What will we do?" asked Meribel, as she dropped to the floor.

A large shadow emerged from the gloom. "I will take you away myself."

The mob burst from the darkness of the forest, running, yelling, and brandishing their weapons.

"There it is," one man called out. "The lair!"

The steam from the entrance was almost invisible now that the sun was peeking over the hills in the distance. On they ran, bearing down on the opening in the ground.

"Where's Taar?" another asked.

"Dragon must have got him too."

"We'll teach it a lesson!" a third man exclaimed, with no thought as to how they might actually do that.

Then they all stopped, half from shock, half from the rush of air as the dragon vaulted from its lair, spread its wings to their full length, and soared over their heads. The villagers pointed, for they saw Meribel held firmly in the dragon's claws.

But then the dragon came to a sudden halt, its bellow of surprise blending with the sound of straining wood. For a noose had been laid around the opening of the lair and was now around the dragon's neck at one end, and a thick oak at the other.

And in its surprise, the dragon dropped Meribel, and she fell several feet to the ground. Then, stepping from the wood, came Taar, his giant bow held at arm's length, an arrow held taut against the string. He released the arrow, sending it straight and true into the neck of the dragon.

The dragon roared, sent flames hither and thither, and scorched the rope that held it, so that it was free. But it could barely sustain its flight, and skimmed the leaves of the trees. A moment later, there was a gigantic splash, and Taar knew that the dragon had plunged into the lake.

But he thought no further of the dragon. His sole concern was Meribel.

Though stunned and bruised, she was otherwise unhurt. Taar gathered her in his arms and carried her to her father's cabin, where she slept like a child. He also used the herbs in Meribel's sack to restore her father's health.

In the days that followed, Meribel told her story to Taar, and he saw to it that the men who had attacked her were punished. She was angry with them, and, despite his help, angry with Taar for his part in injuring the dragon. When she was strong enough, she searched the lake but couldn't find its body. Then her spirits lifted, for this meant that the dragon must still be alive.

Taar longed for a way to make up for injuring the dragon. When Meribel returned from the lake, he vowed to find it. Closing his store and arranging for Meribel to take care of his affairs in his absence, he set out.

While Taar was away, Meribel spoke often to her father about what had happened. Over time, she came to realize that Taar had acted with great courage and out of concern for her, and she also realized that she loved him.

After a year, Taar returned. Meribel leaped upon him and kissed him and wept, and asked that he never leave her again. Taar was unable to speak for a time, but when he could, he told Meribel that his journey was a failure. He had not found the dragon.

For a moment, Meribel was downcast. But Taar had seen something special. It would give her cause for pleasure, and he took her by the hand to show her.

They were soon married. A year later they had a daughter, and when the daughter was old enough, Meribel took her for a walk in the woods and pointed to an opening in the ground from which white smoke rose, twisting up to the sky. Then Meribel told her the story of the dragon and obtained her promise to tell it to her own daughter one day. And she did. And so did her daughter's daughter, and for generations, the story was passed from mother to daughter, until my mother told it to me.

And now, Alice, I pass this story on to you.

Daddy closes the book and says, "And that's the end of *Where the Dragons Sleep*, by Katherine M. Draco." Then he kisses me and turns off the light.

"Mommy has the same middle name as me."

"Yes, that's right. Now have a good night's sleep. See you in the morning."

Daddy and I blow each other kisses, then he closes the door.

As I lie in bed thinking about Meribel and the dragon, I hear a funny sound outside. Getting out of bed, I climb on the chair and look out the window. It's Daddy, outside. There's lots of snow falling, big thick flakes, and he's busy shovelling the driveway.

I watch him for a while, then my nose starts to get cold. But before I can start to get down, I hear another noise, a truck, a big one, going down the street. It sounds like it's coughing. That's what happens when you drive a truck in cold weather. It gets sick. After it turns the corner, I look at the sewer again. There's more steam coming up than there was before.

The steam reminds me of something, and when I remember, I do nothing, just stare at the sewer for a long time. Then I go downstairs, where Mommy is drying dishes. I take along my Pooh bear and let its head go bump, bump, bump down the stairs.

"Mommy," I ask as she turns around, a plate in one hand and a towel in the other.

"Does Daddy know?"

Mommy smiles. She always smiles when I ask her a question. But this time she's trying not to cry. She puts down the plate and towel, kneels, and holds me so my head rests in my favourite spot, on her shoulder

.

Acknowledgments

The beautiful cover art is by Johannes Chazot, who can be found on Twitter @ViiiJohannes.

I'm grateful that Rachel Small was available to edit this book, and for her numerous, helpful suggestions. You can find Rachel on Reedsy and on Twitter @FaultlessFinish. I've since revised the manuscript slightly (Writing is like eating peanuts: it's hard to stop.) and there are a couple of new stories that Rachel didn't see. Any errors are my own. If you spot an error, please let me know on my errata page: https://selimpensfiction.com/something-special-errata/

I'm also grateful to Ichabod Ebenezer for his speedily delivered and insightful comments on a draft of the eBook manuscript, and to Hilary Andre for reviewing the paperback version.

Finally, thank you, Matt Willox, for designing the front cover lettering.

Printed in Great Britain
by Amazon